Last Fight of the Valkyries:

Sirens of the Zombie Apocalypse, Book 4

E.E. ISHERWOOD

ISBN: 0692717196
ISBN-13: 978-0692717196 (Isherwood Media, LLC)

Fiction / Science Fiction / Apocalyptic & Post-Apocalyptic

For my readers. Without you, there would only be three.

History has all the excitement of a haunted jack-in-the-box.
A few turn the handle. A few try to stop it. Most just look away.
And sometimes, what comes out surprises us all.

GRANDMA

Six months before the sirens.

The phone rang.

Marty woke with the feel of electricity coursing through her body. She wrote it off to how she fell asleep in her soft chair—her neck was tilted to the side a little too far. She let the call go to her answering machine as she always did.

"Would you like me to pick up?" Angie yelled from the kitchen.

"Oh no, dear, let it go to the computer."

Marty knew it wasn't really a computer with a keyboard and a fancy monitor, but she thought anything "hi tech" was a computer of some sort. The little box had buttons and a screen and blinking lights—a lot like a computer.

It beeped as the announcement played, "Hello, this is the residence of Mrs. Marty Peters, please leave a message and she'll try to call you back." That was Angie's voice—the woman in the kitchen and also Marty's full-time live-in nurse who stayed in the flat above her. She agreed to do the greeting message for Marty because her voice was getting so weak. Marty had recently turned 104 years old, and was starting to feel her age catching up. Last year, she might have tried to get out of her comfortable chair and pick up the telephone, but now—it was just easier to let the computer do all the heavy lifting.

Normally she'd have the handset of her cordless phone sitting next to her, but it was still early in the morning and Angie hadn't been able to get all her morning chores done down here yet. Getting Marty set up with all her sewing equipment, reading glasses, and even the telephone, were still on her to-do list. She was currently making breakfast.

As the answering machine clicked over, Marty listened in, "Hello Grandma. Uh, listen, I need to talk to you when you get a chance. I got a call from my mom and she has some things going on in Colorado that concern all of us. I don't really want to talk about it on the phone." The voice hesitated for several seconds. "Just being safe is all. I'll be over this afternoon. Love to Angie. Talk soon."

A beep closed out the transaction.

Marty stared thoughtfully across the room to the machine now flashing a little number one at her. Her eyesight was still quite good. The man on the call was her grandson, and he was referring to her daughter-in-law, Rose, who had just won an election to a congressional seat in her home state of Colorado. Marty had about as much interest in politics as she did computers, but something in the tone of Jerry's voice told her this would be no ordinary meeting.

Just being safe.

She pulled out her rosary and began to pray for guidance, but before she got into it, she had a premonition of a sort. A *deja vu?* No, it felt like the *start* of something, but it made no sense though it continued for a minute like a daydream.

I saw Liam and three young girls. All with guns!

"Will Jerry be stopping by, Grandma?" Even Angie, her 54-year-old nurse, called her Grandma. Everyone did, and she was OK with that.

The question startled her out of her reverie.

"Oh. Yes. Jerry will be stopping by after lunch."

"Will he have his tools? My door is sticky again." It was a running joke between them. That door would never be straight.

Marty couldn't reply right away. She felt that surge of energy leaving her. She gripped the beads a little tighter, worried her time had finally come. The vision of her great-grandson and those girls was unlike anything she'd experienced in her many years. It was like a waking dream. Her thoughts turned dark as she recalled horrible scenes of kids with swords, guns, and lots of dead people. She was a spiritual woman to the core. How such evil scenes could come from inside her was a mystery.

The end is coming for me.

"He's always prepared, Anj."

"He sure is," she shouted, "you're lucky to have him around."

Angie cooking. A call from her grandson. A vision of her great-grandson.

She couldn't imagine a busier morning.

A DAY AT THE BALLPARK

Liam Peters was shirtless and soaked. He'd just survived a perilous swim in the Mississippi, followed by a harrowing escape from a massive pile of wreckage floating in that river. By his estimation, they consumed quite a few miracles as they made it from a boat on one side of the river, into the water, onto the wreckage, then to the safety of shore. For most of the journey he'd hauled his 104-year-old great-grandmother Martinette (Marty) Peters on his back. He was assisted by Victoria Hennessey, his girlfriend. In fact, they'd all been running, dodging, and escaping one problem after another for the past couple weeks. Pretty much every moment since the sirens ended the world and the zombies poured forth.

But that was all in the past. They'd reached this moment when rescue was finally at hand. As part of their recent tribulations, their friends had come into the possession of a military truck called an MRAP. Built for the wars in Iraq and Afghanistan, it was a large six-wheeled vehicle structurally designed to deflect improvised explosive devices left by insurgents over in those hellholes. Here in America, it was nearly invincible. And it was waiting for them half a football field away.

"Grandma, we're saved."

As he said it, a sheet of newspaper drifted up and over the edge of the bridge when a stiff breeze caught it and blew it directly toward him

—along with the stench of death from the city below. He swatted it with his free hand, but missed. It planted itself on his chest.

The newspaper was a single sheet—the front page—and it was filled with headlines, but almost no descriptive text underneath. The only photo was a black and white snapshot of the Gateway Arch, from a time that had to be before it was overrun with refugees and zombies. The edition was obviously rushed.

The biggest words were at the top. The headline caught his attention, as intended. "CURE FOUND!" It was one of the few articles that had any text. "CDC promises vaccine. Stay indoors. Stay calm."

He laughed. He had the inside track on that imaginary vaccine.

A cursory look at the other articles gave him similarly curt titles. "Domestic Terrorists Blamed." "Stocks Fall." "Pols point fingers over failed response." "Pope says not Rapture."

"I guess the zombies won." He tossed the paper away. The wind carried it down the highway. Too late, he wondered what date was on the paper. It seemed trivial, but he was curious how long the papers still managed to print.

The sheet floated over the MRAP to points beyond. It drew his eye as it fluttered.

"Liam, look ahead," Victoria said with a quiver in her voice.

It didn't need to be said. All three of them could see the mass of zombies coming onto the raised highway, not too far beyond the MRAP. The infected were coming up from the city, which had been swarming with them. Now, as if released, they began fleeing the downtown—heading anywhere but there.

Liam and Victoria held Grandma Marty between them as they walk-ran her toward the truck. Ahead, the rear doors opened and a few men piled out. And a few boys.

Liam smiled broadly when he saw the Boy Scout uniforms. He'd recently spent a lot of time in a camp built around a Boy Scout property in the southern suburbs of St. Louis, and the fact they came to rescue him warmed his heart. He half-expected his mother and father to appear, but he couldn't see them.

The chatter of gunfire prompted him to move faster. The big chaingun on top of the truck remained silent. It should be easily chewing up zombies.

Like so many times of the past few weeks since the zombie plague began, he ran for his life. He turned to look at his tiny grandma and her hideous pinkish-red pantsuit. Her white hair was a stark contrast to her lower body—which was soaked and muddy like his own. Victoria ran along on her far side. He admired her long brown hair, also filthy with mud, and her normally pretty face. It would have been much prettier had it not been covered with bruises from some earlier mishaps, and soaked with dirty river water. Her white shirt was torn at the midriff and stained with both coal soot and river water. None of them was a model of hygiene at that moment.

The passenger door of the MRAP opened and Phil Ramos, ex-police officer, popped out.

"Come on, Liam. What are you waiting for?" he shouted as he ran to the front bumper, knelt down, and began shooting the increasing numbers of infected coming their way.

They reached the rear doors, and he helped Grandma climb the stairs to get inside. He had no weapons to assist in the defense of the vehicle, so all he could do was watch the battle. Given all that he'd been through of late, he was content to sit this one out. He climbed into the passenger area and took a seat on the long bench next to Grandma. Victoria remained on her other side, as if to prevent her from sliding too far in either direction.

For half a minute, the shooting continued, until a command was given and the rescue team all clambered back into the relative safety of the metal beast.

"Go!" one of the Scouts screamed.

An older man, likely his dad, put his hand on the kid's knee as he sat next to him. "We're good. We'll be OK," he told the boy.

The engine was already running, so the driver threw it into gear as soon as the last door shut. The vehicle lumbered down the road in a direction Liam knew was wrong. They were all pointed toward the river, but the bridge was out. It was lying in the river.

He shouted, "The bridge is out," just as the truck began to decelerate and turn. The driver expertly rounded four lanes of traffic on the empty highway and then gunned the engine as it headed back toward the zombies.

"Grandma, will you be OK? I have to see this."

"I'm fine, dear. Sitting is...heavenly." Her head was already nodding in the hot and stuffy truck.

He'd gotten up, but noticed she snapped right back awake as if she caught herself dozing in class. Something about the look on her face gave him pause.

"You sure?" he asked in a tentative voice.

She looked at him, but was already tipping over again. Her head fell to Victoria's shoulder, who held her steady.

Must be the exhaustion.

He tilted his head to Victoria with a weak smile, then held on to the tie-downs and moved forward. As he arrived in the space between the driver's area and the rear seats, he saw who was driving the truck.

"Mel!"

Melissa was a fellow survivor—a shoe saleswoman by her account—he'd met a week ago in front of his own house. She and Phil were a tag team of sorts when it came to driving the MRAP.

"Yep. Good to see you too. Now hold on."

She aimed the truck into the crowd of zombies on the pavement ahead. Beyond the first loose cadre of zombies were an endless sea of them. They used the entrance ramp to flood onto the interstate from the city's center.

The hull shook a little as they ran over the first few. Liam saw men and women of every shape, color, and dress shambling up the ramp. Most had bloody messes on their faces and necks. They diverged east and west on the highway as they came up onto the bridge, ignoring all rules of the road.

He thought Mel was going to punch through the initial clump of them to try to continue on the raised bridge, but there was a big roadblock less than a quarter mile away. This segment was mostly free of dead vehicles because cars couldn't pass the distant barricade. She veered directly into the exit ramp going faster than Liam thought prudent.

"Hang on!" Mel shouted, just as they got into the thick of the undead.

Liam, unprepared for a collision, fell into the space between Phil and Mel. The truck shuddered and swerved as it pounded the pedestrians. The engine roared as Mel kept their speed just above reckless.

"This ramp was empty when we came up. They must have followed us," Phil offered.

By the time Liam got to one knee so he could look out the front, she had them most of the way around the sweeping left turn of the ramp. The end was in sight.

Mel had the steering wheel in a death grip. It was vibrating badly as more of the plague victims fell under the high front cross bar of a bumper. Blood splashed all over the hood and was beginning to reach their windshield.

Still she kept her foot on the gas, taking them to the bottom of the ramp. Liam almost relaxed, until he saw the new roadway. They'd left the raised highway of the east-west interstate and entered the north-south highway below which should have taken them out of St. Louis. Except it was a parking lot.

When the city collapsed, people got in their cars and tried to head out into the country—anywhere but a city awash in a growing problem of neighbors biting neighbors. In hours, the interstates were traffic jams of Biblical proportions. It was entirely appropriate for the Apocalypse. Even the burly MRAP couldn't push its way down an endless highway of parked cars.

Mel turned hard to the right. Dangerously so. The MRAP jumped a high curb while simultaneously slipping on the...remains...of the crowd of people outside. More blood shot onto the hood. Liam tried to hold on, but fell to the left and bounced off Mel's seat. He knew she wanted to say something to him about getting back in his seat, but she was unable to take her focus from the road.

"I have—"

She turned hard to the right again, and put them on a north south road going *into* downtown.

"—to find somewhere without so many infected."

Like most adults, Mel was reticent to use the term "zombie" to describe the people outside. He'd had philosophical debates several times over the past few weeks with people who shared her view. Zombies were from the movies. These things couldn't be categorized so easily. So people used what terms they could. "Infected" was most common. "Plaguers" also gained favor, mostly because the source of the infection was a disease sort of like Ebola. It was officially called Extra-Ebola, an understated and simplistic name for a very complicated disease process which made the victim bleed like they'd caught the worst equatorial disease imaginable. The joke was: twice the Ebola and one-half the life expectancy. In fact, it killed people—though the resulting dead bodies just kept walking around like they didn't get the memo. And they sought the blood of the living.

After Hayes and his research team had drawn in all the zombies, the roads nearest the center of the urban core were now thinning out. It was the direction Mel had them going. As the engine continued to strain against the still considerable crowd, she tried to plan her next move.

"We can't afford to stop. If we do, we're dead. We'll never get this thing moving again against such numbers. I'm going to head north, then turn west as soon as a street looks passable."

It took her many blocks in the urban grid before she took a chance and turned left. The rear end drifted as she made the corner. In seconds, she had her foot back on the gas and they continued into the dead.

"My God. It's impossible." She spoke just loud enough to be heard over the road noise.

Ahead, the road she'd chosen was arrow-straight for a mile. In the distance, the number of zombies only grew. To plow through, they'd need a locomotive. Even that might not be enough. Maybe a tank could do it. Liam had seen a tank on these streets weeks ago doing that very thing.

"Oh no." Mel pointed ahead. Liam followed her finger to some people on the roof of a small building ahead. It had big numbers and letters, as if it was the home of a TV station.

Phil replied with equal measure. "We can't help them."

The people desperately waved their shirts, large sheets that looked like something a photographer would use for a backdrop, and many flailing arms. They needed rescue.

"What do we do? There are too many." Mel seemed to be considering a rescue, despite Phil's statement against it. Liam wondered if they were asking him.

This is what he often called the gamer's dilemma. Fight or flight? To fight is to invite trouble for their group. Any rescue would be dangerous. Flight...sometimes it was better to survive another day without getting "involved." He'd just rescued Grandma with the help of Victoria. He'd felt he'd risked enough for one day.

He said nothing.

Mel made up her own mind in the absence of input. The MRAP crushed more bodies while it crossed the median. It fell down into the next set of lanes and then bounced up on the sidewalk. Mel ran over several parking meters, a blue mailbox, and sheared off her rearview mirror while slamming the truck against the concrete wall below the balcony. She had pulled up directly under the waving people.

"It's up to them if they want to get on. It's the least we can do for them."

Liam understood the risks. "But you said we couldn't stop. Won't we get overrun?"

She looked back at him while taking a pull from a water bottle. Then she spoke quickly to them all. "I'm giving these guys a chance. We aren't going to let them in. They can ride on top. We'll be moving before we get surrounded."

Liam guessed that would be in about ten seconds.

Far from being a rescue, the pit stop became a horror show. The people up top were desperate. Their footfalls from jumping the ten feet from the low balcony were constant. Then people started to fall off...

While they listened, a pair of men in dress pants and white shirts fell over the windshield, onto the hood. They threw punches at each other. The look in their eyes was pure malice even as they slid together over the blood-soaked metal, then it turned to abject panic as they slid off the side, out of view. The stomping on the roof continued as Liam sat frozen on the inside. One of the men who slipped off the front tried to hop back up near Phil's door, but the swarming zombies pulled him back down.

"What was I thinking?" Mel asked guiltily.

They'd been parked for thirty seconds. More people fell from the top. Anyone who slid down the windshield ended up sliding off the hood too. Then someone figured out they could hold onto the edge of the roof and fling themselves over the windshield. Mel's view was about to be obscured. Sure enough, others jumped down and held onto the legs of those above.

"Lord, forgive me." Mel stomped on the gas. A few of the people on the front, those hanging on for their lives, lost them. One woman lost her grip above them, and she and several people holding onto her legs went tumbling off the side. It opened up enough space so Mel could at least see where the truck was going. Her hands were white with pressure on the wheel. Liam imagined others continued to fall from the top, but he refused to look out the little side windows or those on the rear doors. He'd seen enough of the bad side of humanity to know the desperate survivors would do *anything* to secure their place on the roof.

Mel ran down a few more parking meters, a score of walking sick, got off the sidewalk, and turned the truck sharply to the right. Instead of continuing west, she headed back to the east. To downtown.

"We can't make it guys. There's just too many that way. We need to find somewhere we can wait while all these things clear out."

If they clear out, Liam thought.

He knew the zombies had been manipulated during the outbreak so that when the big tornado sirens all over the city went off, the sick left their homes to try to escape the noise and the signal within. It was part of the plan of those responsible for the infection. They claimed they were worried the sick needed to be motivated to spread the infection, and the best way to do that was to get them moving. But those same people also conducted research in a secretive facility in downtown St. Louis which used that same technology to *bring them back.* This was why, weeks into the catastrophe, the city was full once again with those same infected souls.

"Any ideas where we could go would be great, guys." Mel's tension was infectious.

Liam turned around to the audience in the back part of the MRAP. Grandma was still lying against Victoria's shoulder, though he wondered how she was sleeping through all the bouncing and...the screams. He could still hear people up on the top arguing and shouting obscenities at each other. He guessed none of the group had firearms, primarily because no one had used one yet.

There were three older Boy Scouts, and three Scout dads—or at least men old enough to be fathers. He didn't have the time or inclination to assign dads to each of the boys in the back. Right now they needed everyone to be focused on the only thing that would keep them alive: somewhere to hide.

One man suggested the Arch, as it had a large park surrounding it, as well as a subterranean museum which seemed to offer ample protection from the undead, but Liam reminded him that the Arch grounds had been bombed heavily during the early days of the plague. It was now more hellish-looking than Hell's Half Acre. The remains of the zombies, and the real humans who were caught up in the attack, littered the place. There was no way Liam would go back there.

They settled on trying to get into Busch Stadium. Liam suggested it because it was obviously a large flat area that, if empty, would provide a good way to ensure no zombies were anywhere close to them if they stopped.

No one could think of anything better. All the roads and highways out of town would be crawling with the outward bound zombies, as well as the derelict cars facing into town—relics of that last wave of refugees trying to find safe harbor at the Arch.

That didn't turn out so good.

2

Mel continued to knock over the zombies as she drove around trying to find the stadium. Everyone knew it was close, but the city looked different when sick and bloodied people were on every street corner. She drove until she found the stadium and then the service entrance, when a decision needed to be made.

"How do we get in? I can ram through the gate, but then we're vulnerable inside."

Phil seemed ready to offer a reply, but shook his head in the negative as he peered out his window.

When he didn't offer up any ideas, Liam turned around to those in the back.

"Just ram it," was the consensus. In various ways, and with different reasons, many in the back waved off the idea of any of them getting out to open any doors. Liam could see outside. They were right to be afraid. Though that gave him an idea.

"Hey, why don't we use the gun," he pointed at the roof, indicating the big chaingun mounted on the roof the MRAP, "and eliminate these zom—infected—before we open the gate by hand?"

Phil answered, while Mel drove. "We only had a few rounds. We ran out of ammo shooting zombies back on the raised highway just before you came into our view. It's basically a big decoration now, unless we can somehow get some replacement rounds for it." He laughed, knowing it was impossible.

Unless they could find an armory. Liam searched his memory for one of the zombie books he'd read in the past. He recalled a scene where the heroes found an armory in Denver and liberated some ammunition. It would be like gold in a world where it was required reading to kill innumerable infected to stay alive. Maybe someone he knew had a line on an armory in St. Louis. Now wasn't the time to ask.

The only way for a vehicle to get into the stadium was to ram the big gate which linked the road with the deep outfield. It was the entrance used regularly by the Clydesdale's—a huge horse team that pulled a wagon full of beer around the ballpark to fire up the fans.

Mel had been driving in circles on the streets near the ballpark. "OK, I'm going to push us through the gate and hope I can break the lock without ruining the gate itself. If we can get through, and if the gate can be closed again, we'll need someone to jump out and swing the gate shut and then I'll park just on the other side of the gate so that nothing can get through." She shouted her plan so everyone in the back could hear her.

Liam heard some low groans. He knew no one had any desire to open those back doors. Even if it meant they'd be making themselves safer—eventually.

Short of getting out first and trying to open the gate by hand, it was their best option among a precious few.

Phil craned his neck to look out the window up into the walkways and balconies of the stadium above. "I don't think the stadium is empty. Not that we can stop now."

Mel had been keeping the speed steady, but hit something that made the whole truck bounce a foot or two off the ground and sway dangerously side to side. Several more people slid off the top and windshield.

"Dammit! I don't know what that was. Maybe a motorcycle on the ground. I keep killing them..." Liam could tell how hard it was to see anything now with zombies thick in the streets, people hanging on the windshield, and splatters of blood drying and smearing on the glass. There weren't as many zombies on the street as they'd seen at the TV station, but it was still suicide to stop or consider getting out. Except someone had to do just that if they were going to reach a safe harbor.

"That's it. I'm going for it. Hold on guys, I'm hitting the gate."

Liam held on while looking back at Grandma to be sure Victoria had her. Victoria looked in his direction with a tight-lipped smile. She gripped Grandma as best she could. He returned the smile and focused on the action up front.

Mel did as she said. The MRAP sped down the street next to the ballpark, but as she approached the gate, she braked until she was moving at walking speed. When she hit the big metal gate, she gave it some gas to push on through. The gate made a loud plinking sound as the padlock shattered, and it seemed to be slightly off kilter, but it did open.

She proceeded beyond the gate and then stopped.

"OK, guys. You have to get out and shut that gate."

Liam looked back. He could see the reluctance. But one of the older men braced his rifle and held his hand on the rear doors.

"You guys ready?" the man asked.

The response was tepid, but they too readied their weapons and leaned toward the back gate.

With a flourish he opened the double doors; they swung outward. Zombies were everywhere beyond the open gate, but the very first thing that came inside was a living person.

The man looked like a professional acrobat. He must have been hanging on the rear portion of the roof. When the door opened, he flung himself downward and shot inside the compartment. The man who opened the door got a shot off, maybe thinking it was a zombie.

"Holy crap!" he cried as he fell under the weight of the other man.

The zombies outside were unable to laugh at the improbability of the scenario. Instead, they advanced.

"Zombies. Shoot them!" cried one of the Boy Scouts. He too was armed. But he wasn't at the back of the truck. Another man was at the end of the bench seat opposite Victoria and Grandma. That man had been watching the tumbler on the floor, and he took his eye off the outside world.

Liam saw it all happen in slow motion, unable to shout or otherwise warn the victim. First, the zombie closed the distance to the truck, like he'd been watching the man on the top and was ready for the doors to open. Next, he mounted the rear steps—there were three of them below the back doors. Finally, he flung himself onto the man sitting by the door.

These zombies defied classification. Liam had been trying for weeks to put them into the pantheon of zombie types. They seemed to crave blood, rather than the stereotypical "brains" so preferred by zombies of old. If they had their druthers, they always struck for the neck.

Somehow they knew it was the easiest way to tap into the blood supply of the victim. Liam imagined it was an ingrained superstition in humanity about Vampires. However, if an open carotid artery wasn't immediately available, the zombies would gnaw on any open flesh they could find. The one thing they didn't do—and something Liam never understood when he saw it in the movies—was tear out the insides or destroy the literal brains of their victims. How could the virus spread if the primary means of transmission was eating the victim? As with so many things the past few weeks, reality was much more mundane than the movies.

The zombie bit into the final man's wrist. He screamed in pain, and tried to pull away, but the zombie had gripped onto his forearm with both hands—staking his claim on the prized flesh.

The man underneath the guy from up top saw what was happening and made an effort to kick the zombie back out the door, but the weight on him made him ineffective in that task.

The tumbler, an unkempt twenty-something man dressed in long gray suit slacks and a filthy white t-shirt, realized the situation and he too began kicking—but instead of kicking the zombie, he kicked the man who was bitten. He too was tangled with the guy below him, but he supported himself with one arm and one leg and executed a powerful kick to the victim's face. The Scout dad didn't see it coming. With a dazed look, he let himself be pulled out the back by the zombie on his arm.

That was bad, but one of the Scouts—probably the man's son—tumbled out after him, shotgun in hand. The rest of the people in the back were momentarily stunned to silence. They heard five or six shotgun blasts before there were too many zombies for the boy to fight. Liam started moving at about shot four.

He was still unarmed, but he pushed himself against the tumbler man. He used his own modest girth and the element of surprise to catch the man in an awkward position. Liam couldn't lift him on his own, but the man underneath used the relief to grab the killer's neck and push him backward.

Liam kept going. His anger at what the man had done, fused with the fear he felt at being so exposed, gave him the strength to shove the guy right through the rear door. The man fell to the pavement, very near the dying boy and his dead father. There were about ten zombies hovering over their finds, and a hundred or more within a stone's throw. Liam just hung onto the latch of the back door, trying to comprehend it all. Closing the gate was not possible now.

Someone pulled him back in. One of the dads. Another man was on the other side, bringing his rifle to bear on the moving targets just yards away. Everyone was screaming now.

Liam focused on the most important voice in the confusion: Mel's.

"Hang on!"

3

Mel put her foot on the gas and the MRAP lurched ahead. If Liam hadn't been paying attention to her voice, he might have taken a dive when it happened. He looked at the bodies on the ground behind them, thinking how easily it could have been for him to get pulled out.

The truck ran right through a second wooden outfield wall gate. Mel didn't wait to see if they could close it. She went through much too fast. It shattered. There were too many zombies behind them to contemplate a fast fix.

"We'll do a loop and—"

Liam struggled to get over the legs of those sitting in the rear, aware the rear doors were swaying back and forth in the open position. He gave Grandma—finally awake—and Victoria a quick look and a thumbs up as he got to the front of the compartment.

Ahead, barely visible through the blood stains on the glass and the last two survivors clinging to the hood, Liam recognized the two U.S. Marine Corps V-22 Ospreys. But it was difficult to ascertain what was happening until Mel turned to the right, toward left field, when they got a better look through the clear window on her side.

The Ospreys had their propellers spinning, but the rear doors hung open like the tongues of two tired hound dogs. They were near first base and third base, respectively but turned so they unloaded toward each other. He saw no movement inside the cargo areas. Outside, on the dirt of the infield, a handful of Marines pointed weapons at a large group of survivors near the dugouts.

"What the hell is going on here," he asked anyone who could see the action.

"It looks like the Marines aren't here to rescue these people," was Phil's answer.

Liam knew where at least some of the Marines had gone. They died in the cavernous circular hotel near the Arch. It was the same place he, Grandma, and Victoria had escaped that very morning. He began responding to Phil when Mel veered sharply toward the planes.

"We have no choice. Our only hope is to get on one of those and get out of here."

Phil gave a quick sigh. "I doubt they'll welcome us with open arms." He thumbed toward the crowds ahead. "Doesn't look like they're letting anyone in, and I'm not sure I want to fight the U.S. military. In fact, I know I don't."

That gave Liam an idea. Was he listed as a fugitive from his brief visit—and evasion—from the Marines? He could turn himself in. It was a smarter play than fighting.

"Get me close. I think I can get us in."

Mel and Phil looked at him with the "he's just a crazy kid" eyes, but didn't second guess him.

Liam met the commander of one unit of Marines back at Camp Hope—the base of operations for the Boy Scouts in the south suburbs of St. Louis. The commander had been looking for the man who was responsible for kidnapping his great-grandma, so Liam was inclined to help him. However, Liam couldn't absolutely trust him, so he and Victoria slipped away and rescued Grandma on their own. Liam hoped they'd also welcome him because of the information he carried about the fate of the Marines in the Riverside Hotel: all dead.

"OK, Liam, I'm going to park us just beyond that one on the left. Since the doors are already open in the back, we can practically jump right onto their ramp." She was gracious enough not to mention they might be shot on sight as a threat to the Marines guarding the planes.

There were so many things going on at once Liam could hardly keep up. A Scout in the back shouted a warning that the infected now poured through the ballpark gate—they were following the MRAP like hungry Piranha to a ham hock. Phil said he saw people in the stands surging for the aircraft too. Ahead, the Marines holding back the crowd turned uncertainly as they had threats in every direction. Getting surrounded wasn't what it used to be...

Liam thought, "At least no one is shooting," just as a shot rang out.

The ballpark exploded in gunfire.

In the rear of his truck, men and boys shot at the zombies as they approached. Mel had swerved right as she drove into the stadium, but many of the zombies made a z-line for the noisy Ospreys rather than follow her. The MRAP and the fastest zombies arrived at the first base Osprey at almost the same time. The Marines defended their patch of dirt, but diluted themselves to absurdity in the face of so many hostiles.

"What do we do now?" Liam asked the crew cabin.

Mel turned off the engine and looked to him with a grim smile and a raised eyebrow. "We pray."

He took that as his cue to backtrack to Grandma and get her out the rear door along with everyone else. He hunched over as he made his way to her. The men and Scouts needed no invitation; they charged out the back. The four of them formed a loose firing line just behind the truck so they could shoot the incoming zombies. They looked tiny in the face of the ever growing crowd of infected coming through the broken rear gate of the ballpark.

We did this. Phil warned us. We brought down this sanctuary.

There's always someone around who ruins it for everyone else or for themselves. Liam assigned the name *that guy* to the bumbling character from all the zombie books he'd read over the years.

That guy who bungles holding a key to get him into his sanctuary.

That guy who shoots so many zombies he creates a stack of them, allowing them to walk onto his otherwise safe railway car.

That guy who needlessly brags to CDC employees that his Grandma is 104 so they spend the next week hunting her down.

The examples were legion, yet the three he'd just imagined were from his own experience in the Zombie Apocalypse to date.

Yep, that's all me. My streak continues.

Liam watched the handful of Scouts and men outside and recognized he had to move fast. He grabbed Grandma's arm, thankful that for once she didn't argue with him. She had a penchant for asking him to leave her behind and save himself, but she likely had heard Liam demur so many times she knew not to ask again.

The gunfire outside was incessant. When he and Victoria had Grandma on the dirt, he could see the fighting was more serious than he'd imagined. The crowd of civilians converged on the thin line of—at best, a dozen—Marines, and weren't stopping, even in the face of gunfire. In fact, they were firing back. Several of the Marines fell as he guided Grandma to the Osprey. There was no one standing on the ramp so they just kept going. Several of the people they rescued from the TV station had jumped off the roof and ran in. They moved with grim determination as far into the plane as they could, as if *nothing* was going to stop them from reaching safety. He doubted even the Marines could dislodge them.

He put Grandma on one of the jump seats near the middle of the plane and motioned for Victoria to strap her in. Someone in charge had to be on the plane. He walked by the eight or ten men and women who had taken refuge in the leading seats and stepped from the cargo area into the cockpit. Two Marine aviators sat in front of a dizzying array of buttons, switches, and display panels. The man on the right had a pistol pointed at his chest.

"I'm unarmed!" he shouted.

"What do you want? How'd you get on board?"

Liam thought it was obvious. "Your door was wide open," is what he could have said. Now wasn't the time for jokes. Instead, he played his only card in this rigged poker game called the Apocalypse.

"I'm here to see Colonel Brandyweis. He's the commander of 2nd Marines...or something." He'd met the colonel, but he couldn't recall the man's unit. He was only half-sure of his rank. He continued, talking fast. "I'm here with some Boy Scouts and my elderly grandmother. The colonel was looking for her." That was mostly true.

The co-pilot looked at him for a long moment, then lowered his weapon.

"The *lieutenant* colonel isn't here. Go back and take a seat and I'll contact him. If you're lying, I'll throw you off myself. Clear?"

Liam had seen enough war movies to know the proper response: "Crystal, sir." He thought about throwing him a salute, but opted for restraint. He trotted back to the large cargo hold. Grandma and Victoria were secure and belted, but the other men and boys were still at the bottom of the ramp, firing and reloading as fast as they could.

He proceeded to the top of the ramp, and squatted down so he could see through the side gap in the bay door. Hundreds of infected plodded on the green turf, walking and speed-walking toward the planes. On the other side, Marines were falling back to the planes, downing civilians who were doing their best to get themselves shot. Liam recognized the desperation in their eyes.

The Marines were doomed if they didn't fight back. Opportunities for cooperation, and survival, had passed. The civilians would overrun the plane and make it so overburdened it wouldn't be able to take off. That's how the story ends...

He was in the process of turning around to go back to Grandma when something caught his attention on the top of the MRAP. A child was still alive up there, but wasn't coming down.

"Ugh, that just figures," he thought. Once he saw the person, he couldn't look away. He judged his chances, ignored them, and ran toward danger. It reminded him of "rescuing" that travel Bible for Victoria, but that was different. That was something he did to impress a girl. Now he was only thinking of saving a life.

Victoria screamed his name behind him, overpowering the engine noise, but he couldn't listen to her. He plowed through the small cordon of rifle-wielding Boy Scouts, unaware until it was much too late he didn't inform them he was coming through. He waited to be shot in the back, but was pleasantly surprised when he wasn't.

He judged his distance, speed, and destination and timed his jump perfectly. Getting on top of his MRAP wasn't that difficult because the thing had numerous appendages, grills, and guards on the side which facilitated his climb. He mounted the rig just in front of the driver's side door, pulled himself onto the top part of the hood—away from all the blood—then hopped over the windshield to the somewhat flat surface on top. He got around the automated chaingun, disheartened by all the blood—that was from survivors hurting each other to get their ride on his truck. He took two seconds to see the crowds on both sides of him eating away the Marines by sheer force of numbers. He didn't have long.

It wasn't child, but she was a very small older teenaged black girl. She was prone on the metal surface. Her white blouse carried the typical apocalyptic grime of someone who had worn it for too long. Her long black slacks were shredded below the knees and similarly filthy. Her exposed lower legs were lacerated with what looked like a thousand scratches. Her arms were also smeared with blood from numerous injuries. When he bent down to let her know he was there, she turned her face toward him and it too was blood-strewn. But she *was* alive.

He said nothing, but grabbed her hand and pulled her from the deck. She let him lead her, though she was in a daze. The smell of gunfire was powerful. Clouds of it were everywhere below him, adding to his own wooziness within the chaos.

Still saying nothing, he pulled her forward, and motioned where he wanted her to go. She gave a weak smile and drug herself toward him as he stood on the hood and beckoned her.

"That's right. Just follow me down. We're going to get on the plane."

She looked terrified. A perfectly natural emotion given what she'd just been through. He corrected himself. She was *still* going through it.

He took another look around, felt the crush of time, but knew he couldn't show it to her.

He tried to convey hope instead. "The Marines are here to save us."

A thousand thoughts swirled through his head. His mind landed on a sour one. He expected her to respond with, "And who will save the Marines?" but she remained quiet.

He held her hand as she shimmied down the windshield, and he turned to put his foot on the fender so he could step there. He let himself get distracted by the action below and he slipped on the blood covering the lower half of the hood.

His vision accelerated as he spun.

He became aware of himself sometime later. He opened his eyes while lying in the dirt. Victoria was in his field of vision, running to him. Another woman ran the other way. He recognized her from somewhere.

"Victoria, sweet Victoria," he thought. "Are we going for a plane ride?"

A zombie jumped into his field of view. It ran up the ramp, but was shot by a soldier at the top.

"Not a soldier. That's a U.S. Marine," he heard from deep in his memories.

Screams everywhere. Some Boy Scouts turned and ran into the plane. One looked back at him with terror in his eyes.

"How nice to have them here," he thought.

"I wonder what game they're playing?" His mind was adrift.

He next became aware of himself sitting in one of the Osprey's seats. More gunfire. A deep hum of an engine. He was surrounded by many desperate-looking people. "Wow, they look like they're late for work," he joked with himself.

The already whining engines pitched faster. The plane lurched.

From his left, he heard a swell of gunfire and watched with placid calmness as the Marines shot everyone they could from the ramp of their plane. Most were blood-covered zombies. Some weren't. The noise was deafening, but Liam wasn't bothered.

"EVERYONE GET DOWN!" shouted one of the Marines over the roar of the accelerating engines. Most complied. He physically encouraged the few holdouts.

With everyone off their feet, Liam had a clear view of the other Osprey. It still had its ramp open too, but no one was shooting, and a massive crowd tried to get in from the infield side of the baseball diamond. Another group was on the outfield side of the ramp and they pressed in too.

Isn't this nice. I love coming to the ballpark with Dad.

In slow motion, the other Osprey lifted off, ramp open and all, and tilted dangerously to the left. People clung to the ramp even as it lifted several feet above the crowd. It was too much.

The Osprey continued to tilt and move forward at the same time. It snapped the wires behind third base and tried to correct itself, but it was too unwieldy. It drifted into the lowest seats, and seemed to settle itself onto the incline filled with terrorized and fleeing people. Liam waited for an explosion that never came.

"Nothing is ever like the movies," he complained.

The Marines continued to shoot both the living and the dead at the end of his bird's ramp. It began to close. Before it got too high, Liam had the misfortune to see a man throw his tiny daughter in the air toward the Marines, only to have her pulled down by an incredibly lucky zombie who had his arm above his head as he too reached for the ramp.

"He whiffed it," was his in-game analysis. "I feel ya' buddy."

The whole plane rattled maniacally, then seemed to settle as it rose. In sixty seconds, Liam appreciated they were alive, and hovering. His head cleared, though his confused ramblings were gradually replaced by a similarly disconcerting din of screaming, shouting, and wailing from inside the now-cramped cargo hold.

A grim-faced Marine covered in red blotches on his gray camo walked by. He looked at everyone in the seats as he picked his way through those sitting on the floor. Liam couldn't read his face, but thought he saw anger in his eyes.

He turned to Victoria in the seat to his right and was surprised to see the shock on her face as she looked at him.

"Liam! You fell and hit your head!"

"I fell and hit my head?" he mouthed back.

She nodded vigorously.

"Just rest!" she screamed.

"I lost my shirt," he said with less enthusiasm. But she was no longer looking at him.

He reclined his head on the seat. The Marines shouted at the civilians. The civilians shouted at the Marines and each other. Children —many parentless—wailed relentlessly, as was their right. No one showed the least inclination to heed to sanity.

He leaned forward and over to Grandma. "Hey Grandma, you forgot your cane. You want me to turn the plane around to go get it?" He smiled as he said it, unsure if she even heard him. Ignoring the shaking hand, he used two fingers to wipe at the blood dripping into his eye, then he crushed himself into the back of his seat to steady his body. He'd said it as a joke. He forgot her cane back when they first left her house. He turned around to retrieve it for her; it was among the first of their many trials together. At the time, he had no idea how many adventures they'd have together. Now he was safe inside a military plane, above a city filled with zombies, while thousands of abandoned survivors below cursed him for being so damned lucky.

Grandma smiled, though her eyes were closed—like she had a fear of flying. He let it go.

The ballpark, home to so many friendly competitions over the years, was now witness to the ultimate struggle between the diminishing number of healthy humans and the increasing number of infected. He saw it as a microcosm of what was happening in the whole city, the whole country, and the whole world.

"Ms. Bunting would be so happy to know I remembered what a microcosm is." He giggled to himself as his head swooned. His science teacher was probably de—

"No! She made it. They *all* made it," he thought. "Everyone I ever knew made it to safety, until I'm proven wrong." He didn't want to go crazy thinking of all the people who potentially didn't make it. *Someone* had to make it.

Somehow, he won the lottery again and was one of the survivors.

He agreed with those below: at that moment, he really was the luckiest boy in the world.

GRANDMA DREAMS OF BLUE

While riding in the back of the MRAP, Marty felt light-headed as energy surged in her head and throughout her body. The incidents increased over the past few months, but they usually happened when she was waking up from a bad dream. It had become more pronounced as she dreamed of Al these past weeks, but this "jolt" felt stronger than ever before. And she hadn't dreamed yet.

She still had all her memories of Al and what he told her a short time ago about the mundane nature of all the "miracles" she'd witnessed. Her faith in God was unwavering, but her faith in miracles and Al's role as an angel had been dowsed as sure as her swim in the muddy Mississippi today. The notion she could hear the thoughts of the kids, or could control any zombies was just... She put two and two together now: Al wasn't real. Couldn't be. He was part of the breakdown of her mind under all the stress. Maybe an aneurism was responsible for her mental issues...

Or the infection they put in my veins.

The rocking in the back of the big truck was lulling her to sleep. Her last thought was that she was so glad Victoria had allowed her to rest her head on her shoulder. She'd nap, just for a little while...

She recognized the girl as she entered her dream.

2

The girl came back to life, or it felt like it anyway. Air rushed into her chest. She sucked in the stench of death, and was tempted to cough it back out. But not yet.

"Am I safe?" she wondered.

Her eyes were open, but the darkness was absolute. Her imagination placed her inside a shipping container, or an old walk-in freezer, or maybe on top of her Catholic school church altar. Those were places constructed from her memories, though she'd never woken up in or on any of them.

Careful to listen for clues, her body remained rigid—willing itself not to give away its master.

"Scare much?" She tried to recall the time *before*, but drew a blank. Only her long-term memories were intact. "My name is...Azure, but I go by Blue now. I came here... Then the zombies..." She lamented her memory failed her on the most important questions.

What she did know was that zombies ruled the darkness. It was time for action.

Below her, something was wet. Viscous.

"Why blood? Why can't I wake up in ice cream or ketchup? That way I'd know this was all fake."

Sitting up was difficult in the confined space. Things were stacked on her feet and legs. Bodies. Not one. Not two. Many. She felt the tangled hair wrapped around one hand. She slid herself from underneath the dead weight and got into a crouching position.

"I bet I'm covered in blood."

Her ears were attuned to the dark. The muffled silence indicated an interior room, but she also detected a wisp of distant gunfire.

Testing her body, she rose and made contact with an object leaning against the nearby wall. It slid and rattled to the floor with a muffled clang. The sound was unfortunate, but oddly comforting. She reached down and lifted the cold combat shotgun. She ran her hand along the stock, taking note of the shells affixed to the side. She came up with six plus whatever's in the barrel.

"Someone was very thoughtful to leave this with me," she thought.

Feeling the front of her shirt, it was covered in the red stuff. She just knew it. Her pants were similarly smeared. The only question now was whether any part of her was free of it. She tried to wipe her hands clean when she heard a sound she recognized—the stutter-shuffle of zombies.

"No. Not happening." Her brain tried to establish an action plan. Fighting zombies in the dark was lose-lose. That she ended up in this room under a bunch of bodies proved that.

Crouching, she searched the corpses near her feet for a flashlight, lighter, or pack of matches. Surely one of the dead had been a smoker.

"Don't call me Shirley!"

"Why did I just think that?" Her mind dug deep for a second and an echo of a man speaking popped into her mind's eye. "When you start your new life, echoes of the old will bounce around like the embers of a fire, burning one final time."

The first body she searched was a man. He had nothing in his pockets. The second body was a woman. She wore a pleated skirt. She had massive trauma on her left side. Blue put her hand in the mess before she realized what it was. She stifled the shock of revulsion as if her life depended on it. The third body was intertwined with and below the other two. It was also a man, but it was *jittery*.

She pushed off the two people stacked above him, and found a small throwaway lighter. Working fast, she struck the tab and the thing sparked, providing a snapshot of the wider room—like a bat using sound.

"No. I didn't just see..."

For the first time, she lost hold of her fear response. She gulped air.

Flick. The entire space was lit, for half a second.

Men and women stood nearby, inside—whatever it was she was in.

Flick. She looked at the wall closest to her. It was a good-sized room, not the confined closet her mind constructed. She was in the corner of the larger space, so it felt tighter than it really was. Glad she wasn't in a tiny coffin, but distraught the room could hold an undead football team, she tried to stay positive—she was alive.

"Am I? If I was still dead, would I know it?" It seemed too fantastic to contemplate, but she took inventory and was comforted by her breathing. "Of course I'm alive." It was the kind of thing someone says when they wake up in a room full of dead people. The kind of dead people that want *you* dead.

"Not this girl."

Flick. She could see a door handle—five feet to the left.

She ran the numbers on a) getting to the door and b) getting through the door. These were very important because c) was getting eaten by zombies. Her goal was to do everything possible to avoid option Charlie.

"Charlie Mike. Continue Mission." It was another ember.

Flick. Shuffle.

Flick. Movement. A groan.

She was almost within reach of the handle, standing among bodies in varying states of death. Some were writhing on the floor. Others were already on their feet. She tried to stay on task. The metal hook looked industrial. The kind you'd find in a hospital, an office building...or a hotel.

"Yep, there's the little hanging sign. 'Do not disturb.' That's irony right there." The only remaining question was whether the door was locked. Then it would be an easy out.

Long experience told her nothing was *ever* that simple when Death was standing behind you.

Flick.

The door had a deadbolt sixteen inches above the main handle. It would have to be tossed before the wooden door would swing inward.

She chanced one last look over her shoulder.

Flick.

They were only a couple feet from her now.

"Screw this!" she shouted while tossing the lighter; she'd either escape or die trying.

She lunged, turning the deadbolt—though it wasn't locked—while swinging the handle in a fluid motion. It swung inward, and hit a body on the floor, but her adrenaline gave her the strength to slip through. An attempt to shut the door behind her was thwarted by her slippery hands and the arms of the undead already grasping for her. She tumbled out of the cavity into natural light. The checkered carpeting of a hotel walkway rose up to meet her face—along with scores of dead zombies scattered about. A massacre had taken place here.

On her feet like lightning, she ran the numbers. What were her chances of survival?

"Hello computer?" An ember of a man talking into a computer mouse.

Her vision blurred for just a moment. She became aware of something near her face—inside her goggles—just outside her field of vision. It was fast-moving green text on a translucent background. Her first impression was of a computer interface. Just thinking the word "computer" brought the interface directly into her field of view. It was distracting as she ran in the hallway.

"So I went crazy in that room. Wonderful."

The multitasking began.

"I'm in a silo? No, a hotel." She was inside a circular hotel with a hollowed out atrium from top to bottom. Must be thirty floors. An elevator shaft on the far side went all the way up. The walkway ran all the way around the hotel with a railing to prevent accidents on the inner side, and the doors to the rooms on the outer side.

"Of course I'm at the top."

She looked back at her pursuit. There were six of them. They weren't as fast as her, but she knew they were relentless. The closest zombie—a woman dressed as a nurse—had a shimmer around her. It tripped something inside her brain, and the computer interface identified the runner for her.

>>Subject: A. Beckitswith. Nurse. Last known residence: Atlanta, GA. Employer: Center for Disease Control. Deceased.

The interface threw gigs of data at her—online photos, data streams, social media feeds. None of it relevant to this moment.

"Turn off!" She willed the computer to stop. It merely paused, and moved to the side of her awareness. She almost pulled off the computer goggles, they were already very loose, but she didn't want to lose them.

Her confusion allowed A. Beckitswith to catch up. Blue stopped and planted her feet. She maneuvered the gun in her hands, gripped the barrel like a baseball bat, and swung as hard as her pixie-frame would allow. The synthetic stock made contact with A's temple, splitting the skull with a satisfying crack. Blood splashed everywhere from the wound, dousing her front side and a wide swath of the brand new carpet.

A. Beckitswith fizzled to the floor as zombie number two approached. Another four were closing behind their leader. Fighting was in her veins, but "better part of valor" was an ember from deep inside; it insisted she run.

While fast-jogging, she reached down to the stock of the Mossberg A590A1 shotgun—a model she knew just by looking at it—and pulled shells off the ammo attachment and pushed them into the feeder port. She only needed two because it was already carrying four shells. She put the extra back into the strap and racked the slide in one powerful up and down motion. Since it was already primed with a round in the barrel, the unspent shell popped out, bounced off the wall, and Blue deftly caught it and fed it back in.

"Seven shots ready to go."

The pursuing zombie had the shimmer as the interface displayed stats.

>>Subject: N. Dawes. Nurse. Last known residence: Chicago, IL. Employer: Center for Disease Control. Deceased.

"I think I see a pattern here."

The four other zombies were quite a bit behind on the walkway, but they were also dressed like the two nurses. They were far enough back she could ignore them, for now. The lone chaser, Ms. Dawes from Chicagoland, was hopelessly outclassed in a footrace. Seeming to realize this, she flung herself over the edge of the balcony.

Still moving, Blue veered to the interior edge and looked over. The zombie was there, propelling herself—itself—along the edge of the stout steelwork of the railing. She wasn't going faster than Blue, but it was a new variable that troubled her.

"What other tricks do you have?"

The red glow of the EXIT sign blazed away ahead. She could leave this whole episode behind her. Blue plowed into the steel door of the stairwell with her shoulder—and bounced backward with her head bobbling. Even the computer interface wandered haphazardly.

Blue stumbled around, yelling loudly at the pain—and her stupidity —as she tried to regain her senses. It was only a few moments of delay, but it *was* a delay.

Ms. Dawes came over the top of the railing, five feet from her. She didn't perch on the top like a cat, but she very nearly did. Blue could see the ruined skin of the dead nurse. If she were in a cartoon, her neck would have a very distinct chomp outline. The carotid artery was messily severed, and the resultant blood splatter had covered the nurse in brackish liquid, now dried. Her eyes carried the tell-tale sign of the Double-E. Bloody eyes with gobs of it pouring out the bulging sockets.

They collided, and both careened off the hard metal door. On second glance, she knew why it hadn't opened. Some *wanker* had welded the damned thing shut.

The shotgun squirted out of Blue's hands. The nurse had a hundred pounds on her and pushed her to the floor. Blood bonded with blood as the pair splashed across the carpet. Blue was smaller and faster, and infinitely smarter. She played her hand at just the right time, pushing herself off the slippery nurse before she could take a cartoon-sized bite from her own neck.

She tumbled to her gun and grabbed it as she sprang to her feet. Moving fast, she eluded the sprawling zombie and resumed jogging around the loop. Another EXIT sign was on the far side. It was the only obvious course of action.

Chancing a look over the side again, she was dismayed to see movement on many of the lower levels. Zombies made the most noise when they knew victims were around, and the z-cophony of undead was unnerving inside the large structure.

"Makes me want to toss myself over the edge."

She stopped running at the thought. She *did* feel as if throwing herself from the ledge was a viable plan. "I can't be more than two hundred feet up. I could land on a tree down in the lobby." It made perfect sense. "I'm superhuman, after all."

Blue smiled as she imagined herself getting up on the railing, leaning over...and then she'd just keep going. The feeling was palpable. The desire to escape. Escape *downward*. It was the fastest way.

She looked straight down and caught movement on the walkway below hers. A teenage girl in a bloody blue raincoat looked straight up with her blood-drenched face. She had a shimmer around her. It was both horrible and beautiful. She *wanted* Blue to jump...

The computer spun up, providing real-time analysis.

>>Subject: T. Lowry. Offspring of Z. Lowry. Last known residence: Kansas City, KS. Employer: State of Kansas. Deceased.

"Deceased? A zombie?" Looking at the data brought her out of her glamour. Jumping from the 29th floor was now the *last* thing she wanted to do.

Ms. Dawes nipped her heels, but was a fraction of a second too late. Blue knew she was coming and had time to push herself off the railing. She vacated the space even while the zombie filled it. Recovering, Blue planted her feet, lowered her head, and threw herself into the bloodied woman.

Caught mid-turn, the zombie was off-balance. It was Blue's opportunity to push *her* over the edge. She watched her fall for a moment, but was distracted again by the girl below. She was now screaming bloody murder in Blue's direction. All that was missing was the shaking fist of rage.

"Why I outta!" An image of a Stooge. An ember.

She resumed her run and finished with a sprint as she reached the door under the EXIT sign. She didn't need to look back to know the chase would be close.

This one wasn't welded shut. In seconds, she was through. The door opened inward and there wasn't a chance to get it blocked. She ran up to the next floor, pulled open the final fire door, and forced it shut once she was through. The powerful hydraulic compressor resisted her, almost as if it wanted her to get caught. The zombies nipping her heels reached the door a tense second after the satisfying click. As far as she knew, zombies weren't smart enough to turn handles or pull open a heavy door. "God help us if they do."

Sun beat down on her from above. The penthouse level was a restaurant or lounge of some kind, with a glass ceiling and a glass-like floor. She took a few tentative steps and devoured the horrible scene below her.

Each of the levels had at least a few zombies meandering around. Some levels had many.

"Let's look up top, shall we?"

The access door for the roof was nearby. There was no drama walking up a single flight of stairs to the glass door at the top. It was designed to allow visitors to explore the roof of the hotel. She should have breathing room up there.

"Again, as long as zombies can't open doors."

To Blue it was a joke, but something deep in her memory told her to be careful. It was often fatal to underestimate an adversary. No matter how ridiculous the notion.

The sunny skies and warm breeze greeted her with cheer. On any other day, a tour of a hotel observation platform like this one would be filled with smiling faces and running children. The clicks of photography equipment would be complemented by the know-it-alls providing the names and history of the buildings in the St. Louis skyline.

"Here's Busch Stadium. That's where the Cardinals play."

"That one there, that's One Metropolitan Square. It's the tallest in St. Louis."

"And if you look the other way, you can't miss the Gateway Arch. Tallest structure around, topping out at 630 feet. Robed in shimmering stainless steel so it will last forever."

"Pffft. None of that matters anymore. A structure's value is only measured in how well it can keep out zombies. And *nothing* lasts forever."

Her computer interface activated, as if knowing she would need it here.

The roof and platform were unfinished. Construction equipment —including a huge crane anchored to the building—and various types of building materials were scattered everywhere. The hotel was brand new, and sat at the southwest corner of the verdant parkland underneath the Gateway Arch. The vibrant green of the grass and trees met the dull brown of the Mississippi on the far side of the park. The main area of downtown was to her left—the west. A brand new football stadium was north of the Arch, providing a stark contrast to the ancient brownstone buildings nearby. East, across the river, were factory smokestacks, railyards, and dilapidated buildings as far as she could see.

Normally the view would be rated as "spectacular," or "must see," but Blue leaned in despair against the retaining wall of the viewing platform. Below her, as far as she could see in the park, people huddled together, well behind a line of armed men and women protecting them in the park.

Her memory flooded back as the scene before her helped jog some of her missing memories. She fought her way through that swarm, into the hotel, and up to the top level. She couldn't quite recall the circumstances that got her shut into that dark room, but it was trying to come back.

>>Subject: Battle of St. Louis. Computing...

Unlike the data on individual zombies back inside, the interface took a long time to call up the information requested. Blue could sense the mainframe accessing exabytes of data. Geo-locations of tens of thousands of phones. Police radio frequencies. The Arch website. Shipping manifests of barge towboats plowing the Mississippi river. Automotive maintenance schedules of the cars in her field of view. Construction blueprints of the buildings facing the park to her left, and of the Arch directly in front of her. The number of cups delivered to the coffee shop in the lobby of a nearby building. Ballistics data for the .50 caliber shells littering the streets below.

She raised the goggles, on a hunch. None of what she saw on the computer screen was actually happening below. Instead, there was just bombed-out wreckage and countless bodies being picked over by birds. Though the sea of zombies everywhere else was consistent in both versions.

She put the goggles back on, watching what she figured out had to be a replay of what took place down there.

An M1A2 Abrams tank's engine whined in the canyon of the street below.

"Rock n' roll." *That* was a replay she could appreciate.

The lone tank drove through crowds of zombies almost directly below her. Sixty-eight tons of steel crushed the dead as it cruised along the few streets not packed with abandoned cars. Even from thirty stories up Blue could see the armored hulk was bathed in blood as it created a furrow in the zombie horde. It paused and the automated machine gun on top came to life; it punched into the mass of zombies around the tank—those still standing—and elicited more bloodletting. For a beautiful moment, there were almost no upright zombies within a cone fifty yards wide near the slayer. The pause didn't last long. As soon as the engines revved up to move, the inexorable wave of the undead sloshed back into the cleared space, though more than a few tripped or slipped over the entrails of their fallen brethren. Many dropped down to lap up the pools of blood.

Blue's stomach tried to hide.

The tank was the main attraction, but the rest of the park was no less impressive. A cordon had been created around the entire green space. Almost a mile long and half a mile wide, the island of green was filled with refugees. The air carried the lamentation of children, likely afraid of both the zombies at their door and the loud cracks of gunfire keeping the monsters at bay. The police had created a thin blue line of protection around the park. On this side, untold infected. On that side, a remnant of life trying to escape the city.

The computer spewed out information. As she thought about certain elements of the picture, the interface called up facts of relevance. She was catching on.

"Tell me about the bridges. Why aren't people going across to Illinois."

>>Bridges: Order given, General Hodges, II Corps, United States Army. No civilians allowed to transit bridges from Missouri to Illinois. Preventative to stop infection. Additional data: Secret order, General Hodges, from CENTCOM. Terminate groups of 50 or more zombies by any means necessary. Collateral damage of human civilians authorized. All bridges to Missouri to be destroyed.

"That figures."

The computer seemed to return to its original query, listing every piece of minutia it could find in the landscape in front of her. It was too much.

"Computer. Where can I get safe?"

>>Safety. Negative infection. Computing...

Reams of data spun in front of her once more, revealing an answer.

She ran from the north side of the building to the south. The computer had a green haze attached to an MRAP currently plowing through an ocean of zombies.

"So I have to get off this building, get through those zombies, and hitch a ride?" She looked down at her ruined blouse and pants. "And all I have is one lousy shotgun and these bloody clothes." Thinking for a long while, she realized she had the most important survival tool already on her person.

"Computer, show me a safe route."

Her eyes studied the maps and data, absorbing as much as she could on the fly. She was happy the computer showed her a way that *didn't* involve going back inside.

"Time to improvise." In a few minutes, she assembled enough construction rope and fire hose to get her down the side of the building. She threw it all over, but noticed another wire was already hanging down the exterior. It came out an open space only a few floors below. She wondered if that's how she got in.

The thought spun up the computer interface.

>>Path of ingress. Blue.

She watched herself on surveillance cameras. She didn't climb the wire, but instead entered through a window from the roof of the parking garage far below. Another much taller woman entered with her. At the sight of the mysterious woman, an ember of a past life floated by.

"Let's jog Forest Park, huh?"

The next scene showed them sneaking into the hotel atrium. With weapons slung, they carried long metal stakes. They planted them on the floor when zombies ran at them. The tips drove into the skulls. It was bloody business.

They reached the open stairwell; small flashlights were out. Camera after camera showed them ascending. As they neared the top, an interior security camera showed several zombies standing on floor 30. As if they were waiting at the door.

"Impossible. Zombies can't plan." A pause. "Unless someone put them there."

Even watching herself she felt the dread of what was coming. There had to be twenty zombie men and women standing behind that door. Did chance place them there? She couldn't decide—didn't want to believe it was a trap set by someone.

Level 28.

Level 29.

She queried the computer, desperate to jump ahead.

>>Subject: Ms. Juvy Manzano. Status: Deceased.

"Oh sweet Jesus."

At the thirtieth floor, the two of them stepped out. Blue noted she was toting an AK-47 and the other woman—Juvy—carried the Mossberg. She watched the replay as the trap was sprung.

Blue rolled through the door. From one knee, she began firing at the zombies standing ten or fifteen feet away. Juvy emerged from the darkness at about the same time. She swept both sides of the open door, catching the closest zombies before they could spring at Blue. A body fell into the doorway.

The scene went on. They systematically swept the remaining zombies in a well-orchestrated display of gun handling. One shot at zombies close up, the other aimed for those in a ring further away. Together they brought down a considerable number of the attackers with little direct threat to themselves.

The scene shifted. Another camera showed scores of zombies climbing the stairwell. It was a mixture of every size, shape, and state of decay. The snippets of camera footage in the stairwells was a horrible kaleidoscope of zombiedom. Little kids in happy-colored clothes ran with large men wearing basketball uniforms. All rising in the tube of the stairwell. Heading for her and Juvy.

The first of the undead tumbled out of the doorway. The dead body had kept that door from sealing. She remembered it all now that she saw it. She was scared when they came through. They were both surprised. That *never* happened before. The two women on the camera looked stunned. Distracted.

From another camera view, Blue realized why.

"That little bitch." The young woman in the raincoat was there, on the floor below, looking up at the action. She had some kind of hold on her and Juvy.

More zombies tumbled out of the darkness. Juvy snapped out of it first, grabbing Blue's arm and pulling her along the walkway. Toward a room she knew.

The scene shifted to one last camera. Both women stood at the doorway to the hotel room where she'd woken up. Her own figure was trying to hold off the increasing number of zombies coming out of the stairwell while Juvy worked at the room's door. Some crept along the railing, out of their view in the replay, as Dawes had done.

As Juvy opened the door, a zombie from inside met the push of zombies—and the girls—from outside. At the last moment, Juvy tried to push Blue inside and shut the door, but the swarm carried them all in. For a full minute, the scene showed the mass of zombies standing outside, excited at the prospect of food. There was no room for more to go in...

Blue broke into tears. It was clear now what had to happen.

"How did I survive?" She said it without emotion. It seemed impossible.

The computer threw up a crap ton of data, but didn't answer the question. There was no camera in the room. Blue took it to mean the computer didn't want to admit she had asked the impossible of it.

There was Juvy at the door. She had taken the AK-47. She lined up each shot in rapid succession at point blank range, felling the zombies at a torrid pace. It was an impossible display of skill and luck. When she had created a little hole for herself, she turned around and used both hands to pull the hotel room door shut. How many bodies were lying in that space?

Blue fast-forwarded the camera in her mind, getting past the horrible end of Juvy. Her body must have been in that pile outside the room where she woke up...

Her anger at what the zombies had done—what someone had made them do—burned like a tiny sun in her chest. But for now her mission was much more basic than revenge. It was survival. The computer showed her the location of the MRAP moving around the nearby streets. If she timed it right she would have a shot of catching it.

Blue cinched up her pants. She didn't understand who she was, why she went into a hotel filled with a horde of zombies, or how'd she survived. All she knew for sure was she had to catch that truck.

Blue held the shotgun as best she could, and started over the edge. She pulled up the goggles so they wouldn't distract her. She didn't need them anymore, anyway. She could hear the engine of her target.

CAIRO

Liam woke up in a dingy room draped with tacky wallpaper showing little toy soldiers. The small bunk bed mattress sagged sadly as he tried to sit up. The top bunk sagged in a similar fashion above him. He ran his fingers through his wild hair, expecting to pick out pieces of mud and debris left from his swim in the Mississippi, but he was surprised to only find clean hair.

He looked at the pair of cargo shorts he wore—not his—and became concerned that if he couldn't remember a shower or how he got dressed, someone had to have done it for him. He was pretty sure it wasn't Great Grandma.

Well, that's embarrassing, he said to himself.

His arms were sore, and scraped up one side and down the other. Bright sunlight shone through the small, bare, wood-framed window. It drenched his skin as if he were under a microscope. The scratches were souvenirs from his days of travel and survival since the sirens went off...he didn't know how many days ago. The most momentous event in human history and he had no idea how long ago it happened.

Grandma would probably say it doesn't matter. Just live in the day. Or some other platitude that was both generic, and true. He didn't quite have the same knack for positivity she did.

The room contained nothing but the bed and a small desk, with no chair. Several bottled waters sat on top of the desk; they called to him.

As he gained his feet, he felt pretty good. He had a hard time remembering the details now, but he knew he hit his head when he fell on the hood of the MRAP. And then—it got fuzzy. As if to acknowledge his memory, he touched the side of his head. It was tender with a small pliable scab, but he must not have come out too bad if he didn't have a bandage.

The water invigorated him. He downed a whole bottle and reached for another, but checked himself from grabbing it. Voices carried from beyond the room. He went for the cheap brass handle on the wooden door. He had to know his situation.

He opened the door to step out, but once opened, he hesitated in the entry for a long time. The tiny undecorated living room was part of a small residential house. There were many people lounging about.

Grandma thumbed through a magazine as she sat next to a pretty young girl on a squat cloth sofa. A half dozen other people sat on old metal chairs or sprawled on the wooden floor. Most appeared to be about his age. Their heads were buried in tablets, smartphones, and laptops. Many wore headphones, and none looked up at him. The detached companionship reminded him of any number of school functions over the years.

"Grandma," he called.

Grandma Marty turned and gave him a big smile. So did her friend.

No way.

"Victoria?"

She stood up and moved the four paces across the room, and gave him a tight hug. When she pulled away, she kept her arms around his neck as she spoke. "I'm glad you're OK. The wound didn't look bad, but it did bleed something awful. I was afraid you were going to be out a lot longer."

He had a million questions. But only one thing was on his mind in the moment.

"Victoria, you're gorgeous." As he said it, he had a momentary flash of embarrassment. Paying compliments to girls was brand new territory for him, and doing it for a girlfriend in front of a room full of peers was cutting edge. But after all they'd been through together, he had no plans to spend his time navel-gazing about his feelings for her. No one else seemed to care.

She had cleaned up. She wore a perfectly white tank top with a modest neckline. Her shirt bracketed her cheerful silver cross necklace. She wore a pair of dark blue jeans, and even still had his belt around her waist—along with his leather holster, though it was currently empty. She found a relatively new pair of running shoes—they were white and bright yellow. But mostly he was impressed by how well she cleaned up her face.

Almost since they'd met, her face had suffered extensively. First when she was beat up in the Arch by looters, then when she'd fallen after getting shot, and finally when she lost her tooth jumping in a creek. The tooth was still missing, but it didn't detract from her image. Now those bruises were nearly healed and she had a chance to comb her hair and put it into a ponytail.

Her emerald eyes pierced his blues. She stood on her toes, gave him a quick peck on the lips, and separated. Liam was aware again of all the other young people in the room.

And Grandma. He moved to the sofa with great cheer; he sat next to her while Victoria scrunched in on his other side, with her legs folded under her.

"Hi, Grandma. How ya doing?"

"Oh, Liam. I'm so happy to see you all right. You gave us a fright on the plane."

"I don't really remember the flight." He looked around, trying to look out the windows to the street beyond. He saw other houses; his first impression was he was in some beat down little subdivision in the suburbs of St. Louis. "We aren't at Camp Hope, are we?"

"No, I'm afraid not."

Victoria jumped in, "We're in Cairo, Illinois." She pronounced it like care-oh ella noise.

He looked at her and she returned a smile. She was being silly.

Grandma continued. "That's right. The military brought us here, along with everyone who made it from that terrible stadium." She paused while she appeared to swish her tongue around inside her mouth. To Liam, it reminded him of a stereotypical thing an elderly person might do, but he did it himself as he watched—suddenly aware he was still very thirsty. "When the plane was airborne, I thought they were going to open the hatch and throw us off the back. The Marines weren't too happy we helped bring the infected onto the field."

"We killed all those people." He said it, echoing himself from inside the MRAP while still in the city, though he couldn't decide if it was absolutely true. He hoped Grandma would tell him he was being dramatic.

"Well, we did let the infected into the stadium. I guess we have to take the blame for it." She crossed herself.

No, we can't have really killed them. All of them.

He looked at Victoria, hoping she would argue the point, but she stared at the floor in front of them, suddenly very quiet.

Liam kept going. "OK, so we killed them. We didn't ask to be there. We didn't know they were there. We just wanted to survive."

Once he'd said it, he knew what was coming. He stepped on every landmine in their short discussion.

He waited for it, but neither seemed willing to rub it in. "Of course everyone would want to survive. Some would do more than others to make that happen," he imagined they'd say. "And Phil tried to warn us," they would add.

Wanting to move past the ugly truth, Liam asked, "So what do we do now? Grab Mel and Phil and get back to my parents at Camp Hope?"

The strange silence continued. While the rest of the people in the room continued to push buttons and play games, Grandma and Victoria were both uncharacteristically quiet. The fashion magazine idled on Grandma's lap.

"What? My parents are coming here?" He smiled, but he could tell by their faces that wasn't it.

"Come on guys, you're freaking me out. That's not funny when zombies walk the Earth."

He had a hard time looking at both of them, since they were sitting on opposite sides, but he did catch a nod between them.

"Liam, when we got off the plane we didn't find Melissa or Phil." Victoria held his arm as she continued, "We don't know for certain they didn't get off the plane when it landed, but nobody remembers seeing them. They wouldn't just run away. The only thing that makes sense is they never got on in the first place."

Liam had been with Phil almost since the beginning. He'd come to think of him as part of his A-team of survival experts. Melissa had been a good solid addition too. He thought she may even have been more valuable than Phil for her military prowess.

"OK. So we go out and look for them. Scour the camp." He looked at Victoria, knowing Grandma wasn't going to be doing much search and rescue at her age.

Victoria gave him sad eyes. "Liam..."

"What? What am I missing here?"

Holding his arm tighter, "Liam, that was two days ago. You were exhausted. Injured. We didn't want to wake you up for this. If they were here, someone would have found them by now."

He flopped backward into the cushion of the sofa. Now Grandma held his other arm. He felt like his head was spinning, even though he felt fine. He thought Mel and Phil had been harmed by the survivalists back at Camp Hope, but he left before he was forced to see that truth. Then they showed up in the MRAP and saved him, Grandma, and Victoria in the city. And then...

"Two days? A lifetime of things could happen in two days. We have to go look for them. And then we have to find my parents." He said it without conviction. His whole life recently had been a series of rescues. How many more could he endure?

On the other hand, sitting on his butt was the last thing he wanted to do.

2

Liam's compass spun wildly. Here, he was elated to be safe with Victoria and Grandma. Over here, he was angrily accepting that Mel and Phil were almost certainly dead. Finally, as the compass finished its sweep, he was terrified his parents sat back at the Boy Scout camp worrying about his fate.

He reached for his phone. Two days ago, it was waterlogged and presumably broken. Today...

"Um. My phone's gone."

"No, I have it." She pointed to a nearby table. "I charged it for you. They have everything here for techies. I also put it in a sealed plastic bag. For the next time you go swimming with it."

She chuckled.

"It's working again?" he said excitedly. "Thank you!"

He jumped off the couch, grabbed it and removed it from the bag, and thumbed through the screens to get what he wanted. While he worked, he continued, "Victoria, get in there with Grandma. I'm going to take this photo if it—"

For many days he lamented he never took Victoria's photograph with his phone. In the Old Days, he would take pictures of urinal cakes as goofs to send his friends. Now, taking such pictures seemed the height of civilization. But before he could get the camera app loaded, he saw something else.

"Oh no. I have a text message. I'm not sure who it's from."

Victoria hopped up to get a look at his phone's screen. She looked at the message and the phone number where it originated, but said nothing further.

He looked up and saw Grandma with a patient face. As always.

"OK, Grandma, this is what it says, but I don't get it." He cleared his throat as if it were an important radio announcement. "Liam. Need to go to Koch Hospital Quarry. See research." The number was prefixed by the 435 area code. It was from the day before.

"Grandma, did you send this? Like you did the other one." Back at the Riverside medical lab, a strange message had appeared on Victoria's phone, supposedly sent by someone using Liam's phone. Grandma was holding it at the time, though the message could have been sent hours earlier based on how frequently the cell phone towers dropped service.

"Oh, I'm afraid it wasn't me. I don't know how that other one was sent to Victoria either. I only barely managed to contact you, Liam."

It was true enough. She had gotten one message through to him, giving him an X to mark the spot where she was being held captive. It was by far the most important text he'd ever gotten—and it came during a gunfight to boot. But now...

Victoria finally spoke. "I should tell you this town has the internet. It even has cell service, though the people who run the place say most of the other towers are down in the surrounding states, so there aren't really many people to talk to."

"Wait, internet is working? How?"

Victoria sat on the arm of the sofa. "From what I've gathered, this place is a hub of sorts for all the surrounding country. When the zombies came, local governments and some military retreated here and brought as much tech as they could. There's a huge parking lot with nothing but tractor trailers and generators humming next to them. But," she heaved a large sigh, "like the cell towers, there's not much to do on the internet because lots of the cities are completely offline."

Liam wasn't exactly sure how the internet worked, but he knew there were transmission lines between cities which carried data—they were always laying more fibre cable next to highways. But if the cities were dead, there'd be no one to manage the hubs, and with no one to manage those, it was only a matter of time before they either went offline because of power loss or even something as dumb as a zombie tripping over a network cable. Not many techs would be on duty either.

"So we have cell phones but no one to call, and internet but no websites to visit."

Victoria nodded solemnly.

"Children, don't fret. Liam, I'm sure your parents are fine. We're safe. That's what they'd want for you. For you both." She winked at Victoria; her smile was reassuring.

Liam studied the area outside the home's windows. Again he saw the small, squat houses nearby, and appreciated how forlorn they seemed. A few people milled about on the tiny street—there were small weed-strewn sidewalks, but people studiously avoided them. The yards were unkempt, and judging by the age and condition of several derelict cars and trucks parked under huge shade trees, were that way even before the Apocalypse. He peered out as far as he could and saw some multi-story stone buildings a couple blocks over. Mostly he saw grass though. Like houses had once lined the streets, but only one or two out of ten still managed to survive.

Kind of like us.

"Are all these people," he turned to those sitting in the room with him, and quieted his voice, "are we all refugees here?"

Victoria answered, "When we got off the plane, they took you to a large tent. It looked like it was for the Army or something. Most of the Marines from those planes went there too. They all had something wrong with them it seemed," she chuckled, "though they weren't complaining as much as you."

He put his hand to his head wound without realizing it. "Well, I wasn't right in the head."

With a smile, she continued, "They wouldn't let me stay with you, and I needed to take care of Grandma. They walked us all a few blocks from the landing area and handed us off to some town officials for temporary housing. We got in a golf cart and they ferried us here and told us to get comfortable. They said the residents of this street had all gone and we were welcome to stay wherever we could find room. Grandma and I chose this house because...it had the least blood inside."

Liam gulped. His stomach was legendary for betraying him in the sight of blood, though he was getting better about it.

"They gave us some clean clothes, a bar of soap per house, and told us we could get water over at the courthouse. And...we haven't heard anything for two days."

"How did I get here?"

"I ran back and made sure you found your way to me. To us." She pointed to Grandma, though she smiled, too.

Liam didn't want to ask the next question. It had been bothering him since he woke up and it would forever burn bright until he knew the truth.

"So how did I get in these clothes?"

Victoria's face turned red, but said, "What are you, five? Would you rather Grandma got you out of those filthy clothes and cleaned you up a little?"

As he thought about it he came to the conclusion that no, he really wouldn't prefer Grandma handle that particular chore.

As was common with the trio, they all had a good chuckle at Liam's expense.

3

Liam and Victoria left Grandma in the refugee-filled home and walked toward the center of town. Victoria knew the way. He wanted to see things for himself, and she seemed happy to get out with him.

As they walked, Liam tried to reply to the mystery text, but nothing came back.

"I have service. It should be going through."

"Yeah, well maybe *they* don't have service," she looked over to see the phone number again, "in the 435 area code. Where is that anyway?"

Liam shrugged, ready to write it off, until he remembered where they were.

"Hey, I can look it up!" He giggled as he tapped the browser for the internet. With a few swipes and clicks he had his answer. The biggest search engine survived the zombies, so far.

"This is what I've been missing all these weeks. The ability to answer simple questions." He held the screen in front of Victoria's face as they strode down the middle of the car-less street.

"Utah." She said it in a deep voice, as if it revealed a mystery.

Liam brought it back, then looked at it for several paces. "OK, that tells us nothing." He couldn't help but be disappointed, but he didn't know why. He had his answer, after all.

On his mental map, Utah was a veritable black hole. He knew Colorado as mountainous. Nevada had Las Vegas. But Utah?

"I don't know about Utah, but I do know about Illinois." She pointed ahead. "I don't think we're going to get in there."

Ahead of them, at the large stone building being used as the command center for the town, a large crowd of people hovered about. The diverse group appeared agitated.

As they approached the outer fringes, Liam took Victoria's hand. She gave him a smile, then put on her serious face.

"Excuse me," she called to a smattering of people on the outer edge of the crowd, "what's happening here?"

A middle-aged black woman dressed in black slacks and a long-sleeved black shirt with a sequined cat outline on the front answered her call. "You don't know?" She made a pointed effort to look Victoria up and down. "You folks come in here and take our houses and you don't know what's going on?" She ended with a very deliberate "humpf" sound.

Victoria looked taken aback. Unsure. So Liam tried his hand.

"Sorry ma'am. I hit my head and have been in the hospital. My girlfriend has been watching over me. We really don't know."

The woman's mood softened, but just a little. "You two little kids don't have to worry about it, but us older folks do. Food rations is being tied to work on the line. Can you believe that shee-it?"

Liam and Victoria both looked at each other with blank faces.

"Are you kidding me? How long you been out?" She began speaking very fast. "When the Army came in here, the first thing they did was clear half the town and put us all together like sardines. Then they watched us like hawks. Next thing they began burning all the trees north of town. All of them! Finally, they began digging *the line.*" She said it with dramatic flair, but seemed disappointed it didn't elicit a reaction from them. "Oh fine. The line is a big ditch they been digging up north of here to cut across from one river to the next. Ohio to Mississippi. We'll be on an island. Get it? They gonna keep them zombies out of here completely once it's done."

"Wow, that's a really good idea," Liam volunteered.

"Yeah? Then you go up there and dig! I'm too old and tired to be digging holes."

"Ma'am, why don't you want to dig? Isn't it going to protect all of us?"

Victoria added a soft hum in agreement, as if it were perfectly obvious.

The woman turned hostile. "Oh sure. You come in, take my house. Take over my town. Interrupt with all your comin's and goin's with those awful planes. And then you bring those infected people to Cairo's doorstep. Dontcha' know we've been getting' along jus' fine until you'all show'd up." Her dialect seemed to change the angrier she got.

Victoria pulled his hand, moving him.

"Oh yeah! You two gonna go back home and sleep while I gotta dig yo' damned hole!" Other agitated people turned their direction. Many, but not all, were black. Victoria whispered that the town, until the sirens, was a sleepy and predominantly black community.

They moved around the crowd for several minutes, but there was no one in the middle giving work assignments or otherwise signifying someone in charge. As they walked, they saw the crowd was actually a queue, and the line went inside a large three-story building that looked like something out of the 1800's. It was made of large stones, ringed by a low black metal fence, and even had old-looking decorative cannons at the corners of the small patch of grass surrounding the structure. On the backside, people walked out with shovels, and headed north.

Liam wondered if they were going to hand *him* a shovel.

As if reading his mind, Victoria spoke quietly, "I think we better head back. I'm not sure what we can do here. This wasn't happening the last time I was here." They'd gone around the building and came back along the other side of the angry residents. "Though I vote we take a different street to avoid that mean woman."

"Agreed. Though if someone came in and took over my street—" He hesitated as it dawned on him someone *did* come in and take over his street. They were dead when they arrived too. "Follow me."

When they reached the area where the lady had chided them, she was still there, yelling into the air at no one in particular. He didn't know why it bothered him so much, but he couldn't walk away without responding to her accusations.

"Ma'am?" He got her attention quickly, as she'd been eying him as he approached, though she tried to feign surprise.

"You two again?"

"Look, I appreciate what you said. I lived south of St. Louis up until about two weeks ago." Actually, he thought, even that wasn't true. He lived in the city of St. Louis two weeks ago. But the story was the same everywhere. "I lived in a nice little subdivision, a lot like this place," he swept his hand behind him, "but if they're digging a ditch to keep out the z—the infected—you better be out there digging."

She looked taken aback, but he kept going.

"On my street, when the infected arrived, they came by the thousands." He began to speak louder. "First in ones and twos, but they never stopped. And my street was filled with refugees, just like your town. People who came from the north, hoping to outrun the sick."

He was aware a few more people were listening.

"They came into my backyard. They broke through my window. We ran to the basement. They *filled the entire house*. To the brim. Anyone left outside...was dead." He left out most of the grisly details of his rescue: blood dripping through the floorboards, pieces of the zombies strewn over his lawn, the loss of Victoria. "When we finally came out of our home, the sick had moved on. But my house was destroyed. My neighbor's house was burned to the ground. In fact, my whole neighborhood looked like a war zone. And almost no one else survived."

He knew he was exaggerating for effect, but the end result was perfectly true.

"I can never go back home." He paused, amazed that he had a considerable number of people listening. "It was wiped off the map by the zombies."

He felt he had them. Surely the message was clear, though he didn't intend anything more than convincing the lone woman. But she pulled the wrong message from his speech.

"Zombies?" She said it loudly, as if to bring the listeners back to her side. "Look child, I appreciate your fantasies, and I'm sorry your house got burned down, but I'm not scared of no zombies. Nuh uh. Last year I had a robber break in and I shot 'em dead, yes sir. If these zombies make it to kare-roh, you can bet they gonna get what's coming to 'em."

Then, with a flourish she turned away from him and yelled, "And I ain't digging no damned ditch!"

Liam let himself be pulled forcefully by Victoria.

4

They were halfway back to their temporary house when Liam finally stopped.

"All right, that didn't go as planned." He looked at her and couldn't help but smile in her presence.

"What? What's so funny?" A crooked smile hung on her face.

Liam's smile grew bigger. Most of his smile was because he just liked being around her, but a not inconsiderable part was because of what he saw in the yard behind her.

"You know, you may regret joining up with me for the Apocalypse." He nodded to the pile of bikes under the massive tree in the unkempt lawn behind her. "I'm going to take one of those bikes and go look at this ditch they're digging. I'm not going to spend my life lounging in a house like those kids back there and I'm not going to push a shovel either. Not when there are bigger problems facing us all..." His speech petered out.

Her smile didn't diminish. "So, what I'm hearing is that you suffer from ants-in-the-pants syndrome, and it just won't let you settle down and watch the grass grow. Maybe enjoy a lemonade on a quiet patch of backyard? Stuff normal people do?"

Liam wanted to be a writer. He had more or less took an oath at the dying figure of Agent Duchesne that he would document the destruction of the world, if for no other reason than ensure the proper people were blamed when the history books were finally printed again. He couldn't tell a story if he was thumbing a smartphone with other teens, or "shoveling shit in Louisiana" while a war was going on. He would have to give credit to General Patton for that bit, if he remembered.

They walked through the yard and Liam reached out and touched Victoria's side. "You're it!" He took off running through the tall grass, laughing. He made his way to the bikes.

She sauntered along to the pile as he was pulling one out. "Not in the mood for games?" He grinned.

"You'll know when I'm in the mood for games, mister." She was stern, but she was seldom able to pretend to be angry or mad, which was something Liam loved about her.

Fortunately, the bikes they selected hadn't been there for very long. The tires were low, but not flat. Liam didn't even flinch at the need to ride a bright lime green women's cruiser. Victoria's was pink.

The town of Cairo was smaller than he thought it would be. He could see most of it by looking in all directions along the gridded road system. The central building they'd just left was about midway between the north end of town where there was some kind of metal gate, and the south end of town where there were lots of trees. Beyond and above the trees he saw two metal-trussed bridges. It was a mystery where the bridges went, or what they crossed. He assumed it was the two rivers.

Riding through the town, he saw many more refugees. If he didn't know they were there, he might have missed them. Most were faces inside the dark interiors. Hiding.

Others were bolder, like them, and stood on the stoops or walked in the nearby yards. Some waved. Most kept to themselves. By and large, they were white with a few rare other assorted races, leaving Liam to wonder whether the woman back at the building was telling the truth. Did all these people come in and kick the native residents to the curb? He didn't doubt it would be done by "the authorities," but the biggest question was why. Why go through the trouble of kicking people out? Why not just have refugees live with the natives?

Once again he turned introspective, remembering how he felt when those refugees came up his own street. Or when they were on the highway. Everyone wanted the refugees to *keep going*. For several minutes, he churned the pedals as he followed Victoria.

She pointed to her left. "Let's go that way. It looks like there's a way to get up on that levee."

The levee wasn't obvious from inside the town, but as they neared the edge he was struck by how big it was. It was basically a miles-long huge pile of dirt, covered by grass. "It looks like a prison wall. The town is a prison."

Victoria replied, "With walls like this, I wonder why they need to dig a ditch?"

Liam had no idea.

The grassy slope was too steep to ride. They hopped off and pushed their steeds up the incline. With a huff, Liam pushed his onto the flat gravel service road on the ribbon of levee above the town. Victoria was a moment behind.

"Wow," he said.

She repeated him as she saw the same thing.

They were at the highest point of a narrow peninsula. From his position, the levee road receded into the distance to the south, toward the two large bridges. Looming large to the West was the Mississippi River. The ugly brown water moved fast. He could see that from several hundred yards away, across some newly planted farmland.

"What in the heck is *that*?" She pointed to a side channel of the Mississippi river. It was about a mile long and completely filled with barges, barge towboats, and smaller watercraft. At the head of the inlet were two bright white towboats pushing drifting boats and other debris into the protected harbor.

"It looks like they're junk collectors," he replied.

Across town, to the east, lay the Ohio River. He couldn't tell if the locals had a similar operation on that side, but it was similarly filled with barges, towboats, and a multitude of other boats.

Victoria pointed north. "Let's go up that way." She didn't wait for an answer, she just started riding.

"Hey! Wait up." He jumped on his bike, steadying himself as he tried to get the pedals moving, and rolled after her.

He didn't catch right up. She was pumping hard to stay ahead of him. She turned back once with a wry smile, daring him to catch her.

They both laughed as he rose to the challenge and tried in earnest to catch her. The sub-par inflation of the tires and the uneven surface of the gravel road made it hard going for both of them. When they reached the junction where the levee going north met the one crossing the north boundary of the town, Victoria stopped with a skid.

Liam was only a few seconds behind her. "I was going to get you," he shouted with joy.

The mirth drained away when he saw why Victoria had stopped.

She turned to him. "I think we found *the ditch.*"

He took in everything and had a new perspective on the geography of the town. It was bracketed on three sides by the waters of the two big rivers. The land pointed like a finger to the south. At the very southern tip, the two bridges spanned each river. On the north side, where they held their bikes, the levee provided one layer of defense against the farmland and patches of forest to the north. However, the authorities had taken it several steps further. The levee was the first layer. About a hundred yards north of the massive levee was a similarly impressive trench. It was filled with heavy equipment and hundreds of people with shovels. On the western edge, where it would have met the Mississippi, men were crawling over large wooden beams drilled up and down in the mud. It was a check dam to keep the water out until the ditch was ready. Liam could see the plan was to create a type of moat in front of the levee. On paper, it was a very formidable barrier of entry to the town.

North of the ditch was a swath of destruction of charred and barren land. The woman had mentioned burning. All the trees and vegetation had been stripped from the land—giving the defenders clear visibility up to the interstate miles to the north.

All told, this town had used its unique geography to maximum effect.

Liam reflected on every book about zombies he'd ever read. No matter how strong the fortress, no matter how dedicated the watchmen...

"I give this place two weeks."

5

Victoria gave him a knowing look. "This is where you tell me what you're thinking, right?"

He laid his bike on the gravel, and tentatively felt his head wound after it was down. "Did you know today was my birthday? When I checked my phone earlier I noticed a little reminder." He walked off the pathway to sit on the upper incline of the levee, facing the Mississippi and the workers at the ditch. He spoke as Victoria did the same.

"I've decided I'm going to be seventeen from now on." He looked at her as she sat next to him. "Do you think people will believe I'm seventeen?"

"Why? Why seventeen?"

He took a long time to look out over all the work being done on the defenses of his new home.

"Because of *that*. Because of zombies. Because of people like Hayes. The survivalists. The military. I can't be a kid anymore. This place, this situation we've found ourselves in—it requires someone older. And, because no one is going to be checking ID in the Apocalypse, I figure I can get away with it."

He'd made the realization about identity many days ago. He just never imagined he would be one to capitalize on it.

"Well, I *guess* it makes sense."

Feeling the need to justify himself, he continued, "That woman back there, she's wrong. She can complain all she wants about digging and losing houses. But you've seen them in action. If the zombies come through here in the numbers we saw in St. Louis, even the ditches won't help them. Then she'll wish she'd been out there to make the ditch a foot wider or deeper, instead of causing trouble."

He pulled at some grass, then turned back to her. She was very close. "I hate to admit this, because I've spent two days in recovery, or whatever, but I want to leave. I want to find my parents. I want to—" He slid his phone from his pocket and showed it to her. "—find the reason for this text message. And to do that...you and I can't get stuck in this place handling dirt. The woman did have one thing right: there's no way she should have to dig if all those people in our house are just sitting around playing video games. That won't last long. When the military comes calling, we need to be gone."

"Hmm. Well, then it sounds like we have a few pieces of housekeeping to take care of before we get started." She coughed to get his attention. When he turned in her direction, she notified him of her intentions by puckering her lips.

When their kiss was over, she pulled away with a broad smile. "That's for the big one-seven. Happy birthday."

Thinking fast, Liam shot back, "Actually, why don't I say I'm eighteen instead. Happy one-eight?" He puckered his lips, but she gave him a mock slap on the cheek instead.

"No way you're getting past me. If you're gonna be eighteen, then I'll have to change my age to nineteen. Pretty soon we'll both be thirty and I don't want to age that fast."

She tried to fake a stern look, but relented under his puppy dog eyes. "Oh alright. I'll give you one to grow on."

Liam and Victoria kissed for a length of time well short of what he wanted, but given the hard labor being done on the fields below them, he grudgingly admitted she got the time exactly correct. They both stood to leave.

"Wait a minute."

"We should leave, there's a truck coming." She pointed the direction they'd come from. A white pickup truck was slowly driving along the gravel road on top of the levee. It was still far down the line.

His phone was already out, so he had no problem calling up a map. Much of the internet was down, but luckily he was able to access the map service of one of the largest online search engines. In fifteen seconds, he had what he was looking for. "Wow, the internet is fast when no one's on it."

"Koch Hospital Quarry. That's what the message said." He paused, looking at the data. "Oh crap. I know this place."

He held up his phone to show her, but she didn't recognize it. He pocketed his phone and talked as they gathered their bikes.

"Let me take you back in time...oh, about two weeks...a young boy and his hot, overdressed Apocalypse Friend took a ride on a train to escape St. Louis. Ringing any bells?" He knew it would, she was there. "And on that train ride, they happened upon a pit quarry where cars drove off the nearby highway into a loop the loop going down into the mine—"

He was trying to be funny, but made a sad observation that tempered his humor. He ended it abruptly with, "—it's the place where Jones died."

They walked down the inside slope of the levee, into town.

"The place was crawling with zombies. You really expect to go back there?"

Liam thought about the irony. They took a train out of the city on a rail line that ran along the edge of the Mississippi River. Later, they paddled a boat up the river right along the same route. The big difference was they were too exhausted paddling the boat to dwell on the fact they had been there before. Now, the thought of going back to the place Jones sacrificed himself by driving a large dump truck over the zombie horde wasn't sitting well with him.

"I don't want to. Thinking about all those zombies from that train ride gives me the creeps. But we know the zombies have been moving around, called by the sirens downtown and then chased out again when they shut off. We might be OK."

Liam expected her to point out the weak link in his plan: "might."

"Well, step one of your plan was kissing me. What's step two?" She paused, but caught herself. "And you can't say kissing again." She laughed as she sat up on her bike, ready to pedal back to the house.

"In that case, step two is finding weapons and food. Step three is finding transportation north. Step four is..."

As they rode and discussed their goals, he realized how flimsy the whole thing sounded—when spoken out loud. On the thinnest of clues, he was going to head out into the wilderness with his girlfriend, on the off chance something was going on at the very quarry where he witnessed thousands of zombies attacking living people trying to escape the city. At best, they might find clues as to the origin of the plague as the text message suggested. At worst, they might find themselves dead.

None of the alternatives were attractive though. Being put to work, used up, on a futile effort to forestall the zombies from kicking this place into the river. Or put in prison. He wondered if he was a wanted man by the Marine Corps.

As he rode, the part of his brain where he compartmentalized the concept of "hero" spilled out into his psyche. It tended to get him into danger, but he looked into the small homes as he rode by. Each was filled with refugees from somewhere else. Memphis. St. Louis. Cincinnati. And he couldn't help but think each and every one of them was going to die soon, unless someone did something more than dig ditches. They need someone to be the hero.

He wanted to be the guy to look ahead for them. See the big picture. He could think of plenty of examples of literary heroes even younger than him. He wasn't just going sit around and wait for someone else to be heroic for him.

Thinking back to the crowd complaining about the digging, and the crowd of wretched people already doing the digging, he understood that just because there was a Zombie Apocalypse in progress, it didn't mean everyone magically joined hands in a mutual effort to survive. The old problems remained: mistrust, allocation of dwindling resources, self-defense, food, water, power, internet. There were ten thousand things the good people of Cairo, Illinois had to deal with on any given day. All of it was tactical—local.

Liam thought of himself as a strategic thinker. His books all said the hero would have to break out from the rest of the population. It would take someone with foresight to save mankind by finding the cure.

It isn't down in that ditch. But maybe it's down in a quarry.

He tried to convince himself it was a hero's plan.

GHOSTS OF THE COLONEL

Liam was willing to travel anywhere if he thought there was a chance they'd learn something new about the crisis afflicting the world, but he liked to have as much intel as possible when he put his life on the line. The text message was cryptic, to be sure. The only other possible clue was the data chip he carried—

—he slapped his pocket, worried the photograph had been taken when he...was stripped...of his old clothes. Victoria had indeed replaced it.

Phew.

He'd been thinking about the data chip during their bike ride and was struck by something so obvious he'd almost missed it.

"When we get back to our house, we should see if any of those guys have a laptop we could borrow. If we can find one with a card reader, we might be able to read what's on the colonel's data chip. Then we might know more about what we're dealing with."

"Sounds good!" Victoria reveled in the breeze as they cruised through the squat houses of the residential area. He let himself go, just a little, and simply enjoyed his time with her having what, in the old days, was called "fun."

By the time they reached their destination, Liam had already prepared his speech for the other kids inside. As he laid his bike in the grass in front of the house, he noticed some downed branches and small trees on the side of the property.

"When we leave we can check out those trees to see if we can make some spears. They look like the size we need." Victoria nodded as she parked her cruiser.

"And also," he continued, "if we find a laptop, and if it has a card reader, and if we can borrow it, we should go somewhere private to look at this." He patted his pocket. "As much as I would love to get a group of friends to go with us to investigate that mine, I don't want to be responsible for anyone."

He saw her look. "You are all I can handle."

"Handle? You think you can handle *me*?" She hopped around the back tire of her bike and stretched out to capture him, but he sidestepped her and started to zig zag across the yard. She gave chase and for a few moments they ran in crazy circles, laughing and giggling.

It ended when Liam slipped in the tall grass, and Victoria tripped and fell over his legs. They both ended up on their backs as they caught their breath.

"Oh man, we're going to have chiggers out the yin yang," he said. He looked at his legs below his cargo shorts. The grass was thick and unkempt.

"Chiggers?" she replied.

"You don't have chiggers in Colorado?"

"You mean mosquitoes?"

"No, much worse." He stood back up, sticky with sweat, and brushed his exposed lower legs. She wore jeans, so she focused on her arms. "Everything is always worse, these days." His mood turned sour. "We can't even enjoy five minutes of fun anymore."

"Hey." She looked at him while she held her arms in front of her so he could pull her off the ground. "I had fun on our bike ride. That was nice."

A tour of our zombie defenses; every boy's dream.

He smiled, partially mollified. It *was* fun. Her smile cut through almost all his other worries, save one.

"Do you think Grandma will be safe here? Will she be OK without us to look out for her?" He scanned the neighborhood. A few people walked up and down the street; they looked lost. He imagined each house had a similar group of strangers trying to get a handle on what they were going to do next to survive. His path led back to St. Louis, but Grandma's days of travel were likely over, at least until she had both reliable transportation and somewhere safe to go.

"I think you worry too much, Mr. Peters." She gave him a playful push and took off around the side of the house. He was left standing there. An older couple happened to be walking the street nearby and he felt their eyes on him. They gave him a little wave.

He returned a clumsy salute, then gave chase.

2

Victoria volunteered to go inside and secure a laptop. It took her about five minutes and she came out and sat down on the back porch steps next to him. She handed him a very thin silvery model.

Liam's expression presented a question for her.

"I just flashed my eyebrows and a young lad about your age surrendered his laptop for me." She giggled playfully.

He had no idea whether she was telling the truth. The look on his face said exactly that.

"Oh Liam, you're too gullible. Do you think I'd do that?" She didn't give him time to answer. "No! I told Grandma what we needed and she asked the other kids. A youngster gave up his laptop for her, along with this funny card reader, just like you asked. Lucky, huh?"

He tried to mask his naivete with a laugh. He truly had no idea what she was capable of doing with her charm, though he had no doubt she could make a formidable opponent when she put her mind to it.

"OK, let's see what we've got." He pulled out the chip from off the back of the photograph. He punched it into the tiny card reader, pulled up the hard drive, and saw it was filled with video files. He was tempted to start at the end, but decided if they were going to honor the man's memory, they should at least view them in the order he'd labeled them.

The first video showed Colonel McMurphy at his desk inside the dingy tent where Liam had originally met him. He was the administrator of the Elk Meadow research camp. In the video, he had set up the camera in the back corner of his tent so it put him in the center of the frame, but whoever sat at his desk would be in the frame too, facing the camera. His first reaction was to wonder if his first visit was in this list of videos somewhere. Was he that important?

"Test. Test. Test. I'm Colonel Rufus McMurphy, recording this for anyone I deem important enough to need to see it." He laughed like he just told a sad joke, then stood up and moved toward the camera, apparently to turn it off.

The video was short and sweet.

The next one was just as short.

"I don't know how to use this video editing software, so I just have to put whole movies into my folder. The next video is when I first met Ms. Jane Spencer. Health and Human Services."

Liam had heard that name before. When he saw her on the video, he knew for sure.

"Our friend, Jane!"

"Shh!" was Victoria's reply.

In the video, the red-headed woman walked into the tent wearing a white button-down blouse, with the top couple buttons undone—not unreasonable given the apparent temperature in the scene. She also wore a long black skirt and a military-style cap which looked completely out of place.

He'd never seen Jane wear clothing like that, so he thought it was kind of funny. "Wow. She's dressed like she's in a music video."

Victoria elbowed him to be quiet, but he heard her laugh too.

Jane walked in and reached across the colonel's desk to shake his hand. She leaned over, giving the colonel an inappropriate view down her shirt.

Victoria gave a curt whistle. "Wow, she's workin' him."

"Welcome to the Elk Meadow Camp, Ms. uhhh?"

"Spencer. Jane Spencer. HHS." She held his hand for a moment, looked pointedly in his eyes, then pulled back. "Thanks for inviting me here."

"Please, sit down. I'm afraid we don't have all the creature comforts yet, but we do have chairs."

She took a seat.

"Colonel, I'll get right to it. I'd like this camp to be the first fallback position for our main operation in downtown St. Louis. As you've been briefed, we're expecting a large number of—let's call them immigrants—who will be residing in our—hotel—down by the Arch. The facility is very secure, so don't concern yourself with worry there, but we can't control what happens in the streets outside that facility and it could make operational security of our personnel very difficult. I like to plan three steps ahead in everything I do, and I believe having this delightful country retreat as my first fallback will be advantageous to us both."

"Both?"

"Of course. You see, my group has access to all manner of government equipment. Even some cutting edge stuff they haven't sent out to you Army-types yet. If you take care of protecting my refuge here, I'll provide you with as much gear as you require."

"That's very generous of you. I guess HHS is pretty much running the show now, huh?" He tried to be friendly about it, but Liam detected a deeper question there.

"Strictly speaking, I'm not with HHS. More of an adjunct working with the Centers for Disease Control, but for the purpose of placing me in an org chart, HHS is close enough. I was told I could count on your team to execute our mission though; does that sound right?"

Liam saw through her conniving ways. Did the colonel?

"Yes. I've been instructed to give you every accommodation here."

"Thank you, Colonel, I really appreciate that. But don't worry, it's not like I'm going to take your air conditioned tent or anything, I'll just be looking for a dry space on a rainy day. I can depend on you for that, right?"

"Won't be a problem." His tone was neutral.

"I'm going to leave one of my assistants here to discuss the details with you. I have to be getting back to my main office to continue the preparations there. Time is growing short." She paused for a moment, studying the colonel, as her demeanor changed from pleasant to inquisitive and then back to jovial. "However, in the next week or two, I insist you come downtown to see what we're doing. I think you are the type of man who would like to know what he's fighting for. And fighting against. Deal?"

The colonel nodded.

"Work it out with my assistant." She stood up and moved closer to his desk. She held her arm out for a handshake, and waited this time for the colonel to reach across his desk to her.

Liam spoke up. "Did you see that, she made the colonel lean over to shake her hand. She put herself in charge." None of it came as a surprise. Hayes and his wife had run around like they owned the Apocalypse. It was because they were part of the National Internal Security organization, or were, and literally *could* do whatever they wanted.

She was gone in moments.

In the video, McMurphy slumped in his chair. He picked up the same photo he would later give to Liam. He held it as long as he could until one of his helpers walked in.

The video ended.

3

Liam's finger hovered over the button to start the next video. "So we know Jane was over the colonel, but this doesn't really tell us anything new, right?"

"Not that I can see. Let's check out the next one."

The colonel began with another introduction video. He was at his desk. "I'm not proud of this next one. I acted like a teenaged boy, but it's important I show the world what we're dealing with."

The intro ended and Liam clicked the next one. Instead of a view from the corner of the tent, this one was obviously a hidden camera. It looked like it was a view from the front of the colonel's face. Liam could imagine a camera on the rim of his cap, or possibly on a pair of glasses. The scene re-focused as he changed directions with his head. It opened with him walking behind Jane inside the Riverside Hotel. Liam and Victoria both knew the place as a dark stinky place full of zombies, but in the video, it was bright and fresh.

"Welcome to my secret lair, colonel. Moo ha ha."

Spencer was laughing hysterically and pretending to pet an imaginary cat. She wore another white blouse, and with the improved camera quality, Liam could see it was wildly inappropriate and revealing. She also wore a tight pair of khaki shorts.

Victoria had no comment on her obvious flaunting of her...assets...in front of the colonel.

"Oh, lighten up. I'm just having some fun."

"With all due respect, there's nothing fun about this virus."

Spencer switched gears in one fluid motion.

"Shall we get right to it?" Her alternating demeanor was unsettling. Taken with her dress code, Liam wondered if she was trying to keep the older man off balance.

She began walking across the large open room. Liam recognized it as the top level of the hotel.

"Colonel, what do you know so far about the virus?"

The colonel had to talk to her back as they both walked.

"I'm afraid we know very little. My camp has had a few potential infected, but they all turned out to be carrying the actual flu, *influenza*. I've not seen the Doomsday Bug. Not sure I would know it if I saw it."

"Yuck, I hate that name. It should have been named something cool like Terminator Flu or The Fifth Horseman. Something Apocalypse-y. Don't you think?"

He said nothing.

"But OK, whatever. I'll show you the virus. Stay with me through here." Spencer had crossed the room and plunged down another stairwell. It was very dark. She was just a shadow in the video. Liam's eyes had yet to adjust to the switch from daylight to this. He had just about adjusted to total darkness.

Without warning, the colonel ran into something. The camera rattled and flickered.

"Oh, sorry ma'am!"

He had run right into her backside.

"Mmm hmm. The lights in this stairwell aren't working. This is our floor."

He followed as she went out into the well-lit floor, the camera struggling to adapt to the changing brightness. The colonel's camera observed everything on each side, as if he were trying to avoid looking at the woman ahead of him. Other men and women in military uniforms walked around on this level, though none were close. They were on a circular walkway looking out over the wide open interior of the tubular hotel. Again, Liam had recently been in that exact place, though he didn't know what floor they were on.

"My team has been busy in several parts of the world, doing research on this thing. Trying to get clues on its origin. How we might contain it. So far, zip."

She walked along the inside railing, dragging her hand on the metalwork, giving the colonel the opportunity to look over the side with his hidden camera. More workers were on other floors, moving here and there. On a floor very near the bottom, the video showed someone in a neck collar with a long pole attached behind them, being pushed along by two helpers. The person was covered head-to-toe in some kind of mesh wrap. Hard to say for sure from so high up, and the video was unable to clearly identify the situation beyond that.

"What are they doing down there with that man?" He pointed down. She looked over the side as she walked, and answered in a distracted fashion.

"Ohhh, they're probably bringing in another flu victim. Finding a room."

"Ma'am, are all these rooms filled with the sick? Are we safe here?"

She giggled slightly as she replied, "Don't be ridiculous. Even we don't have the resources to fly in that many sick people from across the globe. No, we put a score of the newest victims down on the lower levels. Up here, we keep a few special cases, like the one I'm about to show you."

He tried to stifle his own laugh, but couldn't prevent it from coming out.

At that, Spencer stopped and turned around. She looked right into the camera.

"You think what we're doing here is funny?"

Struggling to regain himself, he replied, "No, ma'am. It's just that if you were bringing these sick people here—well, you've got them in the middle of the city. Surely you see the huge risk you're taking? This is the plot of a bad horror movie. Why aren't you sending them to my camp out in the country where their ability to escape and do harm is minimized? I have a ten-foot fence around the entire place and soldiers prepared to defend it."

"You military men are all the same. Always thinking about the fight. Do you have any idea how many bombs have been dropped overseas trying to squelch outbreaks? How many tanks have ground the infected to paste to reduce the spread? Satellites. Aircraft carriers. Stealth bombers. All manner of killing. And do you know how much that military thinking has helped the cause of mankind?"

"Right here." She held up her hand, making the symbol of zero. "Squat. Sure, maybe it bought you and me some time to prepare our Last Will and Testaments, but the reality is no one will be around to read them. And do you know why, Colonel? Can you think beyond the bullet?"

She took a step back.

"Camps. Cordons. Cities. It won't matter. But maybe I'm being unfair. You don't know what humanity is dealing with. Well, I'm not gonna tell you. I'm going to show you. This isn't patient zero—we've had no luck finding that prize—but this might be patient 100 or 1000. Close enough to the beginning to expose the flaw in your mindset."

She pulled out a key card and moved to a nearby door. The colonel and his camera followed.

"Get yourself together, old man. What I'm about to show you is going to cause you to soil your pants. I hate to be so blunt, but you'll have to prove me wrong."

Liam was on the edge of the seat to see what was inside, but the colonel's camera drifted with Jane as she opened the door and walked with it.

He's checking her out.

Liam struggled to understand why the colonel would be drawn so obviously to the attractive woman—knowing he had a wife and son—but he remembered the girl in the nightgown in the rail yard as well as the strange attraction some of the zombies had on Victoria on floor twenty. Perhaps the colonel was similarly affected.

As the door opened, she drifted with it.

"*This* is where the infection will take humanity."

When she was concealed by the heavy and very open door, the colonel seemed to be released from her spell and he turned to focus on the big revelation.

He looked into the wrecked room, and saw the plague victim standing inside the darkened space.

"Oh my God in Heaven."

4

Liam didn't know what he was looking at. It was obvious to him it was a zombie, but it was unlike any he'd seen since the sirens. He wore a military uniform of some kind, but it had been muddied and bloodied, making it impossible for Liam to identify. The thing's skin was plastered to its bones, as if it had no muscle mass. The skin, where visible, was black.

"The eyes," the colonel whispered.

Off camera, the voice of Jane answered. "Yes, the eyes are haunting, huh? We haven't quite figured them out, but we know they can sense living humans, even in their...condition."

Liam could stare because the colonel was staring. The zombie had no eyes in his sockets, but he—it—seemed to look directly at the camera. His arms and legs were bound in heavy chains to a large metal box behind him. The beds had been removed from the room.

"Where...where did you find this one?"

"Funny you should ask. This is a local—found him down in a quarry of all places. We call him Twelve." Liam hoped the colonel would ask about the name, but...

"This man looks—"

"Dead? Yeah. The infected like him are pretty much dead."

"So, my camps have to prepare. How do I cure *this*?" He shook his head in the video. "No. This has to be some kind of mistake. A prank. Right?"

Liam appreciated that Jane had seemed to keep him off guard whenever they interacted, and she did seem to have a twisted sense of humor. Maybe this was an elaborate prank. Some kind of initiation for the grisly business they'd soon be doing.

"Can I have your sidearm?"

The camera turned to her, then with a series of shakes, it displayed a man's hand holding a large pistol.

"I'm afraid it isn't very modern. I've had this 1911 since I entered the service."

"Oh yeah? When was that? No, I don't care."

A series of loud bangs resonated in the camera's audio, though they came across as impotent pops on the tinny speakers of the laptop. She was shooting the zombie in the chest. Liam didn't count how many rounds she'd fired, but in moments, the camera panned from the zombie's chest to her outstretched arm with the quiet gun, then back to the zombie. Either she'd run out of ammo, or had proven her point.

"You still think this is a prank?" she yelled.

Liam knew both their ears would be ringing.

"Lord help me, I don't. What *is* that?"

"It doesn't scare you?"

He seemed to consider. "I, uh..."

"Let me put this another way. Do you think I should have sent this to your happy little village, now that you've seen it?"

Liam was impressed. The colonel had no response to her relentless attack.

After a few moments, Jane began talking in an almost-normal voice.

"Colonel, I showed this to you, but I want you to know there is almost no one on this continent that knows what you now know. Can you imagine if this *got out*?" She'd said it in a funny way, as if she was goading the old man.

At last, he seemed to regain his composure. But as before, the colonel only went for the questions of consequence. "Why are you showing me this, Ms. Spencer? This isn't about camps or cures, is it?"

She laughed. "You want to know something funny? You had it exactly right. The cure to these things is bombs and grinding under tank treads with extreme malice. The rest of your Army is doing that overseas. Giving you, me, and other scientists the time we need to prepare our country for what's ahead. I brought you here, Colonel McMurphy, because I need to know I can trust you. It's going to take men of your caliber to bring us through this plague and I don't have time to run an extensive profile on you. If I felt you were someone I couldn't trust, I might have just shoved you in the room with Twelve here."

The colonel's camera panned to her face. It was deadly serious, but at the extreme end of an awkward silence, she cracked a smile.

"I'm joking, of course! Health and Human Services would revoke my parking pass if I did that. I mainly wanted to see if you would freak out on me." She turned serious. "Sir, if there's one thing we need, it's people who can follow orders without freaking out. When these things show up in your camp, you are going to need a steady hand at the helm. I need a steady hand out there. Can I count on you?"

The camera turned back to the zombie in the tattered uniform. When he began speaking, he did not look back at Jane.

"Yes, you can count on me, ma'am."

The video stopped.

Liam set the laptop a bit off to his side, and turned to Victoria. "So the colonel knew about this all along. He knew there were these dead—things—out there, but he never showed one to me. He never even mentioned it. He seemed to be focused on..."

He looked out into the yard. It was vibrant green. Alive.

"The colonel stayed focused on curing the other disease. Hayes and Duchesne said there were three viruses out there. This dead, whatever it is, creature is not the same as the zombies we've been seeing all over St. Louis. Or Chicago. Or anywhere."

He recalled the Riverside Hotel had each floor labeled to signify which city the zombies had come from. Hayes said they were different depending on where they found them. But which floor had this particular zombie been on?

"He said something about the regular old flu being the first virus. Then a modified flu virus was the second virus. And finally, the third virus was more like Ebola. But what virus can bring the dead back to life?"

He laughed, going back to his books on zombies. Just when he thought he'd come to terms with the presence of blood-sucking zombies, he was faced with the textbook definition of a zombie. Now, even after seeing it with his own eyes, he had difficulty accepting such a creature existed.

A small window popped up on the screen, asking him to confirm the update of some piece of software. He tapped the no button, then returned to the window containing the videos.

He clicked the next one.

5

It was another introductory video, back in the colonel's tent.

It began with a long pause. He sat at his desk turned away from the camera. Liam couldn't tell for sure, but he believed he was looking at the photograph of his wife and son.

"This next video is what this is all about. Ms. Spencer probably didn't know that I'd figured out where that soldier had come from. She said she trusted me, but I'm sure she didn't fully trust me if she didn't give me the courtesy of telling me the origin of a man who had so obviously been found near a military cemetery. But she'd given me enough. He was U.S. Army, but his uniform was from World War II."

In the video, he turned to the camera as he swiveled his chair.

"Susan, I hope this video reaches you. I think you are the only person who would believe I'm not pulling an elaborate hoax when you see this. I need someone to know about this, or I'll go insane. I'm going to do everything I can to send all these videos to you, and you can decide who needs to see them. You have these videos, the Mile 444 files, and all the research on the more recent infected I could put on this datachip."

The video flicked off.

"Liam, is he talking about the same quarry?"

"Yes, there are one too many coincidences about that quarry. And it's next door to the Jefferson Barracks National Cemetery. That's the exact kind of place where one might find a soldier dressed in World War II garb. Though I have no idea why he would have been found in the quarry."

"Well then, that's where we need to go. This proves it. Those people were doing something down there. We just need to find out what." She seemed chipper.

"You seem to be enjoying this. Did you see the same video I did?" He laughed, but it was insincere.

"Oh yeah, zombies, zombies, and...oh yeah, zombies. So what's new? Look, Hayes and Jane and whoever else they work for are obviously up to no good. You said it yourself. We can either stay back here safe and snug until the zombies come for us, or we can throw ourselves into the impossible task of going *out there* to take the fight to them. They already shot me once. I've got eight lives to go."

I still don't think we watched the same video.

Her enthusiasm took the edge off what he'd witnessed. She had a knack for that.

"OK then, let's see what we're in for..."

But the screen was frozen.

He tried to push the mouse around with the tiny touch pad, but the computer had locked up. Over the years, he'd probably seen ten thousand computer lock ups. He pressed the power, waited several seconds, then pressed it again so it would restart.

"You're right. I am anxious to get out there and figure this out. The colonel was frightened by the sight of the zombie, but other than being way uglier than the zombies we've been dealing with, it didn't look any worse."

He bumped her with his shoulder as the computer beeped during reboot.

"I have to admit, I'm so glad we met. I'm so glad you stuck with me throughout all those weeks of running around and confusion. I wouldn't want to go back out there without you."

He looked at her face, longing for another excuse to kiss her, but the computer was back on the desktop, waiting for him to do something. He almost found the willpower to turn away from her, but she grabbed him.

"Liam, I'm not blind to the danger. Deep down I'm scared to death of what I saw on that movie, and what's out there. Zombies. The dead. People like Duchesne and Hayes and the NIS. But I'm more scared of sitting here and dying with this whole happy town. I'm scared of being told to dig in the mud until the guns run out of ammo. I'm scared of starving to death. I'm scared of pretty much everything."

She touched his elbow with her fingertips.

"So don't take my willingness to seek out danger as recklessness or, God forbid, a suicidal streak. I'm glad too, that I have you with me. We aren't quitters."

He turned back to the screen, biting his tongue as he felt himself get emotional.

She's willing to follow me into the circles of Hell.

He imagined the spiral road of the pit quarry as just that: Dante's nine circles. The rest of the world was the tenth circle...

Finally, the computer was ready, as was he. He called up the file browser, and searched for the data chip once more. He was sure he'd gotten himself back, but was puzzled by what he saw on the screen.

He pulled the data chip out, then placed it back into the slot.

Still, what he saw was not right.

"Um. I think we have a problem."

He clicked the keys, moved the mouse, and cycled through menus. Finally, after many long minutes and several queries by Victoria, he knew what had happened.

"Our data just got erased."

Victoria, not one for cussing, simply said, "Well, poo."

OXBOW LAKE

Liam set the laptop aside and looked out into the yard. He felt as if he'd just been scammed and had his bank account drained. There wasn't a thing he could do about it.

After a suitable reflection period, he spoke up. "We have to go there. To the mine. It's got the answers we need. We know that much from what we saw."

They discussed logistics for a long time, then got into the details. Liam felt better, despite the erasure of his data, the more they talked about tangible advancements of their plan.

"What do we use for weapons?"

"I don't think anyone is going to hand us some guns," though he recalled people handing out guns back in the early days, at the Arch. "We have to get to work making spears. I want us to have something to defend ourselves with if we go back out there."

Victoria seemed to take it in stride. She got up and scoured the yard for the type of straight wood they'd need for a spear. He was pleased to see she didn't need to be told what to do. He looked for his own while they chatted.

"You know, you could stay here. Watch over Grandma." He said it with as much nonchalance as he could muster, though he definitely wanted her to come with him so he wouldn't be alone.

"Oh really? I thought she was going with us." She said it while looking away from him, into a dense bramble. She was in the process of yanking out a large downed branch that had been in there for a long while.

Could they take her up the river, over to the...No, it was madness. He was absolutely sure of that.

"I know you're joking, ha-ha. We can't risk taking her outside the wire again unless we have both a tank for transportation and a destination defended by an army." He laughed. "No, she stays."

He pulled out his knife and got to work on the branch. He felt it was adequate for a nice-sized spear. Victoria dragged over her find.

"Too dry. You need one that isn't so brittle." He could see the wood was too old.

In time, they both found the pieces they needed and Liam got busy with the whittling. They sat under the shade tree as he worked.

Fifteen minutes later, he was satisfied with his creation. "Here we go. My first Hope Spear in Cairo, Illinois." He bent the dialect, just as she had earlier. "May you never need it."

Fat chance of that.

He passed the spear to her, taking her raw stick to begin work on the companion. As he put his head down, he lost track of time. When he looked up, Grandma was sitting inside the screened-in porch, watching them.

He waved, and Victoria's eyes followed to see who was inside.

An awkward silence passed between all three. Finally, Grandma cleared her throat, then began, "I can tell you two are thinking about leaving."

He looked at Victoria with a little smile. Her face said, "She's got us."

"It's OK, I know. I just know. I see these kids inside," she nodded toward the interior of the home behind her, "and I see you two out there. The difference is night and day. I have to say it doesn't please me to see you go, but someone has to do it. I missed my chance by a few years." She gave a hearty chuckle. At 104, she probably missed adventuring by a few decades, though that didn't stop her from being active during their escape from St. Louis.

Liam increased the speed and pressure he applied to the spear now taking shape out of the raw wood. He felt his emotions reaching up to him. He didn't want a sloppy goodbye.

"We'll leave tomorrow. It's getting too late in the day to be doing anything silly like walking out of a walled fortress into—"

He checked his bravado. He wanted to be brave for Grandma, but that was hard to do when there were so many monsters outside. He could claim to be unafraid of what was out there. Explain how prepared they were. But none of it was true, and she of all people knew the truth. On paper, it *was* really dumb to leave.

"—into a world run by people like Hayes and Duchesne." Somehow it felt less intense to think about the dangers posed by men than it did the mindless and insatiable zombies. At least men can sometimes be reasoned with.

"I understand. I'll be praying for you. Do you know how you'll get up north?"

That was a hurdle he'd hoped to tackle tomorrow. There had to be convoys or something going north. Cairo wouldn't have cut themselves off completely from the rest of the country.

But before he could explain what he didn't know, a voice called out from the nearby bedroom window of the house. It was the same room Liam vacated earlier in the day. He thought back and recalled the springs of the bed above him were depressed. Someone was sleeping up there...or listening.

"I know how you can get to St. Louis. But you have to take me with you."

It sounded like the voice of a child, though the dark shadows of the backyard made the face in the window nothing more than a vague outline.

"I won't say anything more unless you promise."

Liam looked at Victoria. She shrugged, mirroring his own thoughts.

He put on the appearance of thinking about it for many seconds while he whittled, but knew he was going to agree.

He felt the drama in the moment, so went with it. "We'll be a terrific traveling triad."

As he waited for the girl to come out, he realized how stupid it was to accept someone into his group, sight unseen. A proper fighting unit, in the spirit he was used to with his online game *World of Undead Soldiers*, included people with diverse skills so any encounter could be tackled by the special abilities of the team. Division of labor, and all that. What skills were they about to pick up? That question was better answered *before* the invitation to join.

Liam did not feel warm and fuzzy when Grandma called out, "No, it can't be *you*!"

2

Liam knew her. It was the girl he'd saved from the top of the MRAP. She was black, but fair skinned. More of a mixed race. She had her hair tightly pulled back in a ponytail. As she turned in the large screen door to talk to Grandma, he could see her hair went all the way down to her waist. It was wound in braids and had an ostentatious blue bow near the top.

"You got a problem with me? Why can't it be me?"

Her tone was forceful, but not malicious.

Liam stood up, holding his spear. It was almost done, except it didn't have a deadly point yet. He wanted to get a better look at the girl. At that thought, he turned to Victoria to see her reaction. She was intently watching the screen door too.

When he rescued the girl from the roof of the MRAP, she hadn't said anything. He was able to coax her from her hiding place, then he fell, then she ran away. Seeing her again forced him to try to recall details about her, but he couldn't. All he could remember was that she was soaked head to toe in blood and appeared small. Nonetheless, the fact she was unable to get herself to move to save her own life did not inspire confidence.

Grandma looked out the screen to Liam. Her face illustrated a question for him, but he didn't know what.

With a sigh, she turned back to the girl. "I saw you in my dreams. I saw you climb from underneath some dead bodies in a pitch dark room. I saw you running from the zombie inside the Riverside Hotel. I saw you looking out over the army of infected down below. I saw..."

Liam could only watch as Grandma appeared to strain hard to remember. He had no idea what she was talking about, or how he could help her. He motioned to Victoria and they both closed the distance to the screen door.

"Oh, I don't know. I kind of lost you after that. But I saw you when Liam got you down off the MRAP. You left him lying on the ground. You ran to save your life. Not his."

The girl turned to Liam. "This is your Grandma, right? Is she messed up in the head?"

Liam vigorously shook his head in the negative.

"Hmm, well she seems messed up. I don't remember any hotel. I think I would remember waking up in a pile of bodies, don't you?" She too seemed to strain her face, searching for a memory, just as Grandma had moments earlier. "But I..."

She turned to face Liam and Victoria through the screen. Liam got his first good look at her. She was about his age—an older teen. She'd been given a bright green pair of jeans; he knew they weren't hers because she had been wearing ripped slacks when he rescued her. The one thing he noticed on her body was all the scratch marks. He assumed they were caused by the other survivors up on the roof during the fighting for position up there.

She was short. She appeared as a normal adult height while standing next to the hunched figure of Grandma, but she was probably quite a bit shorter than Victoria. Under five feet. Her hair was jet black and pulled tightly back over her head, the blue bow peeked from behind. Her face was round and pretty, with soft eyes.

"I can't remember how I got on top of that truck. I just kind of woke up there." She looked at her arms. He could see all the scratches on them, even through the mesh of the screen. Her face had lots of small scratches too, though they weren't as serious.

"And I don't think I would have left you lying on the ground. I just didn't see you."

Victoria made some kind of sound in her throat.

"Look, I'm from St. Louis. My sisters are there. My family is there. I'd really like to get back." As she spoke, she opened the screen and stepped through just as a small orange tabby tried to escape with her.

Liam watched with amusement as the cat pawed at the screen, though his attention returned to the girl when she walked right up into his personal space.

"Please. I'll be quiet. Just get me to St. Louis and I'll get out of your hair."

He wanted to tell her flat out she wasn't going to go. She'd left him on the ground...

Or, maybe she's telling the truth. She didn't see me.

His head was a wreck when he fell off the truck, so he had no idea if the girl was telling the truth. There *was* a lot going on during the evacuation. And, he couldn't overlook the fact she said she knew how to get there. For all her shortcomings, she was one step ahead of him.

"If we go with you, how do you plan to get us there?"

"Oh no, that's not how it works. I tell you now, and then you run off and leave me. That's how it happens on TV."

Liam hadn't thought of running off, but he allowed he might have done it in this circumstance.

Victoria stepped closer to him, too. "You can go, but Liam's in charge." She said it with a commanding tone he'd not heard before.

The two girls studied each other. Liam felt immediately uncomfortable. But it only lasted a few seconds.

"Believe me. I'm no leader. Just bring me along and we'll all be happy."

The girl smiled at Victoria, and she mimicked the emotion, but her eyes told Liam the full story. A wary distrust. He knew trust was a rare commodity these days. There were just as many bad people using lies to get ahead as there were good people willing to believe those lies. He took the opportunity to remind himself to ration out trust like water in the desert.

Liam took a step back, to get himself out of the girl's space. "OK. How soon can we leave?"

She turned to him with a genuine smile. "Get your sleep. We'll leave first thing tomorrow. We'll be in St. Louis by dinnertime."

Liam doubted there was a home to return to, or that they could reach St. Louis in such a time frame, but nothing was perfect anymore. He knew better than to argue.

She was walking back inside when Liam realized he'd overlooked something important. "Hey, what's your name?"

The girl stopped at the door. "My name's Blue."

3

The morning went by in a whirlwind. Liam woke to find a piece of paper had been placed in the collar of his shirt. It simply said to walk east until he reached the water. Blue would be waiting. It ended with a time: 9:00 a.m.

He spent a few minutes saying goodbye to Grandma. The previous night they'd had plenty of time to catch up, share details of their stories over the past few weeks, and prepare for their time apart. Victoria was by his side the whole time. They separated with a warm three-person hug.

"We'll be back as soon as we can, Grandma," were his final words.

He arrived at the docks walking hand in hand with Victoria. When he first saw Blue on the deck of the boat, he was impressed by how delightful she looked. She wore a light blue short-sleeved top with some kind of ruffles on the ends of the sleeves. She still had the same green jeans, but they fit her very well. She got lucky. His own cargo pants required him to super-tighten his belt to hold them up. Victoria's jeans—blue—fit her very well too.

For just a fraction of an instant, he imagined that Blue liked him and was going to try to wedge her way between he and Victoria—bringing drama into their already over-dramatic lives. But the thought receded as quickly as it surged. There was no way on God's green Earth he was going to betray what he had with Victoria. He'd die for her. They'd even agreed that one day—when the current crisis ended—they would be happily married together. No amount of pretty girls was worth the one sure thing in a world of infinite chaos.

He tightened his hand around Victoria's and pulled her to him. He'd evidently surprised her.

He tucked his spear under his free arm so he could hold her with both hands. "I don't know what lies ahead, but we may not have an opportunity to be alone for a while. I want to tell you that I'll be there for you. If you're taken again. Shot again. Dragged away by zombies or bad guys. I will die trying to get to you."

A wide smile. "Why Liam, that's the nicest thing any boyfriend has ever said to me." She was being playful, then turned serious. "But the world is so dangerous I think I'd rather someone tell me that instead of something sappy and romantic."

He thought that was a rebuke. His eyes must have betrayed him.

"No, no. I didn't mean it like that. The only thing we can count on out there is each other. I mean it when I say no one has said anything nicer to me. I've never had someone I can...count on...absolutely like I can with you. Looking back at boyfriends in my life, I don't think any of them would have been able to hang with you in the Zombie Apocalypse. Makes me wonder what I saw in them in the first place."

He didn't think he was anything special. He certainly wasn't that strong. He wasn't a genius. He wasn't a fighter by nature. Most of what made him "special" was his desire to *not* be a dope in front of her. He worked extremely hard at that.

They briefly kissed and then separated before they walked up the ramp to the boat. It was irrational, but he hoped Blue saw them together. He couldn't afford the distraction, but having a pretty girl on his arm stroked his ego in a strange new way.

Is this what married men feel like?

As they reached the boat, he pledged to stop thinking such thoughts and just focus on the mission. He tried to look at it as a military operation.

First, travel. Second, find the quarry and get inside. Third, do something. He called it X because he didn't really know what he'd find. Then, his plan went into the weeds: do Y and Z and then somewhere down the line get back here to Grandma and report the findings.

And it all started with the pretty girl.

No, she's just a girl, not pretty. At all.

"Hi guys. Welcome aboard," Blue said with great cheer. "You can lay your weapons up there," she pointed to open floor near the front. Some other gear was stowed there.

"Thanks."

The boat was about thirty feet long. It had a large compartment surrounding a couple seats right in the middle. A steering wheel and radio equipment was on the dashboard in front of the right-hand seat. The other seat was on the left side of a small aisle to the front of the boat. There were buttons and levers on a dashboard panel in front of that seat too, though its function wasn't obvious.

As he looked around, Blue continued, "This is a Corps of Engineers service boat. They use them to inspect survey markers, buoys, and other equipment up and down the river. This one makes a regular run up to the north, and then it comes back."

"How the heck do you know that," Victoria asked.

"Hospital. I went in with you." She smiled at Liam. "I met the captain while I was there. We got to talking. He lost his partner a few days ago." She looked around at the sound of someone approaching.

"Here he comes now."

The man was a caricature of a salty old sea captain. He was tanned to the point of being cooked. He wore a loose button down shirt that may have been a Hawaiian shirt at one time, but now was faded almost to white. His jeans were covered in grease or something grease-like, though he evidently tried to wash it out from time to time. The large work boots and faded camo boonie cap completed his ensemble.

He had thick facial hair which was mostly gray. His thick eyebrows sat above his angry eyes.

"You said you were bringing soldiers." He looked around dramatically in front of Liam and Victoria. "I don't see soldiers."

"Hi. Yeah. I said I would find fighters. These two pulled me out of the city. See? Fighters."

The captain gave a distasteful look at Liam. He gave a too-long look at Victoria. The sirens in his head began to spin up.

"Well. I guess if they rescued you..." He looked at Blue, and Liam noticed his eyes flitted here and there over her figure. He ran over a mental checklist; a reference dive into his post-apocalyptic literature. Was this going to be the guy that offed him so he could float down the river with two young women as his prisoners? It had happened before, though he couldn't think of a specific instance from his books to give him guidance.

But he had to pull up the big boy pants. He gripped his spear a little tighter. "We may not look it, but we *are* fighters, sir." He didn't think he quite had the hang of projecting an aura of competence in fighting, though he certainly felt confident of his fighting abilities if Victoria was at risk.

"I'm Liam, and this is Victoria."

Oh man! I should have used fake names.

The captain seemed to appraise him once more, but gave him no clues as to his conclusion. Instead, to Blue he said, "All right, girl. We'll go north. But if one of them things gets aboard, they better earn their keep." To Liam, he only said, "The name is Jam. Go sit down."

Evidently manners were a forgotten art on the water.

4

The boat, dubbed *Lucy's Football*, cleared the moorings and the captain seemed to take it slow while he went over some gauges inside the enclosed work area he had in the middle of the boat. There was no room to sit in the front, and Liam wasn't invited into the enclosed cabin, so he chose to stand in the back of the boat. He hung on to a tie-down just outside the plexiglass windows of the captain's area. Blue remained inside with the captain, leaving him alone with Victoria.

She stood next to him at first, but the captain came out and yelled at them to split up so they weren't both on the same side. "You're weighing us down on the starboard," he said in a loud, gruff voice.

Victoria stood on the opposite side, facing Liam. "Are we gonna have fun, or what?" she asked with a big smile.

"Always something to do in the Zombie Apocalypse."

He knew they were going on a dangerous journey, but he couldn't help him but try to take the edge of their nerves by trying to be funny.

"Yarg! You young whipper-snappers are jammin' me garbage scow. Your whale of girl be weighing us down!" He pretended he was smoking a pipe as he spoke, and he and Victoria both laughed. Already thinking of what to say next, he turned to see a motion in the window next to his head. The captain was scowling at him. Liam froze where he was, hand up to his mouth and all.

The captain cracked open the small door. "These walls be not soundproof." Far from being a good-humored response, his face displayed real disgust, seemingly out of proportion to Liam's antics. He slammed the door shut once more.

He was still frozen with his hand at his mouth. He swiveled his eyes just to confirm the captain was looking away, and then he pretended to take one final pull on his imaginary pipe before putting it away. The dual outboard motors throttled up and they both had to hang on as the boat accelerated into the huge waterway.

The most prominent feature of this part of the river was the number of barges. The entire shore was lined with them. As they cleared the other ships near the dock where they launched, the river was almost solid with the rust-red and dull grey shipping barges common on the big rivers of the Midwest. Either every barge captain for a thousand miles decided to dock here, or these people collected barges like trophies. It made for a jaw-dropping introduction to the journey.

The boat raced out into the middle of the channel, heading for a large bridge crossing the Ohio. He'd seen it while in the town up on the levee. It was graced with metallic girders and was painted an ancient sea gray. As they closed the distance, he could see a few people walking the roadway up there, but there were no vehicles in sight. Above it, there were huge sea birds darting in and out of massive nests placed on top.

The far side of the river looked like a popular gravel bar during a college fraternity float trip. Hundreds of barges had been run up onto the shore to keep them from floating away. The only thing he didn't see were coeds dancing up on the mud banks next to their boats. Instead, there were serious-looking men tying off huge ropes or driving excavating equipment to make more room for more barges. Several dredging barges were pulling silt and mud from the riverbed to improve the clearance of the towboats pushing their cargo into parking spaces.

He wanted to ask the captain what all this was about, but he also wanted to keep his mouth shut. As they went under the bridge, he began to understand the scale of the whole operation. The Mississippi river joined with the Ohio at a great junction and full and empty barges were parked over every square inch of that intersection. There were more tows pushing barges in ones and twos as they came off the Mississippi. They pushed them into the parking lot on the Ohio side.

Liam couldn't see any pattern to their machinations. From water level, all he could see was the sides of barges almost 360 degrees around him. Barges were twenty deep on each side of the river.

"Amazing, isn't it?" Victoria spoke loud enough to be heard over the motors.

"What do you think it's all for?" he retorted. It looked like a massive recovery operation, though he wondered what was inside all the thousands of holds. When he was at the top of the Arch, he watched a barge pass by laden with infected souls standing around like they were on a sunset cruise. Did they end up here?

Then he thought of all the barges which broke through the blockade of debris back up in St. Louis.

"Hey, do you think Duchesne's body is here somewhere?"

"Oh. I hope not."

The man had been killed by a barge. It would be fitting if he did end up here.

The Mississippi wasn't quite as filled with barges. They seemed to be using the Ohio side as the corral for all the loose livestock. However, as they sailed along for a few minutes, it became clear there was a complex operation on this river too. They'd seen it from up on the levee the day before.

On the right, there was a long, thin island covered with trees. There was a narrow strip of water between the island and the shore, which Liam imagined was the pit lane of a race track. It was filled with the metal barge cargo haulers. When they reached the far end, Liam was impressed with the recovery operation guiding rogue barges to the safety of the small passage. A few pleasure boats drifted down the river too, and the smaller tows pounced on them like herding sheepdogs.

The larger tugs waited nearby for larger runaways. Others worked their captured boats into the pit area as he watched.

He counted at least ten tugboats operating in the waters near the mouth of the recovery zone. About half of those were the larger tugs designed to push heavy loads on the riverways. There was clearly still a lot of loose boats floating from the north if that many boats were still netting them.

The last thing they saw of Cairo was the dredging operation for the anti-zombie ditch. Much of the dirt for the hole was stacked on the south side of that excavation, presumably so the defenders would have clear fields of fire on any zombies that somehow cleared the scorched flatlands to the north and made it into the ditch. If they managed to survive that long, they'd have to climb the formidable southern bank and then continue up the pile itself.

He turned around to see if Victoria was seeing the same thing. "Do you think that ditch will hold off the zombies?" They'd discussed secure bases before, but Liam always referenced his zombie literature when the subject was broached. His research would say there was nowhere on Earth that was safe from the zombies. But he hoped some places were safer than others. Cairo seemed pretty prepared, and he was willing to revise his previous guess that the place would last only two weeks. He allowed they might make it for longer.

When she didn't answer, he turned to face her. "What?"

Victoria looked at him with sadness. She shook her head no. "The zombies will make it in. Maybe one of these barges will tip over and spill hundreds of them onto shore. Maybe just one will float from upstream and shake himself off in town. Maybe one is already there, just waiting for someone to open the wrong door. I just don't think anywhere is going to be safe until every one of those things is dead and buried. Or burned."

She turned to look out her side of the boat.

His enthusiasm for Cairo's chances waned. The ditch was impressive and the cooperation it took to get it in place was a bright spot in the otherwise blight-stricken world of the plague, but in the end, she was correct. The length it survived was secondary to the fact it *would* fall.

With her back to him, he spoke, but only to himself. "I think you pulled exactly the right lesson from my books. You didn't even have to read them."

5

Liam and Victoria got tired of standing in the hot sun, so they each took a seat on the rear deck, facing each other from opposite sides. They could speak if they needed but, for the most part, they were silent as the boat plowed the waves up the dirty river.

Several times along the way, they'd feel lurches to either side as the boat swerved around and through debris or runaway barges. One item in particular bothered the captain enough to leave his cabin and stand on the back deck as the boat idled. They all stood and watched as a huge tank of some kind floated by.

"It's a propane tank. A big one. A fifty-foot whale!" the captain said. Then he said he'd have to call it in to the teams in Cairo so they didn't miss it.

It gave Liam a narrow window of opportunity to talk to him. "Why are they collecting all that stuff?"

The captain paused, seemed to consider a response, then continued inside. Blue, standing in the doorway, spoke quietly. "They're trying to gather supplies, instead of letting them drain out into the Gulf of Mexico." She closed the door, choosing to stay inside.

Liam broke the rules. He walked over to Victoria.

"Why do you think she's staying inside with him? Aren't we better company?"

"Well, I am. But you? You *did* make fun of the captain after all." She winked at him.

He huffed. "Well you laughed too," he said with a fake hurt voice. Then he thought better of it and moved back to his side of the boat. There's only one rule when taking a boat ride in the Zombie Apocalypse: don't piss off the captain.

A few hours went by with nothing to do but sit and nod off. The sun was high overhead when the motors' pitch changed and the boat slowed. That got them both off their feet.

The captain piloted the boat into another small side channel off the main river. There were no structures or anything man-made anywhere in sight. Liam's mind was filled with years of video games, movies, and books about dangerous times and dangerous men.

"Is this the part where we get killed? We are about as far away from other people as we can be." Then, with a fair bit of drama added, "There are to be no witnesses..."

Victoria laughed, but she looked at him with serious eyes. She looked into the cabin to get a sense of what the captain was up to, but the tinting and bright sunlight made that difficult.

All they could do was watch as the channel began to narrow. In a few minutes, they came around a small bend and approached another, larger, boat that was anchored in the middle of the creek or small river they'd been touring.

More thoughts bounced through his head, speaking only of trouble. They could be gun runners, deviant hillbillies, a secretive medical team —it wouldn't be his first, or maybe it was simply the angry sea captain's club.

The motors were a dull hum as the boat drifted twenty or thirty feet from the other.

Panic swept through Liam's over-active brain as he realized his only weapon—his spear—was in the front of the boat. He'd have to pass the captain to get it.

"Or, he tossed it over the side while we weren't looking," he thought. That would be a hilarious end to his ill-planned mission. "Death by stupidity."

He moved over to Victoria's side, aware he might be chewed out again. Maybe he would push her overboard so they could swim to safety, though the chance of that succeeding were slim when a motorboat was involved.

A few minutes went by and Liam's fear was being bested by his curiosity. To Victoria, he said, "Either kill us or get on with whatever you're doing."

Almost as if on cue, the captain came out of his cabin. Blue stood once more at the doorway.

The captain walked up to him, sharing some of his bad breath. "When we pull up alongside them, I need you two to grab the ropes and hold us in place. I want to make this handoff quick."

"Handoff?"

"You two aren't going to give me trouble, are you?" He reached into a large pocket in his pants. There was something blocky. He started to pull it out.

Liam tried to step backward, but he hit the starboard motor. "We don't want any violence, captain, sir."

The man's hand paused. He looked down at his pocket as if seeing the situation for the first time. He laughed quietly.

Then he pulled out the object. "Reach for the sky," he said with a raspy voice. The banana rocked in his hand and tilted toward Liam. "I know you two aren't going to give me any trouble at the oxbow gas station, right? Cause if you do—" He pointed the banana and made a "pew pew" sound at both of them.

Liam's heart exited the highway of insane fear and decelerated to the normal operating fear he felt all the time. He'd have to think of a way to stop seeing every situation as a trap designed to capture or kill him. Not everyone in the world could be out to get him.

Just some of them.

The fuel transfer operation proceeded without any kidnappings, shootings, or fights between crews.

GRANDMA DREAMS OF PINK

Grandma watched the refugee kids in the living room of the house. They had managed to spend the entire day with their technological devices—phones, tablets, whatnots—while she did nothing but sit and stare out the window into the lonely town of Cairo. More people were coming in as refugees, she assumed, because they were led to this or that house on the street. A few teens found their way to her house, making her wonder if she'd been placed in the wrong home. She was older than everyone else by 80 or 90 years.

She was refreshed for the middle of the day, but felt the drift toward a nap nonetheless. It was as if her body wanted to turn itself off. Another side effect of aging. Or...

The familiar engery surged through her body. Another dream was coming, and she wondered if it would be as horrible as the last.

In the middle ground between awake and dreaming she was dismayed to see the same girl as before.

I should never have let Liam go with her.

2

Ten days since the sirens.

Saffron slammed the door shut, a second before the first zombie made contact with the glass. She felt the steel vibrate, but could be sure of one thing—there was no way through. Needing confirmation, she turned around to look out the small view port into the near-darkness through the glass. More of the undead were stacking up behind the first. She was breathing as if she'd just finished a race, which wasn't far off the mark. She'd just climbed to the top of the Gateway Arch.

"Thank you guys—" She spread the words around her deep gasps for air.

Unless the zombies could organize themselves and pull the door open, it would be impossible for them to get through. That, at least, was good news. Beyond the first landing, there could possibly be thousands of zombies on the stairs of the north leg of the Arch. Two or three for each of the 1076 steps. The bodies of her fellow survivors were lying on about twenty of them.

"—for getting me to the top."

The banging and moaning of the zombies faded as she walked the final steps to the summit of the Arch, out of the tram-loading area. The light from the observation area was a powerful magnet, drawing her out of the darkness. Her legs screamed at each of those final steps. She choked back the sadness to stay alert. Even so, her adrenaline ebbed. All she wanted was to lay herself down and go to sleep.

She froze near the top. Ahead, a lone figure; a silhouette staring out the tiny window. Saffron was unable to tell if she was alive or dead. It didn't matter in the end because she had no weapons.

"Hello?"

The woman gave no clue to her condition. Saffron chanced a few more steps up the slanted deck of the topmost segment of the Arch observation platform. The small windows on each side of the walkway gave her enough light to be sure the woman was alive.

"Are you OK?" As she said it she knew it sounded insane. Of course she wasn't. Nobody was.

The woman was dressed in blue jeans and a light t-shirt. She was covered in the detritus of hand-to-hand combat with the plague victims. Saffron looked down at her own clothing. The gray capris had become red with blood splatter. Her button-down shirt suffered from the same abuse. She unbuttoned it and tossed it back down the canted floor behind her. Her own t-shirt was glowing white compared to the woman's.

She moved behind the her, intending to look over the top of the Arch to see into the south leg tram loading area, and was disturbed to see the woman held a pistol at her side. She kept walking to give the woman some room. There was something wrong with her, beyond the background noise of despair and fear everyone shared.

"My name's Saffron. What's yours?"

The woman remained stone-still as she looked down through the observation window. Saffron looked out her own window, thinking of better times when she was here. In normal times, parents would be holding young children as they lay on top of the slanted windows. She leaned down to get a better look.

Outside, she saw...

"It's the end of the world." The woman spoke in almost a whisper.

"Ain't that the truth." The lush green grass and remaining trees of the park below clashed profoundly with the dead bodies, surging zombies, and running groups of survivors fighting for an extra minute or two of life. To the west, as far as Saffron could see, crowds of infected crammed the streets of downtown St. Louis—heading to the last people left alive in the city. "But at least they'll die out in the sunshine."

Saffron turned back to the stranger, and tried to engage her once more. "I'm Saffron."

After another minute of silence, Saffron brought up the big guns.

"Where did you go to high school?"

The young woman turned to look at her, but remained silent. Saffron took it as a positive sign. "I went to Northwest. You?"

"Where did I go to high school?" It droned out of her, and she seemed to think hard. "I went to Ursuline Academy. I graduated...a few years ago. Why does it matter?"

"I'll tell you why it matters. I know who you are. You think I'm a hillbilly from Jefferson County who shops at Walmart, and I think you're a rich snob from the suburbs who shops at the Galleria? Am I right?"

She tried to be cheery with the stereotypes of St. Louis—she meant it as a joke. It was normally a safe ice breaker. Instead the woman began to sob.

"It's all gone, isn't it? Walmart. Galleria. High school?"

The gun hung like damp laundry at the woman's side. For the first time, Saffron understood what was going on here.

"No, they aren't *all* gone. I was part of a group. There's help out there. What's your name?"

"Christine." She spoke like a robot.

"Well, Christine, it looks like we both made it to the safest place in St. Louis, huh?"

Christine slunk down against the wall below the windows. Saffron sat down on the other side of the tight space, facing her.

Christine explained her situation. "We thought that, too. What was safer than the Arch? My boyfriend and I live downtown—lived—and he was determined to get us here. We found some of his friends, and some other people along the way, and made it to the south leg down in the museum. The doors were blown apart at the bottom, and we were fighting the whole way to the top. The men were armed with shovels and a few guns. They sacrificed themselves to protect me and other women. Eventually, it was just me. I shut the door at the top just like you did." She sniffled. "So who's coming to rescue you?"

Saffron considered sugar-coating it, but couldn't come up with anything that would ring true. Instead, she shook her head in the negative. No one was coming...

Christine set the pistol on her lap, as she silently cried.

Saffron stood up to get a view out the east side. She'd heard through the rumor mill the Army was patiently waiting on the eastern shore, but she saw no evidence over there. If they were over there watching all of her friends die, including her, she was going to be very angry. Unable to decide if she felt better or worse in not seeing the military, she resumed her own survival effort.

"Christine. Is there any way to get down the south leg? You said there were zombies following you. How many?"

The woman looked up to answer, but just shook her head. Tears streamed down her cheeks.

"There has to be another way down."

"There is." With a shaking hand, Christine pulled the gun off her lap, and vaguely pointed it at her head. "I'm going out on my terms. When I'm ready. I'm not going to die of thirst in this coffin."

That's what it was. A sealed stainless steel coffin. Saffron figured they'd both die and be preserved for eternity.

"Hey, your boyfriend wouldn't want you to give up, would he? My —friends—wouldn't want me to give up either. We have to keep trying."

Christine slapped the gun down in her lap again. It was the kind of careless gun handling which got people killed. "Look around. Do you see any doors we can use? Both legs are filled with zombies. The tram cars aren't operational. What else do you want?"

"To live," she thought.

She studied the interior of the observation deck. It was remarkably bare. The only blemishes were the bloody footprints from her own shoes and long-dried smears of blood here and there. The windows didn't open of course...but it gave her an idea. Moving to the very apex of the Arch, she noticed a square on the ceiling above her. It was about as wide as a man, and it gave the lone clue what it was for.

"Hey, help me up so I can reach this." She was pointing up as Christine looked at her. "I think this pops away and there's a door to the outside."

With wild eyes the girl focused on her, and began to laugh. "Are you serious?" As a response, Saffron jumped up as high as she could, and pushed the square covering. It popped out of its channel, revealing something above it. A hatch was up there.

Instead of jumping up to help, the girl merely pulled her knees up to her chest and put her head down. She continued to cry. Saffron was about to write her off completely when she froze. The girl had stopped sobbing and froze as well. The floor panel beneath Christine's feet was *moving*.

"Oh, Christ. They're under us."

Every twenty feet or so on the curved walkway, pieces of the metal were bending upward. *Things* were trying to push them upward.

Christine jumped up, and the panel nearly popped open. The eyes of the zombie peeking through were enough to get them both moving.

"Help me." Saffron was forceful, but tried to remain quiet. Christine grabbed her around the waist as if to lift her, Saffron pointed out that though they were both small women, she was stronger. She would lift. Her back strained in the effort, but they only needed an extra foot or two so she could pull the ceiling panel down, and then see about the top hatch itself.

She couldn't look up, as her strength and focus was entirely on lifting. Saffron could hear the growing moans of the zombies sneaking through the gap beneath them. They became agitated once they knew the girls were above them. Banging under the floor also grew louder.

"Oh shit. There's a padlock on the round hatch."

"Of course. Can't have a tourist stepping out for a smoke," she thought.

"Can you shoot it out?" It worked in the movies, so seemed a worthwhile thing to suggest.

"Put me down. I can't."

She didn't want to drop her. She wasn't sure she could lift her again. With an "oomf" she let her down. The floor panels moved in several areas. The one closest to them was almost off. The zombies were relentless, but not remotely smart.

Christine showed her the gun. "This is empty. I spent them all coming up."

"I thought you were going to kill yourself." She said it without emotion, wishing maybe there were two bullets in the thing.

"Yeah, I probably would have been dead before you arrived if I had bullets left in the clip."

Saffron resisted correcting her nomenclature. It was just a steel boat anchor now.

"Hey! You can use it to beat the shit out of the lock."

They both looked at the gun as something brand new. Saying nothing, they both got back into position. Saffron heaved. Christine began to attack the lock.

The first panel flipped completely up. It was just a little bit too small for the zombie to easily climb through. It must have been slinking under the floor and wasn't able to bend enough to get out. But it would eventually. It was able to contort in ways beyond a normal human body.

"Bang bang bang." The gun battered against the lock. Saffron was afraid to ask for status reports. The banging was its own report.

"Please hurry." She was having trouble holding the girl up.

More panels popped. Hands and arms began reaching up from the floor in many spots. A zombie had emerged from a panel far down the walkway, nearest the tram station on the south side. It was on the smaller side. An infected young boy.

"They're coming through. You have to hurry."

"This lock is really tough. I don't think—"

Saffron tightened her grip. She willed Christine to break the damned lock.

"—I got it!"

Both tumbled to the floor as Saffron's arms gave out. The lock bounced down the incline of the floor.

"Give me the gun," she commanded.

"But it's—"

Saffron took it from her. She stood and walked toward the small infected person—she couldn't use the term "child"—as it moved in her direction. She swung the butt of the gun with as much force as she could muster, ending at the boy's cheek. Her first swing broke the jaw but took another horrible pair of cracks to damage the head for good. She stepped around the grabbing hands of the crawlers as she made it back to the hatch.

"Get ready. I'm going to lift you to the top."

Christine moved as instructed. Other panels were completely off. The biological hazards below were straining in unnatural ways to free themselves from the conduits.

Saffron put the gun in her waistband, then made as if she was going to lift the smaller woman.

"What?"

Christine looked up through the hatch. "What are we going to do up there?"

There was no time to consider whether it was a good idea. It was the *only* idea that would allow them to stay alive.

"Sunbathe." She said it as calmly as she could.

"Sunbathe?" A long hesitation. "Yeah, OK."

She grabbed the other woman around her thighs and hefted her up. Christine was able to gain leverage on the hatch, but Saffron had to really push her to get her through.

From above, "Oh my God. It's windy up here," she yelled.

"Yeah, well, as long as you aren't getting bit," Saffron grumbled to herself.

Another zombie had snaked out of the subfloor. It appeared to be a small-framed teen boy. He'd lost his shirt along the way, but his black chest and side was drenched in fresh blood. A recent victim of the virus —probably from the crowd directly below.

It gained its feet as Saffron jumped for the hatch. She was able to grab the outer lip, but she panicked as she realized she couldn't pull herself up. Not after the exhausting climb and fight in the stairwell coming up. She hung for a second.

"Think girl. Think!"

"Are you coming up?" From above, Christine seemed oblivious.

"Yeah, why don't you come down and lift me up," she muttered softly.

She pulled out the pistol, intent to do harm to the teen boy. She was getting slow, however, and her swing was a second too late to make solid contact with the zombie's head. Rather than hitting it with the gun, she hit the thing's head with her wrist. The gun got loose and tumbled to the floor. The zombie winced too, but kept its feet.

A panel directly below her rattled. She didn't fall over, but the shock almost made her lose her footing.

The teen re-oriented on her. On a hunch, she dropped to a squat and pulled up the floor panel. It was light, probably aluminum, and was about a twenty inch square.

She noticed the woman squished into the narrow space, trying to turn to look up at her. The thing wore a bright red shirt, which did a remarkable job of camouflaging the blood on it.

From a crouch, she swung the panel like a banshee. With a heavy grunt from a place in her soul she was unaware existed, the sharp edge ripped into the teen zombie's stomach. Blood and parts spilled out.

Again the zombie was forced to the side, its muscles damaged but its body unbroken.

She stood, gripped the panel, and swung it again as hard as she could. This time it cut into the boy's neck. It was already damaged from the boy's own encounter with a zombie, and it allowed her to make a good, solid, cut.

"I don't believe it." She panted as her strength continued to wane.

The boy's throat was indeed severed, but the spine held it in place. His noggin was canted unnaturally to one side, but he was still coming back for her.

She threw down the panel. It slid on the floor, loosely covering the red shirt woman. She was close to getting out. Many were close to escape now. Hands reached up from many panels on the floor.

"The panels," she shouted to herself.

The windows of the Arch sit on what are effectively small shelves, so people can look down. Saffron hopped onto one shelf and then pushed herself off with all her strength and grabbed the boys neck—and twisted.

The thing cried out until a satisfying snap occurred on its neck. With nothing left to hold it in place, the momentum carried the head from the body. Surprised, Saffron threw it while the rest of the body collapsed at her feet.

She was mesmerized as the head rolled down the incline of the floor, bounced off the side a couple times, hopped over some of the open panels, and then rolled into the darkness toward the tram loading area. Gone.

She shook her head vigorously to clear her mind of what just happened.

"The panels, girl. Get the panels!"

She found the panel she had tossed down, and pulled it from the red shirt woman—now facing up from the floor—and placed it under the hatch to the outside.

She repeated the process several more times until the panels were stacked about a foot high. She dared not try more as she could see two or three zombies far down the walkway standing up and starting her way. The crawlspace was more spacious farther away from the apex.

"Just a little more time. You got this." She told herself.

Christine's face was up in the hatch, looking down with terror.

With a tentative first step, she placed her foot on the stack of panels. It immediately tipped over.

"No. No. No."

She looked closer at the stack. The panels had a slight curve to them, to match the curvature of the top of the Arch. She didn't notice it in her haste. She rearranged the panels, then chanced a look over her shoulder.

"This is it," she shouted up to Christine.

"Or I'm dead," she said to herself.

The stack was steady. Her legs, thought wobbly from exhaustion, held her in position. She grabbed the hatch above. The sunlight drizzling in through the gap was heavenly.

With a final grunt, she jumped. With her arms, she pulled at the same time. Christine grabbed her shirt and pulled, too. It got her just enough leverage she could get her elbows outside the hatch. For a moment, she hung with her legs dangling inside the Arch. Her torso outside.

The view was spectacular.

Something brushed her below. She spun her legs and was horrified to make several contacts. Multiple zombies were on her. She heard the moans as she pushed them back with a weak kick.

"Help me up," she screamed. Christine looked surprised and frightened by her tone. Instead of helping, she slid away, toward the big warning lamp next to the hatch. She hugged it, looking away from Saffron.

She had no time to plead. She'd have to do it herself.

More hands on her legs. She strained to pull herself up with her arms. She was normally a fairly strong teenager, especially for her small frame, but her strength had been stolen from her.

She swung her leg backward. She made contact with something.

Then she put her feet forward and found something standing almost next to her. She decided it was her last chance. She raised one of her feet, risking a bite, and found the shoulder—or maybe the top of the head of a short zombie—and pushed off like a step.

Her ploy worked. With the extra support of her leg, she shimmied up through the hatch. Rather than hoot and celebrate, she spun around to look down.

A half dozen people looked up at her with bloody mouths, bleeding eyes, and outstretched hands.

"What have we wrought?" She peered down for many minutes as more came out of the gaps in the floor. Soon the entire space was filled. She was about two feet beyond their reach. She didn't think there was any way they could figure out a way up, but to be safe she knew she had to get out of their view.

When she finally looked up, Christine was gone.

She didn't bother calling for her. She took over the spot on the warning lamp. It provided the only handhold on the upper surface of the Arch, beyond the lip of the hatch. The warmth of the metal in the July sun was a firm reminder that she was still alive. Below her, in the Arch, the moans and longing grunts of the infected continued unabated. It was like radio static blaring from the tiny hatch.

She lost track of time. A couple days. A couple nights. The pangs of thirst were as constant and withering as the wind.

"Christine saw this coming. She took the easy way out," she said to herself.

The view was incredible. From her perch on the top of the structure, she could see the entire city of St. Louis for thirty miles in any direction.

"A beautiful way to die."

In the distance, she heard the whine of aircraft. She changed direction and saw a spectacle taking place inside Busch Stadium. Two large ungainly looking helicopter-planes were taking off from the field. The first to rise hovered near the ground, then slid sideways into the stands where it appeared to take a seat. Even from up there she could see the people and zombies scramble toward it.

The other aircraft had similar issues but the people hanging on the back ramp were pushed out by someone on the inside. The machine stabilized, then rose.

Saffron began to yell, though she was terrified to realize her voice was gone. She was so thirsty her throat wouldn't respond. Instead, she wheezed for help.

The beast rose above the stadium, its rotors and wings folded forward, and it began to depart—changing from helicopter mode to airplane mode. It would have been impressive if it didn't represent death for her.

As the plane became a speck in the distance she reflected on Christine's method of exiting this situation. Just one quick slide or jump and it's all over...

Her head was a haze. The wind became unnaturally calm, as if it wanted her to jump.

She stood up, though she was very unsteady and weak. As she gained her bearings, she held onto the light. The moaning from inside the Arch was a reminder she could never fight her way through the interior.

"I'm sorry, Mom. I couldn't save them. I couldn't even find them."

Saffron moved closer to the edge. Despite herself she had to move on one knee. She was too weak to stand on her own. The survival instinct still injected itself into her psyche, telling her to be careful, lest she fall over the side to her death.

At the edge she hesitated. Looking upon the city 600 feet below, she saw fires burning in the distance, people scrambling on rooftops in every direction, and the infected rambling everywhere in the park directly below and the urban nightmare beyond. She was too high to hear the screams.

Willing herself to stand, she trembled on the precipice.

"Any last words?"

She had none.

"Well—"

A small black helicopter ripped between the legs of the Arch, fifty feet below her. She was too tired to be shocked. Two more purred right behind it; they headed for the wall of buildings of the city. The trio of gunships banked hard to the left and swooped back into the park, like young teens at a skateboard park. Machine guns on each side of the birds spewed out tiny sparks toward the crowds of the sick below.

She took a knee.

The helicopters raked the ground as they darted back and forth in the once lush park. The grounds had already been bombed, burned, and befouled by an earlier battle, so the dead fell upon the rotting casualties from that engagement.

Saffron became dizzy at the excitement. Standing after so much time off her feet made her head spin. Now she was in real danger.

"Why should I care?"

The instinct to die fought the instinct to live.

"You have to live. You have to take care of *them*."

"I'm sorry, momma, I can't. They've been lost."

On her knees now, her hands gripped the sun-warmed metal to remain stable as she watched below. But the wind increased. Dangerously so. It beckoned her. It wanted to see her fly.

"I could just tip forward and be done with it."

"No, turn around. Stay alive. There is hope."

"Ha!"

She looked once more below, though her eyes swam in white streaks. The black dots of the copters cavorted with those in her vision. There was nothing to be gained in watching.

All she could do was slide herself on her knees. A little at a time, she turned to move back to the lamp.

When she faced the proper direction, the wind became a tornado. In front of her, causing the grief, was a dark angel.

Inside the windshield, a man gave her a thumbs up sign.

"Well, that was unexpected."

Time faded out once more.

DISTRACTIONS

Liam knew he was asleep. He'd drifted under with the rhythm of the boat on the river. What he didn't know was how he got to *this* place.

The cityscape was from his video game, *World of Undead Soldiers.* It wasn't unusual to dream about the game—he played it all the time. For the past six months or so, he'd been having gaming dreams so much he considered cutting back his game time, though that was a short-lived hope once the light of day caught him. Until today, he hadn't had any gaming dreams since the sirens...

The game wasn't known for complicated story lines or missions. Often it simply came down to how well the characters could aim and how fast they could reload their guns.

He had a gun. A combat shotgun.

"My favorite. Oh yeah!" The thing had some heft to it. The folding stock was retracted, making it easier to carry, but less accurate to fire. With some effort, he extended the stock and pressed it against his shoulder as a test.

"Nice."

He searched himself for ammo and was pleased to find a mag pouch hanging off his belt. He didn't know how many shells were in there, but he guessed about fifty. That was the limit in his game.

It didn't seem safe to remain in the middle of the road, so he trotted over to the nearest skyscraper entrance. From there, like his game, he'd assess the landscape and determine his next steps.

The changing perspective allowed him to look up and see the building across the street was on fire in several places, mostly near the top.

"Eye-candy, put in there by the game developers." It really did feel real, but he saw the little details that were inserted to make the city more dynamic and interesting. The fires, the torn sections of roadway as if bombs had fallen—or sewers had collapsed, and the bodies...

A body lay just ahead. It was propped against the outer glass of the front facade of the building. Blood was smeared in a short streak behind the man's head. Cautiously, he approached the victim. He was dressed as a businessman. There was a hole behind his head, in the glass. It was a telltale sign of what happened to him.

"Zombies always die by a shot to the head. Is that a universal truth?"

They also die if you blow them to bits. Or dip them in acid. Or freeze them and then break them apart. Or...

Yes, there were many ways to kill, but on the open streets, by average people, there was only one realistic method.

Destroy the brain.

He moved on to the edge of the building, and could see down the next street. His mission came into focus. A big yellow school bus hunched on flat tires at the next intersection. And yes, he lamented, it was surrounded by a couple dozen zombies. They pawed at the door and left sickly reddish brown streaks wherever they touched the clean yellow exterior.

"Why does this seem so familiar?" His game had many types of missions for players to challenge themselves. Some required attacking the zombies to force the way to rescue. Others demanded the player survive for a period of time against an ever-growing horde. The most complicated required stealth. Getting around a city crawling with zombies was something he knew a little about...

"There are always weapons up in the buildings." The game allowed players to carry one weapon at the outset, but others could be picked up on the map. If this was a dream meant to mimic the functionality of *Undead Soldiers*, he'd have to go up into the burning building.

He broke the glass next to the dead man. In moments, he was inside and in the staircase. He clicked on his flashlight—players always had one available in the game—and made it to the first floor without incident. It wasn't long and he was overlooking the bus from a corner office.

"Could I shoot them from up here?" He judged he had 50 shells. Their effectiveness was reduced at his current distance. He was maybe thirty yards from the bus. He could hit them, but not be sure he'd damage the heads. That would be a necessity.

He stood and watched, wondering what his next course of action should be. Go up the stairs to find any number of rifles, compound bows, or fire axes, as he'd do in his game world, or go back outside and distract them, kill a few, and make it into the bus just to see what's inside. From there, who knows. He'd learned it was best not to overthink the scenarios. After all, the game was designed to be played by kids, and they didn't have the same game problem-solving skills as a sixteen-year-old.

He felt mildly bad for feeling pride in that statement, but it had to be true.

Nearly about to turn around, he saw movement across the intersection. Someone was crouched behind a column under the building across from his own. The person wore all-black clothing. He couldn't make out anything more.

Studying the scene, he noticed someone else on the diagonal corner. And a third could be seen below the remaining building on the other corner.

In a flash, he realized what was happening.

"Cooperative play!" He had three helpers in the game with him. Together they were challenged to secure the bus. Now it all made sense.

They came out shooting. He watched the one across the street he'd seen first, as that one was directly in his line of sight. He too had a shotgun—

"A girl!"

The player was using a female avatar. Not uncommon in the game. Whether it was an actual girl was less clear, though doubtful. He looked at his own body to see if he was an avatar, but felt relief that he was really him instead of his in-game avatar.

The rules of this place were nebulous.

She led with a shotgun, rattling off six shots with great precision. She only missed one of her targets on the third shot. She put it down with the fourth. She fired slugs. They ripped great holes in the heads of those she targeted to die.

When she ran out of shells, she ran down the street to his right, reloaded, and then began moving back toward the zombies. The small crowd of them around the bus pulled itself apart as the zombies individually pursued the three killers on the three corners of the street.

"I should be down there."

Not knowing what else to do, he squatted down at the door of the office and aimed upward into the glass, intending to make a hole so he could shoot down. He ticked off the safety, then let a round go.

"Crap!"

It put a small hole in the window, but it didn't shatter apart as he'd hoped.

He got back up to look at the girl below. He wondered if, here inside his dream, the girl was Victoria. It would make sense he'd dream about her, since she was literally feet away from him on the boat. But the girl definitely had black hair. It was both darker and longer than Victoria's. He couldn't see her face to be sure.

She had made a lot of progress. More zombies lay on the ground behind her, and he could only marvel as she swung a fire axe at a charging businesswoman. She let go of the axe as it, and the zombie, fell to her side.

The other fighters were similarly dispatching their cadre of infected. One of them had a sword. The last one had a baseball bat with spikes on the end. She swung it and twirled it in her hands like an expert baseball player showing off in the batter's box.

He saw his reflection in the glass. His mouth hung open.

The girl below swung her shotgun by its heat shield at a small male in a bright blue ball cap running toward her. He could almost hear the thunk sound through the thick glass. The hat, thick with blood, popped off his head and fell to the ground.

She ran back toward her building, reloading. A few zombies trailed her.

"I need to get down there."

He ran through the building, retracing his steps. He stepped out of the broken front window and turned to run toward the bus. But when he came around the corner, the action was over. The girl wasn't anywhere to be seen. None of them were.

It was irrational, but he worried they were inside the bus. In the game, all the players had to be on the victory point in order to end the game in a victory—kind of like capture the flag. If one of them was missing, and the game ended, it was considered a loss for all of them.

"I'm here!" He kept his shotgun out, but he ran as fast as its bulk, and the heavy ammo pouch, would allow. In moments, he arrived at the outer layer of dead zombies. Each had a grisly entry and exit wound from the high-velocity slugs.

The going was tough as he closed the distance to the bus doors. He became aware of the blood stains on the sides and the glass on the doors was smeared to the point he couldn't see inside.

Somehow he knew the doors would open.

No one was in the driver's seat. A sign on the top riser said, "Watch Your Step." He ascended the few steps and peeked over the railing so he could see into the seating area.

"Liam?"

"Grandma?"

He rose to the main floor, and looked down at the tiny form sitting in the first seat. She looked as small as the school kids that should be on a bus like this.

"Oh, it's good to see you again. You always rescue me."

There was some truth to that statement. He had rescued her from Hayes and Duchesne, but he got the sense she was talking about something different.

"This dream is very odd, Grandma. What is this place?"

She looked at him for a long moment, her head tilted a little to the side. "Liam? Is it really you? You've never spoken here before."

He returned the confused look, thinking that he'd never *been* here before. Instead of an answer, he looked into the back of the bus. The three players were there, just as he'd expected. They were huddled in the last row of seats, talking to each other.

"I—"

He did a double-take. One of the figures had turned her head, he was sure they were all girls now, to reveal a blue bow.

"I think I'm in *your* dream."

He turned back to her, but she was gone.

Looking up, the girls were gone.

Thinking of his game, he realized the match had ended.

The screaming in his head was real.

2

"Liam! Wake up." Someone shook him hard.

"I'm up. I'm up."

The boat had slowed on the river. He got off the fiberglass floor and looked where Victoria pointed.

A large mud flat ran along the riverbank. It was about a hundred yards wide from shore to open water and ran for a mile in each direction. Up the river, a barge had run aground and tipped in the deep mud, allowing its contents to escape. A hundred zombies spilled out and were waist deep in the quagmire along the muddy bank.

Victoria pointed to a small figure struggling in the mud, well downriver from the bulk of the zombies, and nearly half way across the flats—heading for the water. Several infected struggled in the mud near the figure—they were leaders of the slow motion escape. The animated figure waved arms in the classic symbol of "I'm here. Save me!"

Liam's instincts kicked in.

"We have to save her."

"Her?" Victoria mused. She looked again, as if to confirm his observation.

Banging on the window of the control room, he pointed to the girl, hoping it was understood what he wanted. In a moment, the door opened and Blue came out.

"The captain said we can't get involved. It could be a trap. He also said you shouldn't be standing out in the open like you are."

That got his attention. He looked around, suddenly aware he was standing hilariously upright on the back of a huge bullseye on the river. He began to crouch, but reconsidered.

"We can't leave someone to die. Why did the captain slow down—" He decided to yell to the captain directly. "Why did you slow down if you weren't going to save her?"

"*She* is very persuasive."

Liam could only assume he was talking about Blue. He studied the look on her face. He imagined he saw an agreement there.

"All...right." He let the words drawl out of his mouth, while he thought of a response.

They were about twenty-five yards from the edge of the mud flat. The current wasn't as strong toward the shallows. He saw how it was going to play out.

Sitting down, he took off his shoes and socks. Then, with some embarrassment, he took off his jeans. Then his shirt. He thanked the fates for putting him in boxer briefs today.

"Don't leave without me." He shouted it to the captain, but was looking at Blue. He couldn't quite figure out how she and the captain fit together.

He looked at Victoria, aware he was almost naked, smiled, and then jumped feet first over the side. It only took a few strokes to reach the beginning of the muddy bank. He easily made it ashore, but was disheartened to see how far his hands and feet sunk into the loose mud where it transitioned with the water. It was the consistency of very wet play dough.

Once he was on the edge of the mud field, his struggle began. The mud was hungry as it chomped at his feet and refused to let him pull his legs back out.

Speaking aloud, he tried to calm himself. "How did she get that far in the mud?"

The girl was making forward progress, but the mud got deeper the further she went. The last ten yards for her would be up to her waist if she let herself sink down too much.

Liam took a different tact. He let himself fall sideways so he could get his whole body on the muddy surface. It worked to an extent, though it was almost as difficult to move himself forward. In an instant, he was covered with dirty mud.

"We've got ya!" he shouted to the young girl. She too had become a filthy mess. Her clothes were caked with the mud. Wherever she'd come from, she'd been in mud there too.

"Help me. Don't let me die."

"You and me both," he replied to himself.

The infected were closing the gap. They too were covered in the mud, making it difficult to identify their sex or occupations. A couple had long stringy hair, suggesting they were females. All of them were hideous crawling through the viscous mud.

The boat behind him revved its engines, though he couldn't tell what it was doing. A few moments later, he heard Victoria call his name. When he turned around, he could see the boat had gone upstream and was now drifting back down, closer to the mud than when he jumped.

Victoria threw a spear toward him. Her intentions were good, but she evidently thought she was going to hit him with it, so she under-threw it. Instead of reaching anywhere close to him, the thing splashed in the water and sank.

He sighed.

"It's OK," he shouted back. He was shocked how tired he'd become from just the short distance he'd made it into the mud. He turned his attention back to the girl. She'd stopped. They looked at each other at the same moment, and he saw the exhaustion.

"I'm not going to let them get you. Keep moving. I will too." They were about twenty feet apart. The handful of zombies struggled behind her. One had fallen behind. It appeared as if it had sunk so far in the mud it would never get free. A gangly little man made the best progress toward its prey. It flailed and flopped on the surface, much as Liam was doing. There wasn't much time left.

He pushed himself forward, though it struck him he had no weapons.

"Maybe I can hurl harsh language at them," he joked.

The boat was revving up again. He heard a splash, but he was too close to the girl to turn around now.

"I've got you. Just a few feet more."

He was tempted to tell her not to look back, but it seemed silly to say now. They could both hear the angry moans of the sick chasing her, though only Liam could see them.

As she closed the distance, he had a piece of inspiration.

"I want you to get out of the mud if you can. Lay on top of it. And slide toward me."

She did as he instructed, while he did the opposite. He dug himself into the mud so he was standing in a muddy pit up to his thighs.

"I'm going to pull you and then let go," he shouted.

She said nothing, but her eyes told him she'd heard.

The last few feet were a struggle for her and Liam hoped she wouldn't look back, but when their fingers touched, Liam did as he promised. He grabbed both her hands and pulled her toward him and then kept her going on top of the mud for another five or six feet. It was enough to get her out of immediate danger.

And himself into it.

3

When the girl slid by, she nearly ran into Victoria.

"Victoria!" She had jumped over the boat just like he'd done, but instead of showing up empty-handed, she brought their one remaining spear.

She had stripped down to her underwear, the same as him. Despite all the danger, he found himself looking at her body. During her struggles through the mud along the path he had taken, she noticed his dumb looks.

"Eyes forward, soldier!" She smiled, but it was grim.

Liam assumed she was going to toss the spear to him, but she kept coming until she was next to him.

"What are you waiting for? Get out of here. She'll need help to the boat." There was no ambiguity in her statement.

She stood with her legs slightly spread, a little ahead and behind her. The fighting stance indicated her willingness to engage the first zombie. He'd wriggled through the mud and was only a few feet from her now.

His options were to either wrestle her for the spear, or get the hell out of there.

"You better follow me." He threw himself backward into the deeper mud, behind her. As he righted himself in the disturbed mud, his eyes were drawn to her muddy figure. He noted, with some innocence, that she wore the same black boxer briefs as him. It must have been all that was available at for refugees in Cairo.

Victoria lifted her spear, then let it drop onto the head of the zombie. Liam couldn't see it, because she was between him and the infected, but he heard the sucking sound as the spear came out.

She looked around for the other zombies. He saw them too, coalescing toward her from various angles. Reading the angles, she made a decision to run for it. She pulled a leg out with her own sucking sound, and soon faced Liam.

"What are you gawking at? Git!"

It was all the prodding required. He turned around, and he was confident he could hear her sloshing loudly behind him as they headed for open water.

Victoria did stop once. He turned when he didn't hear her moving, and was impressed as he watched her again lift the spear over her head and slam it into one of the female zombies with the seaweed hair. Victoria caught her looking up from a prone position on the mud, and the spear drilled into her eye. He did not watch it come back out.

The boat remained out on the water, doing the equivalent of a hover. The motor was holding it still against the current. He saw the shape of the captain inside his bubble, while Blue stood in the back with an anxious face. From time to time she would wave, as if beckoning him to hurry back to her.

"Where else am I going to go," he muttered to himself.

When he reached what he judged was the absolute edge of the mud flat, he turned around again. Victoria was pushing herself hard through the mud, chased by a curious group of flailing mad pursuers. Everyone was coated with the mud over most of their bodies, including Victoria. She must have fallen when he was faced the other way. She was still spitting the stuff out as she slid up to him.

Just before she arrived, he dove out into the water. He had a terrible deja vu though, which insisted he look over his shoulder—to be absolutely sure she followed him. Still gripping her spear, and moments ahead of the four remaining zombies, she jumped, or more properly, fell into the slow-moving waters.

They drifted as they swam, and the boat began to drift backward as well. The zombies continued their pursuit as well, unaware they couldn't swim.

"Or, maybe they can swim." He wondered about that, then remembered the zombie under the water back in St. Louis. After a few more strokes, he did absorb the implications. Suddenly he imagined zombies littered the riverbed below him.

He drifted and paddled water while he looked for Victoria. She was nowhere to be seen.

"Victoria?"

Panic swept through him. He'd drifted with the current fifty or more feet from where he'd fought his way ashore. The muddy bodies of the two dead zombies lay like small mounds of dirt over their graves.

On the river side, he saw the girl as she boarded *Lucy's Football*.

But no Victoria.

Then he felt a bump against his upper leg. A grip. Then a poke.

His skin crawled. He wanted to scream in fear, but didn't know how. He was too scared to remember.

When Victoria popped out of the water with her eyes closed, he couldn't have been more shocked. He tried to yell at her, but still nothing would come out.

"I'm so sorry. I wanted to get this mud off before we got back in the boat."

She floated next to him, with a bemused look. "What?"

Should I tell her she almost made me scream like a schoolgirl?

He liked to be honest with her, but that felt a little *too* honest.

"I'm glad you made it, that's all. I didn't see you in the water until just now."

He figured that was a good explanation.

The boat had drifted closer to them, so getting out of the filthy water would be much easier. Liam was glad; he'd nearly reached his limit of endurance after creeping through the glue-like mud.

Blue had tossed a rope ladder over the side. Victoria made Liam go up the ladder first. He didn't know why until he was half way up and his rear was hanging in the wind.

"Oh, right." He tried to hold his dignity as he climbed aboard. Blue's grasp as he cleared the edge was both welcome and a reminder he was nearly naked.

I almost died, and all I can think about is girls.

He wondered if his brain was programmed that way, or if there was something wrong with him.

He sat down hard against the inner wall of the boat, where he'd been sleeping before he was interrupted from his slumber. In moments, a soaked Victoria slapped down on the deck across the boat from him. She looked a lot more winded than she let on in the water. Her chest heaved up and down. Sitting as she was, her toes touched his. For a moment, that was the most reassuring feeling in the world.

That's when he noticed the girl he'd rescued. She was on the floor at the very back of the boat. He'd missed her coming in. But now...

Her muddy clothes were only marginally cleaner after a dip in the water. Her hair was still a mangy, tangled mess of long black locks coated in the thick mud. Only her face was clean. Liam got his first good look at who he'd risked his life to save.

The girl looked just like Blue. As in, *exactly* like her.

4

"Guys, this is my sister, Saffron."

"Pink," the girl repeated.

"Uh, I mean Pink." She laughed, as if it was no big deal. "She came out of St. Louis and got stranded out here. Lucky we came along when we did, hey 'sis?"

The girl huddled on the floor, but didn't say anything further.

Liam had nothing but questions. About ten to be exact, but he started with the most basic.

"Why do you call yourself colors?" He looked at Pink, but it was obviously addressed to both her and Blue. He thought both of the mixed-race girls were very attractive, though both were very short for teens.

The girls shared a look, then Blue answered. "It's from a book we read last summer. Every year, our local library has a reading contest and me and my sister here have our own competition to see who can read the most books. We both got caught up in a series of books about magical Adepts. The main hero is the Blue Adept, so naturally I chose Blue. I think Saffron just likes the color Pink." She smiled at the slouching figure on the floor. The other girl tilted her head up and gave a thumbs up, then tilted her head back to her chest.

He didn't want to bother the new girl, but Blue was fair game.

"But why now?"

Liam heard her response, though he thought he was hearing himself talk.

"Don't you get it? Everything is gone now. No more school. No more libraries. No more nuthin'. We can be whoever we want."

It made sense to him. He changed his age on the fly, for the same reason. But there was one troubling fact emerging from the cloud of his recent incident in the mud and water. One that made him feel chilled to the bone, even though the hot sun beat him from above. He wasn't ready to voice it to the group, though he would definitely be asking Victoria as soon as he could.

Why, pray tell my dear Watson, have I rescued two colored twins from near-certain death? What are the odds?

Grandma had recently said some things were improbable, though not impossible. This seemed to be one of those improbable coincidences.

He was dying to ask Victoria, but she had also curled up in a ball and shut her eyes. He too felt the pull of sleep. It seemed the only safe thing to do these days in the long, hot afternoons. Especially when you are safe on the back of a boat, well away from the zombies lurking below...

He felt himself tip sideways a little as the boat accelerated.

Blue excused herself to return the captain's side. She pulled open the door and stepped into the interior. Then the captain put the hammer down and they began to fly up the river. He shut his eyes, believing there was nothing else to do with most of his crewmates asleep.

Before he knew it, Victoria tapped him on the shoulder. When he opened his eyes, she sat next to him. He had to look away, as she still wasn't dressed properly.

"Oh, grow up, Liam," she giggled. She spoke so only Liam could hear. "Listen, something isn't right here. What are the odds you pull Blue off the MRAP one day, and practically the next day you pull her sister—PINK—out of a random mud bank? This can't be a coincidence."

He followed his heart, and leaned in to kiss her.

When he was done, she wore a big smile. "What was that for? Saving your life?"

"Oh, man. I forgot all about that. I think it happens so often these days, I don't even notice." He laughed, but there was an underlying sadness at the necessity of it. "But no, I kissed the smartest girl in the world. Or, at least the girl who thinks along the same weird lines as me.

I had just made the same observation and I was sad to see you had gone to sleep. I really wanted to ask you that exact question."

"Well?"

He hunched his shoulders. "Dunno." So far he had nothing but flimsy speculation. Blue was almost left behind for dead. If she planned her escape up to that point, she did a terrible job closing the deal. She was smashed to the roof of the MRAP. She would have been dead if he hadn't noticed her.

And Pink, or Saffron, was exposed on the mud flat well before the boat showed up. She couldn't have known anyone would rescue her. She was going to die, too.

Except they didn't. Twice.

As a postscript to their discussion, he continued. "One thing I know for sure, something doesn't smell right here. I don't just mean you," he said with a teasing look at her. Quieter despite the drone of the motors, he went on. "I don't like whatever it is Blue is doing inside this cabin with the captain. I don't like whatever it is that brought her twin to this boat. And now, I'm beginning to wonder if we've gotten ourselves into something more than we can handle by going to that mine. I don't like any of it."

She turned toward him with mock exaggeration. "Liam Peters. Are you saying you aren't enjoying your time here in the Apocalypse? Is that it? ...Cause I will stop this whole thing right now and take us back to the beginning if that's going to be your attitude."

Ah, back to the tree under the Arch. He wouldn't mind going back to when they met. It was as clumsy as it was exciting for him. One of the few bright spots from those early days.

But time marches on. They rocked as the boat sped up the river, the air dried their bodies, and Liam and Victoria both managed to get their clean clothes back on before any more trouble found them. He didn't think he'd like fighting zombies in the open with just his drawers to protect him from bites.

The afternoon wore on into tedium, and sleep.

Nearly out, he sprang awake with an important piece of awareness from his recent dream. Something he missed the first time. He'd assumed the dream represented some subconscious, um, desire, for Blue. That's why he saw the blue bow on one of the three figures in the back of the bus. But something told him he also saw a pink bow.

That's what I'm talking about. I don't like this one bit.

He kept that piece of information to himself, for now. Having weird dreams was Grandma's specialty...

5

Victoria kicked him gently to wake him up.

"Don't you ever sleep?"

She looked down at him condescendingly, hands on her hips and head cocked. "And all you ever do is sleep. What am I going to do with you?" She straightened and smiled as she reached down to help him up.

"You'll want to see this."

When he had his footing, she walked him across the deck to her side. There, across the river, was the bridge they'd seen two times now in their travels. The blown bridge over the Meramec River. The bridge was a couple hundred yards up that river, but they could easily see the downed span where the wrecking ball ruined it. That crane still towered over the ruin.

Liam laughed. "I wonder how many times we're going to pass that thing?"

He was happy to watch it from a distance. He had nothing but bad memories from their first encounter and didn't want to relive them now. Content he was safe and dry, he relished his time standing next to

Victoria. The rocking motion of the boat ensured he rubbed up against her arm from time to time. It made him feel giddy.

His peace was disturbed as the captain kicked open the door. Nothing was said to them, but he was talking in a loud voice to someone on the radio and wanted he and Victoria to hear.

"No copy. Say again." He angrily yelled it to whomever was on the other end of the connection.

"You are entering a restricted waterway. The channel north of Interstate 255 is closed due to navigational hazards. Over."

The captain passed quiet words with Blue. Liam couldn't hear what was being said. He considered going inside the cabin to escape some of the noise of the motors, but he'd received no invite.

"Understood. We have freight to deliver to the Koch Hospital Quarry. We will hold to the south of the interstate. Over."

The radio was quiet for a full minute. The captain made no effort to slow to wait for permission.

Then the voice continued. "Negative, *Lucy's Football*. For your own safety, we require that you turn around. Do not proceed. How do you copy?"

Blue came out of the shaded cabin with several bottles of water. She seemed calm and refreshed as she handed them out. A great contrast to Liam and Victoria, who spent the day covered in residue from the river and the sweat of a hot day. Her sister looked even worse, and she hadn't woken up since the rescue. She somehow slept just in front of the two motors, occasionally sliding side to side as the boat made course corrections in the choppy current.

"Hey Pink," she shouted. "Wake up. There's trouble."

The girl stirred while Blue turned to Liam. "You guys sure you want to do this? The captain said he would try to get you close, but it doesn't look like he can get you all the way to the docking platform in front of the mine."

Liam looked at Victoria, but he knew her mind already. "Just have him get us close and we can walk the rest of the way. We can't be more than a few miles now."

He didn't want to tempt fate. That was always bad these days.

As he turned to Victoria, he noticed a drone hovering about a hundred feet over their heads. It looked like it was attached to the boat because it moved at exactly the same speed.

The girls noticed it, too, as they scanned the sky to see what he was watching.

"Everyone smile for the camera," Victoria joked. Liam laughed, despite himself. The last time she'd gotten her picture taken, it had been by Duchesne—the man who tried to kill Liam's whole family.

Note to self: take her picture!

He waved like he was on a luxury yacht putting on a show for the paparazzi. He was startled when he leveled his head back toward the front and saw the captain. He was in the doorway.

"What's wrong with you, kid? Don't you know they're taking your picture?" He looked at the three girls in turn. "All of you. You shouldn't take this lightly. Never let them see your face if you can help it."

Liam's mouth was open, but Victoria beat him. "Who do you think is taking our picture?"

The grizzled man gave a look of disgust and turned to go back to the controls. As an apparent afterthought, he stopped and looked out of the shaded cabin. His voice was calmer.

"Well, at least you stupid kids make me look more like a party boat than a serious threat." Then he shook his head and turned away for good. The door was still open; it swayed with the turbulence below the boat.

Liam had to practically bite his tongue not to reply. His first instinct was to explain how wrong the captain was about the crew he was carrying, though he felt he learned his lesson over the last few weeks about bragging to strangers. But the real reason he didn't reply was because he *was* a stupid kid in this instance, and it made him realize how fast he reverted back to his old care-free self on this trip.

He looked at Victoria, wondering what she was thinking. Surely she could make the same case to the captain. Did she also understand how right the man was? Her countenance told him nothing. She was playing it cool, like him.

Blue helped Pink in the back. The drone above them had come down almost to eye level. It was black with four fans, one on each corner. The enclosure above the fans was circular, about the size of a small car tire. On instinct he moved to the door and pulled it shut. He slammed it with as much force as he could muster. He hoped the captain would notice why.

Soon they all watched helplessly as the thing lazily hovered next to the boat as they continued up the river. The captain yelled obscenities at someone, probably on the radio.

Liam couldn't eliminate the possibility he was yelling at him.

The boat lurched to the left, into the path of the drone. It easily maneuvered out of the way, and sped ahead of them so it could hover in front of the bow, as if telling the captain to stop. He responded by accelerating.

The four of them standing on the back had to hang on to the sides.

Liam watched ahead as the captain opened the door on the front of his cabin. He brought something up he'd been holding. A gun.

Through the glass he watched as the captain lined up a shot with his shotgun, then pumped off a quick couple of shots. The sounds were loud in the open air.

He missed the drone, and it dipped low to the water's surface and then sped away from them. The captain didn't waste any more shots.

Liam used the opportunity to voice his concerns to Victoria. "I didn't say this at the time, but do you think the people taking those pictures know who we are? Like, specifically who we are and what we've done?"

Victoria looked at the two girls at the back of the boat. Pink was on the ground again, crying. Blue remained on her feet, but was studiously watching the drone as it flew toward the Illinois shore. She then turned back to him.

"I bet whoever is looking at those photos probably has us already figured out. Duchesne said he had bosses over in Illinois. Maybe they had agents down in Cairo watching us leave. Who knows? But even if we weren't on a watchlist before, we have to be now. We're accomplices to this," she pointed into the cabin, "jerk."

He grabbed her hand as he held onto the railing with his other hand. They watched ahead as the land got closer.

DEEPEST DARKEST

The captain ran the boat as near to shore as he dared, but continued northward despite the warnings he'd been given. Liam decided his life was in enough danger so he'd confront the surly man. He shuffled over the shifting deck to grasp the edge of the door and speak to him.

"Sir, uh, captain, I think we deserve to know what's going on. Who was on the radio?"

The man didn't look back. He stood in front of his controls. One large screen to his right showed a rolling script of colors and beeped loudly in the small cabin. He reached over and shut off the screen, and the warnings stopped.

"That is your new lord and master, the kings of St. Louis."

When the man failed to laugh, Liam countered, "I've been downtown, there's nobody in charge."

"Bingo! There *is* no one in charge. But there are groups *taking* charge. This side of the river," he nodded to Missouri, "is controlled by a group of Marines. That side is controlled by some damned fool Army unit that got lost after the Battle of St. Louis. Up north of the city and into Illinois is in the reach of the official US Army fortress—and they've been taking what they want all the way to the Mississippi River from their base near Springfield."

Liam was surprised at the depth of the man's knowledge. "What about the rest of the city?" He'd seen the Marines a few times now, and each time, he saw fewer of them. "The military can't control the whole thing."

"You're smart kid. No, they can't. And they don't. A few parts are controlled by leftovers of local governments. Others are maintained by groups of neighborhoods protecting each other. Even the Catholic Church has organized defensive pockets for their flocks. They had the resources to try it, at least. But most of the city is controlled by the undead."

"You mean the zombies?"

The captain turned around with crazy eyes. "You on drugs? Zombies? No, these are the walking dead. Spirits that come back from the dead." As he turned around, he continued, "I saw barges of 'em tossed out like trash and sent to float the river until some dumb riverboat crew happened upon them."

Liam knew exactly what the man was talking about. He'd been swimming inside just such a ship. But he held his tongue. In a few moments, the man continued on his own.

"Me and Pete ran this boat for twenty-five years. Well, not this boat, but boats like it. We ran the river together. When the Final Day arrived, we were on the river..."

He faded away for a few long seconds.

"After all that...stuff, he and I ended up in Cairo, needing to refuel. Credit cards stopped working, and with no other money, we started working for that town. Our job was to go out and find resources for the city government, until stuff got better. A few days ago, a few miles south of here, we see a large flotilla of loose barges bumpin' and grindin' down the waterway. We picked out one barge to dock with and evaluate its cargo. I had to stay with the boat, but Pete went up and boarded to check it out. He got up there OK, and walked out of my sight on the high deck. Five minutes later, he came back with a gunshot wound to his chest."

Another long pause.

"Someone shot him. He kept repeating the word 'shore' which I took to mean someone on the shore did it. I got him to Cairo, they threw him in their third-rate medical clinic where he died not much later. There—"

"And that's where he found me." It was Blue. She'd come up behind Liam. "I was in the hospital with Pete, and—"

The captain cut her off. "I need you guys to sit down and hold tight. We're going to beach right up here."

Liam was full of questions, but he admitted he *always* had questions.

Back out on the rear deck, he took a seat next to Victoria. Blue and Pink sat across from them. They all huddled as close as they could to the cabin, toward the middle of the boat. Liam was once again reminded how much better he felt having Victoria by his side. She grabbed onto his arm. He smiled at her and was relieved to see she didn't have any fear on her face.

"We're having fun, right?" She smiled big, her missing top tooth a reminder of their prior adventures.

"Oh yeah, flying drones, muddy escapes, and boat crashes are my idea of a good time. I think all our dates should be this fun." He laughed, felt her tighten her grip, and then lay her head on his shoulder.

"You two make a cute couple." Blue smiled, then turned serious. "Thank you for helping my sister, really. But I'm sorry for whatever comes next. I didn't know St. Louis would be this messed up."

That was the story of his life. Never knowing what was out the door, around the corner, or down the river. Well, that was mostly true. The one constant was death.

"I'm glad you found your sister. Is she OK?" Blue's twin had hardly said a word the last several hours, and slept most of the ride in. Liam guessed she was exhausted from her tough crawl through the mud, though he figured she'd be recovering by now. That made him concerned.

Pink wore dirty gray capris and a top that may have been white at one time, but was muddy brown today. He didn't see any bite marks. Just lots and lots of scratches.

"Hold on everybody!" the captain yelled from inside.

The front of the boat ran into the mud and several feet up onto the shore. The captain had found a tiny inlet of a creek that afforded a gentle approach and landing, which was good because much of the shore here was otherwise steep and rocky.

When he'd gotten it solidly on the bank, he shut off the motors and trimmed them up as far as they would go.

Everyone was deathly quiet. By some agreement, no one talked or otherwise made a sound. Liam could hear the birds chirping and the leaves rustling in the trees. Water gently splashed up against the hull.

It was idyllic until a new, mechanical sound drifted on the wind.

A drone.

2

The captain had opened the door to the front section of the boat. Liam went through to grab his stuff.

"OK, who here knows how to shoot a gun?" He looked at Liam first, then at the girls. Victoria was fast to raise her hand, but Pink and Blue just shook their heads. After sizing everyone up, he pulled a pistol out of a cubby hole near the passenger seat and tried to hand it to Liam.

"Sir, you'd be better off giving it to Victoria. She's got a steadier aim than me. I'll carry a spear."

The captain seemed to think about it, then relented and handed the Glock to Victoria. "All right. We need everyone armed once we get off the boat." He rooted around in some boxes stuffed under the consoles and came out with a large wrench and some kind of metal rod. He handed those to Pink and Blue.

"The first thing we have to do is run. We have to get up onto the bluff and into the woods so we can lose our tail."

"Why don't you just shoot it?"

He looked at Liam with a serious face. "We can't waste the ammo."

The captain grabbed his shotgun and slung it over his shoulder. He also grabbed a long metal pole with a hook on the end. When he saw Liam eying it, he seemed to sense the need to defend his choice. "It's aluminum, so it won't last, but I should be able to get a few good hits in with it."

Liam had to give it to the captain, he seemed to understand the zombie threat. All except the part about them being possessed spirits. That was nuts.

As they all made landfall, the drone hovered high above them, unmoving.

"Just run, guys, they know we're here already." Liam watched as the captain's big work boots carried him up the rocky bank into a tight row of trees next to the river. The two girls followed.

Victoria waved him forward while patting the Glock tucked into her pants on her hip. "I've got your six." She smiled, as did he.

In less than a minute, they were all under the relative safety of the first line of trees along the riverbank, but the drone had dipped a little lower so it had a direct line of sight to them under the canopy. There was no way to hide from it. On the landward side of the trees, there was a large field of small shoots of corn. Beyond that, a steep cliff with large houses on top. He realized he knew exactly where he was.

"Hey, this is Cliff Cave Park. We have to get to that gap over there," he pointed to a dip in the cliffs to their right, about a mile away, "because that's where the road comes in." He knew that for a fact, because on his earlier trip on the train escape from St. Louis, the engineer stopped at that road to pick up her husband. Somehow he felt much better knowing where he was.

"All right, ladies, run for them hills!"

Liam wondered if he intentionally lumped him in with the ladies. Did he lose his man card when he refused the gun?

He thought about it the whole run over the bumpy field. Everyone held together until they reached the railroad tracks that ran along the base of the cliff. Liam looked left, hoping to see the train engine called *Valkyrie* parked somewhere in that direction, but the tracks bent out of sight around the base of the cliff. In the other direction, he could see the railroad crossing for the road they sought. The captain and the two girls were already walking in that direction. He hung back as Victoria clambered up the rocky slope of the railroad grade.

"What's wrong?"

"How did you know what I'm thinking?"

She laughed. "Because you're *always* thinking. But sometimes you think more than others, like now."

He was aware one half of their guns was getting away; he didn't want them to get too far ahead. "I just want to get to the mine and see what's there. Suddenly we're hitched to two strange girls and a boat captain without a boat. I just have a bad feeling we're heading into more trouble than we need right now."

He started walking, indicating she should walk next to him.

"Well, where's the mine? Isn't it up these tracks? Maybe we could just keep going. Leave them to go their own way."

"Hmm." He chewed on the idea, but was reminded they had no weapons of their own beside the spear. If they kept going, they'd have to surrender the pistol. Two people with one spear would not do very well in a giant hole potentially filled with zombies. Of course, the closer he got to the quarry, the more he admitted how silly the whole plan had been. He just didn't know how to express his feelings to Victoria without sounding scared.

You are scared, dummy.

They all regrouped at the intersection. A large parking lot and a huge wooden pavilion were the only indicators of the park nearby. A sad looking red pickup truck was the lone vehicle parked there. To their left, the access road snaked up the wooded valley between the two hills that backed up to the cliffs along the tracks. The captain made as if he was getting his bearings, and then tore into the woods, climbing the hill on the north side of the road.

To Victoria, Liam whispered, "He's already heading toward the quarry. It's just on the other side of this hill. We can at least see what's up there. Maybe get a good look into the pit before we go any further."

"Sounds like a plan. Maybe when we're in the woods you can make me a new spear."

Louder now, he spoke as he started up the hill after the others, "Yeah, about dropping that spear. I'm going to need you to pay for that. I put a lot of good time and effort into that one."

"Seriously? Why don't you bill me." She then made a raspberry sound with her tongue.

He paused on the rocky slope, and looked back at her. "Oh, that's how it's going to be? Maybe I *will* bill you. You told Duchesne I blew up that railroad bridge. That's really going to cut into my inheritance."

As he started scrambling up the rocky hillside, he was still laughing as he heard her pass along a sheepish, "Oops!"

3

The access to the cliffs overlooking the river became very steep near the top, but the group made it with only minor delays. Pink needed the most help because she still seemed exhausted from her earlier escape. When they made it to the top, they had a majestic view up and down the big river. To their left, north, they saw the big arched red span of the Jefferson Barracks Bridge. If the interstate was open, cars would be zipping over it from Missouri into Illinois. Now, there was no movement. To their right, the river was visible for several miles before it meandered around a bend, out of sight. It was easy to see why they were spotted in their boat.

With that thought, Liam looked around, wondering if the drone operators were nearby. He only saw trees.

"Is that Illinois?" Pink asked. "Up where we live, Illinois is a dirty place with a bunch of factories chugging pollution in the air. Down here, it looks beautiful."

He looked again, seeing the land as a first-time observer rather than a jaded local. Beyond the river was a line of woodland. A large floodplain sprawled a couple miles further, until it met an escarpment much like the one on which he now stood. It was pretty amazing.

And dead.

Ugh. He ruined it for himself as he looked again and saw only miles and miles of farmland that would never be plowed again. If there was no fuel for the tractors, and no one to drive them, and no one to sell seed, and no one with money at all...

He turned away, continuing the last few feet to the long crest of the hill. He heard the rest of the group gathering themselves to follow. Even the captain lingered.

While lost in his thoughts, he walked by a group of people sitting in the brush to his left. When he heard them, he turned around with the spear pointed at them. A little boy, about ten, put up his hands. Several of his compatriots did the same. Liam dipped the spear.

It wasn't one boy, or one group of people. All around him, deep into the woods, people sat and stood in small groups. They were amazingly quiet.

His own people came up slowly, and fell in line next to him.

"Who are you with?" the captain inquired of the nearest men. They were dressed in dirty khaki shorts or jeans and were either bare-chested or sported sweat-soaked dirty shirts, as if they were at a backyard barbeque that had been going on for a week.

They said nothing, but they pointed further up the hill.

With a huff, the captain spun and walked on. Liam was quick to follow, though Victoria passed a gentle "thank you" to the pointer.

She caught up to him and whispered, "What are we getting into here?"

They walked with the vista on their right and the sad-looking people on their left until they reached a large flat area along the edge. The cliffs continued for a hundred yards or more, but this looked like the summit.

"Get out of the open, you kids," a man commanded from inside the canopy.

For the second time today he found himself making a juicy target to an imaginary sniper. And he was seen as a kid...

When they were all into the trees, they approached a command center of sorts. A dozen men and women dressed in camouflage lazily watched as they came up the path. Many held binoculars as they looked out of the trees, down toward the river. A couple sat near a small wooden table with a radio. Weapons stood against the base of trees all over the place.

"Did our guards let you through? We saw your boat come up the river, and we saw you run across the fields, but we didn't know where you were headed." The blonde man was a hunter, not military. Or at least dressed as a hunter. He had long pants imprinted with a confusing woodland pattern. He wore a short-sleeved t-shirt, but it was the same pattern. He was middle aged, but looked younger because he had little facial hair growth. He had serious blue eyes and a furrowed brow.

Liam opened his mouth, but the captain replied, "We didn't see anyone. We just climbed up from the railroad tracks below."

The man leaned hard against a large black oak. "My God, anyone could have walked into our camp." He remained there, looking at Liam and the others in turn.

He stood up straight again. "My name's Jason." He wiped his forehead. Liam recognized the burden of command under which the man suffered. He was responsible for all these people in the woods. "We have guards watching the flats around this area. The dead don't climb the steep rocks, like you did. But we should know better."

Liam knew there were zombies that could climb. He said nothing to further spook the man. Surely he'd learned his lesson.

"We'll have to put someone over there."

The men and women reminded him of the survivalist group that attacked Camp Hope. It inspired him to be clever, and cautious.

"Hi, I'm Sam and this is Becky." He pointed to Victoria. She caught on immediately and introduced herself as such. He was ready to high five her, and start talking about chickens and guns as they had done back at Riverside, but—

"I thought you said your names were Liam and Victoria?"

Liam turned to the captain, ready to soak him with lava-hot anger, but the man's face held no malice or sarcasm for once. He seemed genuinely surprised.

With a slow turn back to Jason, he was ready to fall on his sword and admit the truth. Jason didn't wait.

"I don't care who you are. If you have food you can call yourself Santa Claus, for all I care."

The captain, to Liam's surprise, pulled out a small bag and handed it to the man.

"Some dried fish. It's all I got, right now."

Liam looked again at the group of people spread in the woods around them. The sallow looks and longing eyes were clues to their status. But something else caught his eyes. Something more troubling. The kids weren't lounging or playing. They were digging. Worse, there were several white splotches on the sides of tree trunks throughout the area. Someone had cut into the bark.

These people were starving.

4

Once proper introductions were made—using Liam's real name—they were given an overview of the camp, confirming Liam's own observations. But the reason the camp was here on this hilltop built upon something the captain said earlier about control of the region.

"We arrived here a week ago after the dead came through our subdivision, followed by the looters. Most of these people live around here, but our houses are either gone or occupied by refugees from inside the city. We've been going out in small groups to ransack our own homes, looking for supplies, but there isn't much left."

Jason then pointed out to the river.

"But the longer we stayed here, the larger the group became. There are a lot of people who want to cross the river, but there are Army units on the far side of the bridge that keep turning people away." He pointed to the bridge, though there was only one. "The Army controls those farmlands over there. But we don't know how many of them there are. But they do have tanks."

Victoria let out a quiet whistle.

"Yeah, no kidding. We don't think they'd actually hurt us, but they probably wouldn't like what we've been doing from up here." He chuckled as he reoriented them to look down below.

"This is the high point around here. Anyone heading east tries the bridge first, gets turned around, then comes up here to plan what to do next. They never head north into the city. Too many of the dead. And no one goes into the pit either."

I know someone who will.

"So, they come here. To my starving friends. Sometimes they offer food, but most people are as bad off as we are. That's why they're trying to move on to somewhere new. When it gets dark, we run small teams down below and we have a couple small jon boats with stout paddles. We help them across in return for whatever food they have left. Sometimes we bring people back."

"Why don't you fish down there? Plenty of fish to be had." The captain undoubtedly knew what he was talking about.

Jason let out a tired laugh. "Gee, why didn't we think of that?" He looked at the captain who seemed to take offense to his mirth. "Oh, I'm just kidding, buddy. We do a little fishing when we can. But people are scared to leave the protective bubble we've got up here. In the daytime, anyone caught out in the open is a target for the undead, or for snipers, or for pirates. At night, it only gets worse."

He turned serious. "Fishing is a great idea. I didn't mean anything by it. I'm grateful you brought what you did to feed the kids. That's why we were hoping you'd be interested in using your boat to help us do some fishing."

The captain took a moment, rubbing his chin. "I'm here on business, actually. I'm..." His voice trailed off, though he came around a moment later as if just coming up with what to say. "I know. I could use some help on my boat. I need to go back down the river to Cairo, Illinois. You provide some help and your men can fish the whole way up and back."

Jason's eyes lit up, then he turned to Liam and the three girls. "But aren't these kids your crew?"

"No. They, ahh, were just helping me get up to St. Louis." A look passed between Blue and the captain.

The camp leader caught it. He had a pistol on his hip in a black leather holster. Liam noticed it earlier, but thought nothing of it. Everyone had to be armed these days. But, he thought earlier the holster had a clip holding it shut. Now it was open...

"Fair enough. But let me give you the lay of the land, just so you know where I'm coming from." Jason pointed over the river. "Illinois is a mess. There's at least one Army unit guarding the bridge. Whatever is beyond, we don't know. The Marines are a few miles south of here. They are on a cliff, just like this one, watching the river and foraging homes to the south. To the north is the main part of the city. The dead own that. But, there are other groups we've encountered. Everyone needs protection. Everyone needs to belong, eh, friend?"

"Yes, friend."

The two stared at each other for several long moments. Liam looked at Victoria and the twins, though they didn't seem to sense the tension as he did. His internal alarms were going off, though he didn't understand why.

The captain continued in a slow, deliberate voice, "Some of those groups a real *thorn* in your side, I take it?"

The tension in the air was palpable and taut. The two men faced each other now, only a few feet between them. The captain's shotgun was still on his back, however. Jason had folded his arms in front of his chest.

Jason turned to Liam and the girls. "Would you mind if I spoke to your captain for a few minutes? I think he and I need to clear the air on something." He motioned for the captain to follow him. Liam was left with his companions. They all passed a look of confusion, although Liam imagined that Blue's was somewhat inauthentic.

He kept his thoughts to himself, desperate to get Victoria away from the color twins so he could share his concerns. Getting that separation would be difficult, he admitted. Ever since they left the boat, he had the sneaking suspicion Pink was becoming enamored with him. It was innocent at first. She ran near him across the field. She looked back at him a little too often as they walked the train tracks. Then she needed his help up the rocks one too many times to be coincidence. And now, just as he wanted to have some privacy, she was right up on his side—opposite Victoria. Blue hovered nearby.

The hero gets the girl, right?

He admitted there was a time, back when he played *World of Undead Soldiers*, that the thought of rescuing a damsel in distress actually appealed to him, but now...

One beautiful heroine partner was all he could handle.

He took Victoria's hand and squeezed.

5

The captain and Jason were gone for ten minutes before Liam found the excuse he needed to get Victoria to himself. They'd taken a seat near the edge of the woods, so he stood up before making his announcement.

"Victoria, you and I haven't had any alone time in a while, will you take a walk with me?" He bent down with his elbow out, as if to pull her along on a romantic stroll.

"Why, I'd be delighted, sir." She spoke in a passable southern accent.

When she was attached to his arm, he looked at the twins. "We'll be back in a little bit." He hoped they got the message.

They walked in and out of the treeline along the cliff's edge for many minutes before he turned around to confirm they weren't being followed. He saw no pursuit, but he kept his voice very low.

"I don't trust those girls. They kind of creep me out, you know?"

Victoria wore a smirk. "And I thought you'd like having a fawning girl all over you."

He stopped, pulling her into his arms. He peered into her emeralds with as much seriousness as he could muster. "I want nothing to do with her, or any girl but you. I only just realized she was sticking to me, I swear."

Victoria studied his face, then looked back toward the camp before stealing a quick kiss from him. "Liam, you may find this hard to believe, but I trust you more than you probably can understand. Not just in a keep-the-zombies-off-me way either." Still quiet, she spoke quickly. "Before I met you, I was...promised...to a real jerk of a young man—"

Liam felt his face betray his cool exterior. He tried to recover, but she read him.

"—No, it's OK, listen. We were promised to one day get engaged and get married. Childhood sweethearts. Foolish high school fantasies." A sarcastic laugh escaped. "But there was something I didn't know about him until it was too late. I was too stupid to realize it. I only figured it out when he…"

Her strong eyes dropped from his.

Liam was frozen, torn between shock and compassion for her difficulty. He pulled one hand from hers and used it to lift her chin. He gave a weak smile, willing her to continue.

"He drove me into the middle of the forest—we were supposed to be meeting friends for a weekend camping trip—and he said something to the effect of 'Oh Vicky, we're practically married anyway; we should *consummate* the marriage early.' He said that word as if it were dirty. I guess in his mind that was what marriage was all about."

She regained her fortitude and was able to look him in the eyes again. "He raped me, Liam. I was so scared and confused, I couldn't fight him. I didn't have a clue how. He was someone I loved. I trusted. Or, I thought I did."

Liam wiped a tear at the edge of her lashes. She looked away again, though off to the side rather than down. She wasn't embarrassed, but looked like she was thinking.

"I never said anything about that night to anyone. I pretended it didn't happen. But I knew right there I was going to escape him. That's why I applied for that pre-medical internship in St. Louis. That's how I came to be in the city when the zombies came. That's how I came to find you."

She looked at him once more, with tears of joy.

"But that sonofabitch never knew I was leaving. I broke it off publicly, I told my parents I wasn't in love and never wanted to see him again. When the time came, I just got in my car and drove. I threw out his ring somewhere in Kansas." She laughed heartily at that.

Liam didn't know what to say.

"My point is that I trust you with my deepest, darkest secrets. You are a good man, Liam Peters. And that's why I think it's cute that Pink is smitten with you. She senses your goodness too."

Again, Liam was speechless.

He didn't view himself as a good person in the religious sense. Hell, he hardly ever went to church before the sirens. He had no idea why God would allow such evil in the world, but he believed there had to be a continuum between good and evil. Victoria's "fiance" was clearly aligned with the latter, while he imagined he would always fight for what was right. She was in a position to judge whether he was good or evil. He was pleased he passed the test. Sure, he wanted to do right by the one person he cared deeply about here on this cliff's edge, but also because he knew the world was broken badly, and it could never be fixed by someone who goes around raping helpless young girls. It was no contest really; he *was* the better man.

He pulled her along while she regained her composure. He was happy to learn about her past, but he also wanted to keep her moving into the future, with him.

"Is it wrong that I want to kill him?"

She was silent for several strides, before she sniffled once and responded, "We've talked about this before. Will we always have to be killing people in this new reality? Is it wrong to want to kill him? I can't say. But I do know this: if he ever saw me again, I can't imagine he'd be too happy. And, if he saw you—"

She stopped, as if making a painful realization.

"Oh Liam, I didn't mean to say it like that. I'm *sure* he's dead. He has to be. You and I have so much to worry about, we don't need to think of some loser in Colorado right now."

They walked a few minutes in silence, and came to a point where the cliff above the railroad tracks met the cliff surrounding the large pit mine he'd been seeking. Beyond, he could see the tracks go under the big red bridge. A line of cars ran from the highway, along a small access road, and into the mine. Just as he remembered, the line of cars descended the mine in several spirals before entering a gaping hole in the wall at the bottom. It was large enough for the big dump trucks to enter, which made the cars far below seem like toys.

They'd reached their goal.

Still holding her hand, he finished his thought from earlier. "I don't want to kill him. I really don't want to kill anyone, not even the zombies. But we have to do a lot of things we don't want to do these days. Killing the evil *things* out there is just part of the deal. I'll do it if I have to, without hesitation, to protect you and anyone else I love. And, I'll kill the zombies too."

He had just taken a seat on a white piece of the exposed rock at the edge of the woods when a military jet passed with silence as it went bullet-fast over the treetops above them. It headed for the bridge—

The crack of the blown sound barrier moved the forest.

SPIRALING DOWN

The sleek fighter jet banked to the south and became a tiny point in moments. The noise and surprise had sent him into the weeds. He found his feet just as Victoria found hers.

"What was that all about?" she shouted.

He took in the mine and the surrounding cliffs and hills. He could see a way down, but they'd have to continue along the cliff for another few hundred yards. Or they could go back.

"I don't know." He grabbed her hand. "Let's go. We can leave them behind and do this ourselves."

She hesitated for a moment, but seemed to relent. "Yeah, I guess that makes sense." But she was clearly torn. She paused after only a handful of steps. "I...I don't know. What if we need help? What if they go looking for us?"

Liam let go of her, appreciating her concerns. "They'll figure we went to the mine, just like we told them." He hadn't even convinced himself.

"No, we have to tell someone. Just so I can sleep at night."

He doubted anything would help him sleep at night, but she was right.

"OK, we'll find the captain and tell him we'll be on our way."

She perked up at that, and she pulled him this time.

They'd walked along the edge of the cliff for several minutes when Blue and Pink appeared ahead, running in their direction.

When they met, the girls pointed in the direction they were already moving. "We're leaving. Just go!" They each carried their crude weapons.

Liam was unsure. "We have to tell the captain where we're going."

"Trust me, the captain isn't who you think. We have to run." They didn't wait. Liam watched them get lost in the underbrush.

"OK, this is weird."

Victoria agreed, but had no brilliant ideas.

"Follow?" He was inclined to follow them, if only because they were more pleasant than the captain. Whatever that man had going on with Jason, the look in their eyes during their brief exchange earlier told him they were both driven men.

She nodded, and they began to trot after the girls.

They caught up at almost the same point they'd been overlooking the pit mine earlier. When he reached the clearing, he searched the sky for more planes.

"We're going down in that mine to look for clues about the zombie plague." The literal truth fell out of his mouth before he was able to stop himself.

The girls both turned to him with a smile. "As long as you keep the captain away from us, we're with you."

"Why? What's wrong with the captain? Why were you so chummy with him?" He eyed Blue.

"Run with us, and I'll tell you." She and Pink started along the cliff edge, heading around the outside of the mine toward the far side where they could descend to the first level of the spiral road to the bottom.

The girls were small for teens, but they were quick. Though Pink seemed to lag, she wasn't struggling. Liam's overactive imagination began to wonder if she was sandbagging earlier just so he would help her up those rocks. When he caught up to them, Blue began to share what she knew, just as she'd promised.

"When I was in the hospital down in Cairo, I listened to Pete the whole night he lay there in a state. He died the next morning, but he told me everything I needed to know about the captain."

She breathed heavily as they jogged.

"And what was that?" He was unhappy to realize he also sounded winded. He'd lost much of his base of fitness after two plus weeks of a horrible diet, high stress, and no training.

Hard to get training miles in during the Apocalypse.

"They're part of some secret group that runs guns up and down the river. They communicate with other groups hidden along their route, like that fuel barge thingy we saw."

More running.

"I got him to take us in exchange for my silence, but he changed the terms on me. I don't want to discuss it, but I'm not going back."

Many thoughts swirled. How would they get back to Cairo? What if the captain was following them? Will he want his Glock back? Out here, a gun was the equivalent of a gold brick. Surely he'd want it back.

They continued to run, though Liam felt worse and worse about it. He checked behind them as often as he could, and didn't see any pursuit. That meant exactly nothing. He knew that from hard experience.

It took them ten minutes to run around the curve of the cliff and reach the gentle slope going down to the top level of the mine. The last time he'd seen this place, it was crawling with thousands of zombies, and a lesser number of human survivors, but now all he saw were empty cars and the dead.

The dead.

Something about that word made him stop.

"Hey, hold up." The twins ran a few paces, but did come to a halt. Victoria ran up behind him.

"Does anyone else find it odd the dead bodies are still down there? How long does it take for bodies to break down or get eaten? It has been two weeks since we were here, and those bodies are all still where we left them."

He could see the biggest piles near the railroad tracks. That's where the most shooting happened, so the most bodies were stacked up there. But he could also see a path of crushed and dismembered zombies lying on the road below. That was where Jones ran over the dead with his dump truck—before falling over the edge.

"Hey, I see Jones' truck." It was a bit of a non-sequitur, but he was stream-of-consciousness now. "And those bodies over by the railroad tracks, Victoria and I helped make those piles."

Pink chose that moment to speak up. "Wow, you are one bad ass, Liam."

He turned to Victoria with a shrug, then Pink. "Uh, thanks. There were lots of people on the train though, not just me."

Victoria, ever helpful, expanded his thought. "But it was Liam's idea to use the dump truck. He helped save lots of people with that one."

He looked at her to find her smiling. He raised his shoulders as if to say, "Why?" She loved to rib him when he tried to play down his heroics.

Maybe he was a hero of a sort, but the real hero died in that dump truck. The mood of the group was already fragile, so he didn't want to use it as an opportunity to dwell any further on the sacrifice of Officer Jones. It steeled him to man up for what was ahead.

From his vantage point, he could see the spiral road full of cars falling down into the mine.

Lots of heroes died there.

2

They drifted among the cars as they went down. He was in front, with Blue. Victoria and Pink were a couple car-lengths behind, quietly chatting.

"Why this mine? What are you looking for?"

The answers to that question were endless. How do you explain you are trying to save the world? But he'd already blurted out the thrust of his mission earlier.

"I'm trying to find the cure to the plague. I was...told...this was the place to look."

"Who told you? What could possibly be down there? You sure you trust them?"

Her questions hit the mark. A random phone text message was a flimsy premise to pack up from a safe city, travel by boat hundreds of miles, and then try to gain access to a pit mine he was pretty sure was packed with zombies. Yet, he'd learn to trust his instincts the past couple weeks. They often—not always—put him on the correct path. Plus, this time, he had no other options if he hoped to do more than sit things out in a safe house.

"A friend gave me a tip. This mine is supposed to have some kind of information that will help Victoria and I track down the people who made the plague so we can get help curing it."

She was quiet for a long minute.

He tried to make the sale, though he didn't know why he should care what she thought. "You probably wouldn't believe this, but we actually met one of the guys who released the plague. We helped kill him."

There was a lot of nuance in the real story, but he didn't have time for a data dump.

Still, she remained silent for another couple minutes while they continued by car after car. They passed the wreckage of the dump truck that Jones drove off the edge. He wasn't surprised to see there was no body inside the cab, even though the superstructure of metal was crushed and ripped apart. Other than one cursory look inside, he didn't make a big deal about what was otherwise a very sad moment for him. Victoria made no effort to stop, either.

"You really think there's a cure for this?" Blue pointed to the line of cars. He almost answered with a snap reply, but he took some time to think over the question. The implication was much broader than he'd given her credit for, initially.

Since the sirens blared, he'd seen things getting worse from one day to the next. There were some high points, such as Camp Hope, but even that had been overrun and he had no idea how it fared today. Or if Mom and Dad were making out OK there. Cairo held out some promise, though he'd already accepted it was doomed. He kept that thought in a locked vault deep inside him, because he couldn't spend his days worried sick about Grandma. If the zombies overran the place, she'd be the first casualty. He was sure of that. But, through it all, his only tangible hope for surviving the zombie infection and all it brought was that he would document everything—with a notebook he'd had yet to find—and eventually play a part in rebuilding once they'd gotten the zombies sorted. He had to believe the cure was both literal and figurative.

"Yes. My Grandma once said something to the effect the cure starts with me. If I'm not willing to go out and find it, the world would die. Everyone thinks someone else is going to do it. Eventually, someone has to do it. So why not me? And Victoria of course, we're partners."

"Is she your lover? I see the way you look at her."

Liam felt his face explode in redness. "I, uh. We? I'm not—"

Blue laughed. "Say no more, Mr. Smooth. I was just asking for a friend." She made sure he was looking; she winked at him and nodded her head backward.

Liam stammered, trying to formulate a reply. Eventually he bagged the idea and just shut up.

About halfway down the spiral, they came to a large white passenger van. They'd been talking in normal voices up until that point, but they all shut up as it became obvious what was inside.

"My God." Victoria had caught up and stood by his side as they looked ahead.

The van was filled with the infected. At least as best they could see. The large windows lining the van were all filled with bloody hand prints. As they watched the shadows inside, bloody hands rubbed in several spots on the glass.

It was like some kind of sick wind-up toy. The longer they watched, the more animated the hands became. They swished faster and faster along the glass, then they began to pound from time to time. The van started to rock slightly.

"Move it." Liam spoke forcefully, but in a hushed voice.

They formed a line as they walked between the edge of the road—and the twenty-foot cliff below them to the next level of the road—and the van itself. The passengers erupted in screams and moans, creating a terrible storm inside the confined space. The van rocked wildly and hands started to pop through the glass. Blood flowed in torrents as flesh was sliced by the glass. The friendly carpool van soon had several streaks of red as macabre accents.

As they all ran, Liam turned back to see the first bloody mass pour out the shattered side window.

"Don't stop, guys. One of them just got out."

He ignored that several other cars also had moving shapes inside. If people were already sick, or bitten, as they made their way down this ramp, it wasn't a big leap to imagine them turning into zombies inside their vehicles, and then sitting there until something drove them to get out. He was horrified to realize they were now bait as they ran past more and more cars with deadly fish in their glass bowls looking for their first meal.

The only creature in pursuit, so far, was the one from the white van. And, because Liam was accustomed to disappointment these days, he wasn't surprised at all when he tried to guess how fast it was moving. It was going very fast.

In fact, one might say the thing was running.

3

Liam tried to get a feel for the land. They were getting close to the bottom, but it would still be many minutes before they covered the distance to the black hole down there. He had no idea what they'd find at the entrance. It could be blocked or stuffed with zombies. They needed to take it slow.

A hundred yards ahead, he saw what he needed.

"Guys! Jump in the back of that pickup truck. We have to fight this zombie before we go further down."

He hoped they'd heard him. It was dangerous to call out, but they were spread out and he had no other option, short of stopping and fighting alone. He knew that was as good as suicide, in most cases. It wasn't that he was scared of fighting any one zombie, but he had a primal fear of twisting an ankle or getting his head stuck in a drain pipe and then dying the death of an idiot.

It was always safer to stay with your team. He'd learned that in video games, and used those lessons now in life.

Pink and Blue were already inside the bed of the truck, their makeshift weapons at the ready. Victoria scrambled up next. He followed her in, spear under his armpit.

When he turned around, the zombie was nearly upon them. It had made good time down the slope of the road. Others followed. He looked across the pit to the road above and saw a few figures here or there stumbling down the road. They weren't moving very fast, but those zombies would go until they reached whatever was at the bottom, now that they had something to chase. If his group started at the bottom, they could have sucked all the zombies right out the top of the place.

If only.

Liam braced himself with his spear. Victoria had the Glock out.

"Don't shoot unless you have no choice." He assumed she understood why.

She turned to the twins, eying the wrench. "Are you going to use that?"

Pink timidly handed it to her. Blue kept her grip on her metal rod.

The running zombie was blood-soaked, but it was once a teenage girl. Thin and slight of frame, it was covered completely in both wet and dried blood, as if it had been soaking in the stuff for days. The fresh blood was undoubtedly from its escape through the broken window. She wore tattered jeans shorts, though he couldn't tell if they were designed that way or had been torn recently. She had on the remains of a tasteful light-colored top, though its color was difficult to guess given the red all over it.

The girl zombie surprised him by zigging behind the sedan behind the pickup truck. She jumped up onto the back and, as she found her feet, continued running over the roof and onto the hood. Then she jumped the gap between the two vehicles and made a clumsy effort to grab onto the tailgate. Her subsequent fall would have been comedy gold if she weren't trying to eat them.

The girl screamed in an unworldly howl.

"That's new," he said to no one in particular.

A moment later, the truck bed leapt up, bouncing him about a foot above metal. Something had slammed hard onto the roof of the small cab.

He looked up. There were two faces on the edge of the cliff up on the next level of the road. Those zombies could continue to walk down the road and reach them in twenty minutes, or they could just jump and close the distance in moments.

The jumper zombie was a mess in the bent metal, but it wasn't dead. It tried to pull itself from the dented cab.

"I got it." Victoria went with her wrench in that direction. Liam had no time to watch as the teen zombie stuck her head over the back tailgate, reminding him he had his own problems.

His feet felt like they were made of worms. He couldn't get a solid footing, but he thrust the spear toward the head of the girl. He could tell it was a bad push as it was happening. Instead of piercing the eye and brain, it went through the left cheek and glanced off her jaw. It sent a splash of blood onto his spear and his hands. The wound was horrific to look at, but not even a bother for the zombie.

She snapped at the spear and grabbed for it. Her hands were a slippery mess, so she couldn't wrest control of it, but with blood all over his end of the spear it became less effective for him, too. It was hard to grip the wood and get another shot.

OK, so these things have a design flaw.

He recoiled at the disgusting scene. He tried to kick her face, though that only bought him a few seconds. He slid in the bed of the truck, more from fright than the drips of blood down there.

Victoria let out a series of grunts as she pummeled the zombie on the roof.

Pink and Blue huddled together in the middle of the cargo bed, seemingly paralyzed with fear. Above, another zombie started his jump. He judged the distance, angle of approach, and position of his friends—and knew it was going to be close.

He made it to his knees, and used his spear to shove the girls toward the cab. They tumbled into Victoria, who had her wrench high above her head in the midst of another killing blow. All three fell against the cab and the grievously wounded zombie there.

In a flash, the zombie from above dropped exactly where the two girls had been standing. The thing had no grace whatsoever; it fell head-first onto the metal. He couldn't look directly at the remains of its head, but he knew it was absolutely out of action.

The teen zombie was over the edge and upon him. Not knowing what else to do, he held up the spear and she landed on top of it. Unlike the movies, she didn't fall on the spear as it passed through her. Instead, the spear entered her chest and got stuck on something. She stood there flailing in anger, trying to reach him.

Victoria, recovering from the interruption from the other girls, turned to Liam's zombie.

"Get out of the way," she shouted to them.

Still, they stood with little movement.

She got around them and swung the wrench with great force. The heavy metal tool fell squarely on the top of the teen's skull, making a sick crunch as it impacted. Liam had to look away as Victoria proceeded to dismantle it from the inside out until the head was more or less a pile of mush.

"Come on Liam, I need you."

He heard it as an echo in his head.

"Come on Liam, I need you."

That time he heard it clearly.

"I'm here." He balanced the dead zombie on his spear as he got up. The thing had slumped down, so he pushed her backward as he drew the spear from her. He had an inspiration to wipe the spear on her clothes to clean it off, but she had no clean patch of clothing on her. Instead, he used his jeans.

A third zombie fell from above. This one landed on the tailgate—another horrible attempt to shortcut the roadway. It fell to the outside, leaving a large dent and a clump of hair on the back of the truck.

They looked at each other, then above. More heads had reached the shortcut.

Together, they came to the same conclusion.

"Run!"

4

Liam tapped the twins before he got out.

He assumed they'd follow him. He was several cars down the road before it registered they did not.

"Victoria, stop!" She was a few cars ahead of him.

He turned around, wishing at that moment he'd just run off with Victoria when they had the chance. He gripped his spear as he'd gotten it reasonably clear of fluids.

"Blue! Pink! Run!"

They were huddled together in the truck bed, near the cab. Just where he'd left them.

"Hey! We have to go." He stood off the side, hoping they'd get the hint and jump the side to him. When they made no effort to comply with his reasonable request, he did the only thing he could think would help.

He turned his spear around and poked them with it.

"Ouch."

Not knowing how to play this—he'd seen people freeze in battle several times the past few weeks, including himself on more than one occasion—he decided to use humor.

He turned on his British voice—he was a fan of goofy British humor. "Pardon me, ma' ladies. Things seem to have gone pear-shaped here. Fancy a walk fer a rescue?"

It had the intended effect. The both turned to him with the look of confused humor.

He held out his hand. Pink was first and took his hand as he helped her over the edge, Blue jumped the side on her own.

He pushed them down the road, willing them to find some haste. He heard the thud of another zombie as it slammed into the pickup truck.

Whatever smart planning he intended to do on the way down had to be sacrificed for speed. They kept running straight ahead on the road, not stopping to look into the cars and trucks, or finding places to fight the growing numbers behind them.

I knew this looked too easy.

When they reached the bottom, Liam looked up. It was a confusing mass of activity on each of the levels of the spiral. Walking zombies. Running zombies. Some jumped the edges, though most did not. Somehow they knew to keep trudging down the road and they'd eventually reach their prey. If it was any kind of intelligence, it reminded him of a bloodhound.

They were far ahead of most of the zombies, though the bottom of the pit mine was filled with more cars. An area about the size of a football field was crammed with abandoned vehicles. Now that they were close, he figured any remaining dead inside those cars would catch wind of them. Then it would all be over.

They stayed away from the parking lot, and headed for the thirty-foot wide black hole of the pit mine entrance.

A huge sign was inset in the rocks above and outside the entrance. It once acted as a friendly reminder for truck drivers and mine workers, but someone had defaced it permanently. It said, "Congratulations! You have had," followed by a blank space with numerous shotgun blasts in the sign, "days since the last injury at your quarry."

Beyond the sign, still near the front of the illuminated entrance section, it looked like someone had lined up a bunch of cars, then blew them all up, then blew up the debris. Large rocks had fallen from one wall, and there was a good-sized hole on the floor of the rocky tunnel. The walls were blackened and scorched. His first thought was that a tank had blasted its way into the tunnel, though that was impossible given all the intact cars on the one road in they'd just descended. He'd seen a tank tear into the zombies inside a similar, if smaller, tunnel back at the Arch. If this place was crawling with zombies, a tank would be a great start to cleaning them up. Or...

He thought of the jet that screamed overhead while they sat up on the cliff. Another piece of random data plopped out of his head, too. Back at the Arch, he'd learned the military attacked large groups of zombies wherever they could find them.

At one time there *were* a lot of zombie here.

They all stood at the threshold of the darkness, unsure.

He turned around and tried to guess how many zombies he could see moving above him on the mine road. Dozens for sure. Maybe a hundred. Enough to require an air strike if someone discovered them? The pilot from earlier had nearly flown over the mine on his sneaky pass above them. It wasn't unreasonable to think he'd be back.

He looked into the blackness, suddenly aware of an important piece of missing survival gear.

"Does anyone have a light?"

The groans gave him his answer.

"How could you have overlooked something so obvious," Blue asked. He heard Pink crying softly.

The zombies from the road were very close now, and other zombies lurked in the parking lot of cars. Whatever he was going to do, it had to be now. He had a notion to go toward the parked cars and try to find a flashlight, but he could easily be cut off by those from the roadway. His team consisted of fifty percent deadweight, further making any decision a potentially deadly one.

He admitted to himself he didn't know what to do. It was a full minute of pacing before Victoria finally asked him.

"You don't have any ideas, do you?"

He pulled her aside. "We can't leave these two behind while you and I go look for a light. They can't fight. I don't know what to do."

"Liam!" Blue called. "We have more trouble."

"Well, that just figures. And here I was worried this was going to be too easy."

Up the road, minutes behind, they could also see the running group of zombies. They were dressed just like the teenage girl from the van. The rest must have busted open more windows, or maybe they hit the button to unlatch a door. Bottom line: they were all out, and heading their way.

He turned around. "I guess it's just like in that *Fellowship* movie. We have but one way to go."

Blue surprised him, as she knew the movie he referenced. "Yeah, but they had Gandalf's staff to guide them. What do we have?"

Liam had no retort.

"We trust in God," Victoria offered as she grabbed his hand.

Behind him, the girls replied with a sound he interpreted as "wishful thinking."

5

They walked about a hundred yards into the darkness. The faint light was adequate to that point because the floor was smooth and they could hold onto the parked cars. Once they'd cleared the entrance, with the destroyed cars, the line of traffic resumed. They walked in silence far into the tomb. Liam thought he heard banging on several of the cars here, but it was too dark to see for sure.

Just keep walking.

Behind them, far back at the lighted entrance, figures moved.

"They're with us now. What do we do?" The question came out of his mouth, but it was directed at himself.

"I guess we could find a car and climb inside. We might be able to hold them off for a while. Or maybe we could hide under the cars and hope they lose interest. Or we could just go into the darkness for as long as we can."

"I vote that one." Victoria's voice drifted out of the deep shadows around him. He thought she was behind him, but she could be next to him, or on the other side of the line of cars.

"Yeah, we aren't hiding and dying in here." Blue seemed to have the most resolve of the twins, but Liam was curious why she even bothered to come if she was so frightened.

"Blue, thanks for helping us get this far. Even if we don't make it, I appreciate that you got the captain to bring us up here."

"My pleasure, I guess."

"But if you don't mind me asking, why did you offer to help us at all? You could have stayed safe down in Cairo and we'd be none the wiser. We might even have found another boat up here."

"I don't know. Maybe it just felt like the right thing to do, after you saved me back on top of that truck."

And then you left me for dead.

It was tempting to remind her of that, but now wasn't the time.

"Well, I'm sorry if this is how our story ends. Dead inside a damp stone quarry tunnel, eaten by—"

"Hey. We ain't dead yet. Just keep going. I'm not stopping, I can tell you that."

From behind him, a hand found his shoulder. Victoria's touch bolstered him in the darkness, which was now nearly complete. The tunnel had begun to turn to the right, cutting any remaining light to nothing.

Sensing they had turned both a literal and figurative corner, Liam offered some advice. "Everyone move as fast as you can. There has to be some survivors, or at least some gear left by survivors. We might get lucky and find a flashlight. Or help. Or anything. Just don't stop."

They used the cars to guide them. He assumed as long as they followed the cars they were heading the right way, though he thought they passed through a few intersections because the cars were parked in different directions. They always went forward.

A couple times, the tunnel was illuminated by the equivalent of starlight by the tiny LED blinking lights of car alarm systems. The soft blues or reds blinked on and off, giving them faint snapshots of the tunnel around them.

One such car had movement inside. The repeating blinks outlined the zombie strapped into the passenger seat. They passed close enough they could see the thing's eyes were fixated on the only light in its world. Liam almost felt sad for it, but he drifted by slowly so as not to call attention to himself.

Far behind, they heard the distinctive howl of another of the teen girl zombies.

"Why do they do that?" Victoria asked. "Just to creep us out?"

Liam searched his zombie lore and couldn't come up with an explanation. He'd have to rely on guesswork.

"I think it's some kind of call to arms. When the other one did it, the zombies above started to jump on us. She alerted them to our presence."

His earlier theory on bloodhounds really troubled him though. He had begun to believe they were using their senses to follow the cars well beyond the ability of any zombies to follow them from outside, but if those howlers somehow tracked them in the dark, then no distance would be enough to get away. They'd be overwhelmed as more zombies followed those howls even if they made it to the center of the earth.

Victoria whispered to him, as if unsure it was something he wanted to hear. "If we get attacked from behind, we'll never be able to fight back in the dark. We could turn on some headlights of these cars and maybe see where we are. At least we wouldn't be surprised."

Liam stopped. With a slap, he smacked his own forehead. "Of course. Argh, I'm such an idiot. We're walking by two huge flashlights every time we pass a vehicle."

He gripped Victoria firmly and guided his lips to hers, hitting her nose first.

"I love you," he whispered. Louder, he said, "You may have just saved our lives."

They waited until they found another car with an LED. It was the only way to see the interior and ensure no zombies waited for a doorman to let them out. It only took a few minutes.

Liam opened the door and fumbled with the steering column until he found the lights. When they turned on, the headlight beams deflected off the sports car in front of them and sent light in all directions. His eyes took a minute to adjust. He turned on the dome light so he could see into the rear seats, though nothing of any value was back there. Some baby clothes and a broken down cardboard box.

He jumped out.

"OK, this is our chance. Search the cars. Turn on the headlights of every car we can find. If we find a flashlight, we can run ahead and leave the zombies behind us."

Until we hit a wall.

He kept his negativity in check, but at some point the mine had to branch off or end or do something. It couldn't go on forever like this.

Then they'd have to fight. Him, his girlfriend, and two scaredy-cats.

A thought flew into his funnel—too many years growing up on a British train show—and it seemed impossible, but he actually thought he'd rather have Grandma with him than these two walking colors.

"At least she made *me* stronger." He hadn't intended to say it out loud, but Victoria was close enough she heard him.

"That's so weird, I was just thinking how much I miss Grandma."

More lights came on ahead as Pink or Blue found another car with working headlights.

Behind, very close, he heard the familiar howl.

"Grandma, I hope you're praying for us."

"Amen," answered Victoria.

GRANDMA DREAMS OF BLACK

Two days since the sirens.

Indigo Hamilton woke up where she went to sleep. In the front seat of her mom's car, in traffic. She wasn't sure how long she'd been out, or how far they'd moved, but she took her nap in the middle of the day and it was now dark outside.

When her mother saw her stir, she smiled. "I'm sorry, we haven't gotten very far."

Indigo looked around, gaining her bearings. "We haven't moved at all, have we?"

She eyed the back seat of the small car, wishing the rest of her family was with them. They'd tried to get out of St. Louis when all the commotion started up—that's what her mom called it—and they'd been separated. The cell phone network had gone up and down, but after a long string of failed tries, they'd finally established the rest of the family was leaving St. Louis with other relatives. The message was short and clear: get out of St. Louis.

They were facing east, toward Indianapolis—home to her relatives. But the highway had been stopped since last night. Her mom's face held back the fear. Only her eyes betrayed her. She was unable to squelch it completely, and Indigo had a sixth sense for the feelings of others.

Ahead, many people had pulled over to the side of the highway and lay in the grass, waiting. She wanted to get out and stretch, but something told her to stay in the car. It wasn't so much the rumors of vicious attacks by sick people, but more of a superstition. As if exiting the car would be the last thing she ever did, so she needed to make it count.

Another hour went by as they sat listening to music on her smartphone. She had it plugged into the charger and the aux port, so they could hear the music through the speakers of the car. As one song bled into the next, the line ahead started to display brake lights in the night. It meant people were starting their cars, and finally, the line was starting to move.

"Hey, lookie there. We're moving." Her mom was genuinely happy. The veil of fear slid away for just a little while. People in the grass jumped up and ran to their cars before the line left them behind. Frantic merging followed, but people were mostly civilized about letting them back in. Her mom even let in a large passenger van, proving that the fear truly had receded.

But a mile along and Indigo felt it return in a wave.

"Oh no. What's this?"

The highway was blocked ahead. The powerful red warning lights on top of the twin spans of the bridge laughed at them from above. They were so close to escaping the gridlock of St. Louis, and now they'd reached the end. In her head, Indigo imagined them smashing through the construction barrels guiding them all off the highway, but just in front of the bridge they could see piles of box-like containers stacked and arranged to create a makeshift wall across the entire eight lanes of highway. The bridge was closed in both directions.

And those left on this side were being directed to an off ramp. When they reached the bottom of the ramp, they could turn left and follow the bulk of the traffic. Or turn right down a narrow road.

"That way will take us back to St. Louis," her mom was talking to herself as she pointed left, but Indigo offered her own suggestion.

"Then let's not do that. Where do you think *those* people are going?" The cars turning to the right were continuing south along a dirty paved road. There were no road signs or other clues as to where they were going.

"What's the worst that can happen? We all get stuck in traffic?" Her mom chuckled, as did Indigo, but she knew her mom was scared. She was getting there too.

The traffic bunched up again, and soon she saw the same white van ahead of them.

A man ran out of the weeds and up to the van. She was only half paying attention until someone in the van opened the door for a moment and then some kind of altercation took place. It ended with the man getting a kick to his chest. He tumbled back into the weeds next to the road, then got up and ran past Indigo without a sideways glance.

"Did you see that?" She felt the panic in her voice, but her mom was in the driver's seat and didn't have a line of sight to the passenger door of the vehicle ahead. All she saw was some crazy guy run by.

"Yeah, hardly the time to be out jogging." Her chuckle was forced. She kept her eyes forward. Indigo fingered the door lock button, thankful it was already locked.

Several minutes passed without a word. The music continued to drone, but she wasn't listening anymore. When one of her favorite songs came on—an upbeat anthem—she ripped the cord out of the radio. The music was replaced with that horrible emergency broadcast loop.

"...we advise you find safer jurisdictions. No emergency services are currently in operation. If you have an emergency—"

She shut it off.

If you have an emergency, no help is coming.

She willed herself to become invisible. She willed the car to become invisible to "the crazies" going for jogs outside.

"There's another one!" She surprised herself and her mom at her exclamation. A man stumbled along the road in the same direction they were going. He was on her side, so she could watch him up ahead. As each car or truck passed, he tried to grab on. He more or less bounced from car to car like a sad version of Frankenstein until he reached the van in front of them. Those people, possibly angered by the last pedestrian, opened the door swiftly. It struck the passerby with a thud loud enough she heard it behind the closed windows of her own car. The man went tumbling off the road.

As her car pulled alongside the downed man, she could see he was covered in blood. At first she believed the car door had done the damage, and indeed it had caused some blood on the man's forehead, but the man's neck was a neckerchief of blood. The top of his tan shirt looked like a red dickie. The thing—she couldn't call it a man anymore —looked up at her from the ground.

She slouched in her seat, willing it to ignore her.

Please go to the next car.

Her car lurched ahead with traffic, and in time, she risked a look out her window. The man was no longer in view. It probably *did* go bother other cars. She thanked her lucky stars.

As she turned forward once more, she was just in time to see the sign indicating where they were going.

"A quarry? This whole line is going into a quarry? Really?"

Her mom clutched the wheel in a vise grip. She rode the bumper of the van ahead of them. "We go where they go. *Anywhere* but here."

Indigo wondered if *anywhere* was always better than here.

2

At one critical junction, Indigo saw they had a chance to divert from following the crowd. There were railroad tracks going next to the mine, they shot off into the darkness toward a cliff face being lit up by the lights of the cars now entering the property.

"Mom, maybe we could drive down those tracks? Get away, you know?"

To her credit, her mom did look where she pointed, but the response was typical. "No, we have to stick with the crowd. Someone up ahead knows where we're going. Maybe they set this up to protect us?"

Indigo felt the car tilt forward as it started down the slope of the mine's entrance road. Once she was into the event horizon, she could see the snake of headlights going round and round the spiral until they disappeared to some point below. Her panic was building.

"Mom, we can't go down there. There's no way out!"

"Oh honey, we have to follow instructions. All these people can't be going down there without guidance. It will be fine." Her tone betrayed her words.

That's the universal parent red flag for "I don't know what I'm doing!" Indigo recognized it, and her fear spiraled worse than the road.

After they were committed, and had gotten through most of the first loop, Indigo was in five alarm fear territory. Several times, men and women had run by them in both directions. Some screaming to turn around. Others screaming the cars weren't moving fast enough. A couple times, she looked out her window into the rocky cliff face of the mine wall and saw dark shapes clinging to the shadows. She imagined they were sleeping.

Yes, of course they're sleeping.

Eventually she stopped looking out her window.

"Mom...do you think A-Z and Saffy made it over the river?" The terms of endearment for her sister's sprang from their mom. The woman loved her nicknames. Her friends called her sissy. Even at the hospital.

Indigo took a long time to respond. Her eyes stared into the back of the white van. She didn't know for sure, but she suspected her mom had a fear of driving along the cliff's edge, though it could also be a hundred other fears in the dark of night. When she did respond, she almost didn't recognize her mom's voice. It had become deep and husky, like she was straining hard to speak.

"This isn't a safe space. This isn't a government help center. This is...a death trap. I've taken my daughter into a death trap."

"Mom!" Her mom jumped, as if she was asleep. "You're scaring me. Quit it!"

She looked at her with sadness in her eyes. "I'm so sorry. I can't do this. I just can't."

Indigo felt the fear bubble over. Not just her, but the whole line of cars. More people ran by, in both directions. The traffic had stopped. The van ahead had gone dark. They turned off all their lights, apparently parking right on the road. Looking down into the pit, many others were shutting off their lights. A great mass of cars at the bottom were already mostly off; they'd lined up to park at the bottom. She could see into a gaping maw at the bottom of the mine. A line of cars poked inside. Their lights remained on.

"I can't. I just can't."

"Mom. I said quit it." She was stern, but she didn't know where this was coming from. She'd never known her mom to act like this.

"This was a mistake. We can't die like this. We won't die like this."

More people ran by, most went down the road now. Several screamed as if they were dying.

Without warning, a man fell from the sky and slammed onto the front hood of their car. He didn't hit it square though, he hit the very front edge. Her mom began to scream. Indigo covered her ears, but couldn't look away.

Slowly, the man got up. His face was a wreck. One eye...was missing. Blood covered his left side. Maybe it was all from the fall, but she didn't think so.

The man was lit by the headlights of the car. With deliberate motion, the man walked to the inside edge of the mine. Without so much as a look either way, he stepped off the edge to points unknown below.

That was enough to break her mom. In seconds, the hysterical woman had opened her door and began running back up the hill.

"I'm not going in there. I have to get out. Go back!" Those were the last words she could hear from her mom before she became background noise among all the other screaming and shouting.

Indigo sat in shock.

The driver's door hung wide open. She stared at it, imagining that someone was going to see it and jump inside at any second.

You have to move. Go follow her. Be a good daughter.

She didn't listen to that voice inside her head.

A minute went by. The door was still open. People ran by. One man clipped it and tumbled over the edge.

Close it. Do something!

The voice was insistent, but her body would not respond.

Another minute went by. She began to imagine it would be her mom that came back through the door. Of course she would come back to save her daughter.

Of course. But where is she? Run, girl.

That voice was new. Could she run? Shouldn't she wait for mom? She imagined the trouble she'd be in if she didn't wait.

"Mom said wait for help. There was help here. Follow the crowds." She talked to herself to steel her soul for what she was about to do.

Still, she waited.

Just one more minute.

And then someone came inside the door. More like she bounced off the door and fell inside. The blood from the thing splashed violently all over the dashboard.

Indigo was no longer herself.

She saw a hand that looked exactly like hers open the door, then slam it shut. The thing in her mother's seat looked at her, but she ignored what it was.

Run girl, run!

3

The first mistake she appreciated was forgetting her shoes. She'd been in the car so long she'd long since kicked off her fancy sandals to stay comfortable in the cramped space.

That, however, was minor compared to her second mistake.

"This is unreal," she shouted.

She had only made it fifteen feet from her car when she looked inside the white van they'd been following. A young woman's face was squished up against the glass near the back seats. Her hair was a bloody, clumpy, mess. Long strands had been pasted with the sticky red glue so as she leaned forward her hair stuck to the glass. It made it appear she had the wind in her hair.

Others inside the van were thrashing about. She'd gotten too close. She didn't dare look at them. Instead, she squatted down and moved past it at a tentative pace. There was so much going on, she didn't know what to do.

"I could run back with momma. Take care of her."

You'd die.

"I could just go back up the ramp, get out of the pit."

You'd die.

"Hide?"

You'd die.

"Well dammit, what do you want me to do?"

She answered her own question when she looked down to the mouth of the mine. Everyone who could run headed for it. The lights of the cars down there were strobing as people ran through their beams.

Even on her section of road, the stream of people running downhill continued to swell. All cars had stopped.

In the distance, she heard a train horn. And, o' happy day, the sun would soon be up. Almost in a blink, she realized the light of day was creeping into the spiral of death around her.

She took off. Down.

A few minutes went by and another man fell from the sky. He landed just short of a large RV parked on the narrow road. He'd come from twenty or thirty feet above and crumpled before her eyes. She slowed just enough to see the man's head tilt toward her. The bones of his legs had shattered and looked like a sick broom with the bristle-shards projecting from his calves.

"Better luck next time, loser." Her resolve improved as she continued to run in the wide circle, nearing the bottom as the light of the sun drenched the upper crust of the far side of the quarry like hot butter on a bagel.

Her stomach complained as she thought about it.

More train horns. It was approaching the quarry, though she was too far down to know from which way. She was near the flats at the bottom, but took the time to look at the road she'd just come down. People continued to enter the mine on the top tier—they ran along the edge for the most part—though some tried to go back out as they saw what they were getting into.

Gunfire had become commonplace throughout the night as well. She couldn't remember when it started. It just *was*. Now the chatter was constant.

She told herself that was her third mistake of the young morning. Without a weapon, she was as helpless as a new babe against the sort of horrible people she'd seen arguing with the people in the van. And now the people *in* the van. And the not-dead jumper. And the person in her mom's seat. They'd been ruined by some kind of sickness.

"Think. You have to think."

She steadied herself against the back of a black jeep Wrangler. The truck had the plastic windows and cloth top, making it dead simple to look inside. The answer stared her in the face.

It took five minutes to scramble inside the unlocked Jeep, figure out how to get into the tight back seat, and then unscrew the bolts to free the offroader's jack. She threw it out the door, and jumped out after it.

It was too heavy to carry as it was, but she figured out how to remove the base and the other non-essentials. The pace of people running by dwindled...which made her body scream in fear. But her mind kept her on task.

"You can do this. This is your ticket, girl."

After too much time, she had what she needed. The narrow metal bar for the jack was about four feet long, made of heavy steel, and it had holes along the length which made it lighter and gave it the appearance of a small ladder. She picked it up and felt its weight.

She was very short for her age, but very strong.

"Look out world, I'm a teen dynamo!"

She swung the metal bar from side to side, testing her agility with it, and felt pretty proud for equipping herself with something useful.

She looked again in the Jeep, hoping against hope for a pair of shoes.

That's when a pudgy middle-age man ran up from behind her and shoved her hard into the open door.

"Give me that!" His eyes were crazed, and only saw the red bar she'd set next to her.

But the man was winded and clumsy in his efforts. Though she was surprised, she wasn't injured. She adeptly grabbed the bar and let it fall to the ground. She then stepped around the door, reached down to the bar and picked it up. In the amount of time that took, another man— one of the sick ones—had run up behind the first.

She stood up, weapon at the ready, and watched in disbelief as the blood splashed all over the glass of the open door. She lurched to avoid it before realizing the window was closed.

She ran from the screams of the man.

She ran from screams of the roadway above her.

Into the earth.

The screaming continued there, but at least she had a weapon. And she resolved that not one person would ever stop her from surviving whatever came next.

The lights of the tunnel were bright into the distance, but a long flicker caused everyone to scream wildly.

Everyone but her.

4

Marty woke from her nap with a start. The feel of the electricity in her head faded fast.

She struggled to find her rosary. The dreams felt more real than ever, and while she suspected all these visions of the girl who left with Liam were merely her imagination playing tricks on her, she couldn't help feel there was something more to it. The girl—Blue, Saffron, Indigo, whatever she called herself—was dangerous.

Sadly, she couldn't pick up the phone and warn him.

VOICES IN THE DARK

"I found something," whispered Victoria.

"A flashlight?"

"No, something better. I think it's a tire changer tool."

She showed it to him by holding it up in the faint light coming from far behind. It was a piece of steel about twenty inches long, shaped like the letter L. On the short end, it had a fitting to remove the lug nuts from a wheel. On the other—

"Oh yeah. It's sharp." He heard the smile in her voice, though her face remained masked in deep shadow. They'd found a few cars with working lights, but as they continued further into the industrial mine's tunnel they had trouble finding vehicles with power in their batteries. They might have been run down back when the cars first arrived. That was his best guess.

"Keep it close."

He didn't want to worry her, but he couldn't temper his own concern. Blue and Pink were many cars ahead. They weren't very good at keeping quiet. Once, one of them even slammed a door shut. Yet he couldn't yell at them. If they found trouble, he didn't know what he'd do.

Behind him, he could hear footsteps and the angry moans of the infected. They should have caught up to them already, but they'd been leaving car doors open wherever they could and that was—he believed —slowing them down.

In another minute, he almost ran into one of the girls. They'd stopped and waited near the driver's door of a late model sedan.

"There's a blinking light in this one, but we can't see inside. It has tinted windows. Should we open it?"

A howl from behind. It was hard to judge distance of sound in the confined space, but he thought it was very close.

A hand pounded on the window of the mystery car.

"Get out of here," he quietly urged them all.

A faint voice yelped from inside the car. "Don't go!" The door latch clicked as Liam hung between running and staying. The others had already moved out, including Victoria.

He pivoted back, but stayed away from the door. "Are you OK?"

The door opened with a loud squeak. The hinge needed some oil. A dim light spilled out from the car. The man held a flashlight.

"Is this a rescue," the man inquired. The light was dim, but the man pointed it in Liam's eyes. He still didn't get out of the car. "I'm not getting out unless you have a platoon of soldiers with you."

Liam moved so he could see inside the car. As he got closer, the stench of the filth overwhelmed him.

"Oh my—" He put his hand over his mouth, cutting himself off.

"I have to know. Is the Army here to rescue me?"

The man on the rear seat wore fatigues. Liam didn't care to ascertain what branch he was with. Instead, he took a step back toward the tunnel wall. He tried to make it look casual, though it didn't look like the man much cared.

"No, I guess not. You're just a kid. Those others were just kids, too, weren't they? Do you have any food?" The flashlight was in his face again. "Just a little? I've been here for..."

The flashlight went to the man's watch.

"A week. A week," he repeated with surprise. "Water drips from the ceiling, but not food."

He's not right.

Louder, the man repeated himself. "Kid, I said, do you have any food?" The beam, weak as it was, landed on his face. But now the man had his feet outside the door.

"N-no, sir. We've been looking for food in here." He was always looking for food.

"Liar. Kids always lie." The man reached for something behind him. The light moved up to the man's head, and he tucked the flashlight between his head and shoulders. That gave him a free hand so he could bring his gun around and spin the revolver's cylinder like he was in a cowboy western.

"Don't really recall how many bullets I got anymore." He snorted, then chuckled, like he'd remembered something. "You feel lucky, kid?" More laughing. He was too loud.

"Let's find out." The guy stood up, but had to lean heavily against the open car door. His light was still wedged in his neck like he was holding a phone to his ear.

"Been a while since I've stood up. Feels good."

Liam wanted to run, but the man was so close he didn't think he could get away. This had all happened so fast, he wasn't prepared for it. As he stood waiting, his mind imagined shapes lurking just outside the reach of the glow of the flashlight. Zombies had to be nearby...

The man was pretty big. When he finally took a step from the support of the door, he straightened up, and Liam guessed he was well over six feet tall.

He weakly held his spear, knowing it was useless in this situation.

Delay. Every second of life counts.

"You can search me. I don't have anything."

"You know what they do with liars in the Army? They shoot 'em!" The man laughed with lots of nervous energy.

Liam didn't think that was exactly true, but he wasn't going to smart back.

The gun came out of the darkness; its smooth outline was well defined by the flashlight behind it.

Smile for the camera.

Liam saw the details of the gun in his face for just a fraction of a second. A flash of light filled the tunnel; during that instant, he saw behind the man.

The soldier's gun went off just as the other burst faded.

He felt something hot snap at his left ear. The pain was confusing, as his head was assaulted by the sound of the two gunshots. He was unable to judge if the pain was due to his ear drums exploding, or something else.

All the gunplay happened in slow motion, though strangely his concern was elsewhere. His eyes focused on something he'd seen during that initial wave of light. The light had gone out like a radar pulse. His mind assembled the data and reported its findings.

A zombie squatted on the roof of the car behind them.

Its head was cocked as it looked right at him.

2

The soldier fell over where he stood. The light flickered as it slammed into the rocky ground.

Victoria, with the Glock, stood in triumph. She spoke, but Liam couldn't hear her over the constant scream in his ears.

He reached down for the flashlight and yelled, "Run!" as loud as he could. In moments, he and Victoria raced along the narrow space between the wall of the tunnel and the cars parked in the long traffic jam. They quickly caught up to both of the girls. They'd been moving as instructed, but were unable to run until he caught up with the only portable light in this section of the tunnel.

They yelled something at him, but he still couldn't hear.

He just pointed and ran, hoping it was obvious what was happening.

The tunnel turned sharply to the right, which he took on the run with the girls in tow. He looked back to ensure they were there; the light was dimming even as he ran.

"No!" He yelled at the light in his hand, knowing it was stupid but unsure what else to do. He saw this expedition ending in the back of one of these cars as they were surrounded by hungry zombies.

He'd almost stopped to check a car door—to find their last redoubt —when the tunnel came to a final "T" junction. It was a confusing tangle of cars, bodies, and rock piles. He swung the light in an arc across the scene, and tried to piece it together.

To the left, the traffic jam continued as far as he could see. To the right, a few of the big mining dump trucks were parked next to each other at the cusp of a larger room. Cars had tried ramming into them, but that clearly failed. The big trucks seemed to huddle together to block traffic in that direction. They most assuredly had blocked the line of cars here.

Liam found a hole between the trucks large enough for people to fit through, and he held the light as he stood next to the crevice—pointing the way. Victoria stood by him, allowing the two girls to get through first. She gave him a hasty smile and began to wedge herself between the trucks. Then it was his turn.

He threw himself into the gap as if his life depended on it. The hand on his arm suggested he'd once again made the right call.

A faint howl made it through his foggy brain. Lots of screams came from the other direction. He was tempted to yell for everyone to be quiet and scream one at a time, so he knew what was happening.

I'm going crazy. That's clear now.

He didn't look back. He felt more hands reaching for him in the tight space.

Scooting along the truck, he absently wondered if zombies could get into tight spaces. It seemed like a pretty complicated task for the dumb things...

Fingertips on his shoulder gave him his answer.

Seconds later, he fell out the back side of the truck roadblock.

With very little breath in his lungs, and a mouth as dry as the desert wind, he yelled, "Fight them here!"

He still had his spear, but it felt small in his hands. He put the flashlight on the ground so it pointed to the gap. With a flourish, he turned with his spear to stop them from coming through. He sensed as much as saw Victoria and the two girls standing behind the next truck. The dim light almost couldn't reach them.

The first zombie squirted through, and had gained its freedom before he could bring his spear to bear. It moved toward the girls.

He hoped Victoria could read his mind, but he yelled the obvious to be sure. "Get that one!"

A second zombie poked its head from between the two trucks. Liam set himself upon it with growing anger. He channeled his fear at almost being shot, and his fear of this dark space, and used that to thrust with all his strength. The spear plunged into its face, though even with all his pent up anger, he was unable to look at the damage he'd wrought upon it.

Rather than fall to the ground, the body of the zombie wedged itself into the space between the two trucks. The next zombie in line behind it comically peeked over the head of its slumping partner and Liam dispatched it—her—as well.

He could see what would eventually happen. As more and more zombies got into the gap they would eventually push their dead comrades forward to clear the space. But for the moment, he could turn his attention to the one that got away...

In the ugly light, he saw the male zombie had on a too-tight fitness shirt and running shorts. He had fallen upon Blue. He imagined she was screaming, but he couldn't be sure. Victoria was over the zombie swinging her tire iron like a mad woman.

As it happened, he added audio to what he was seeing.

"Crack! There goes the skull."

It went rigid for a moment, then dropped like a lead balloon on top of Blue. Victoria struggled to get the man to roll over until Pink came out of the shadows to give her a hand.

His head was still a mess. His ears alternated between a tinny ringing, a high pitched whistle, and perfect silence. Once in a great while, voices would filter through, but he couldn't be sure what was being said.

He felt hands on his arm, and jumped once again. But they were friendly—Victoria picked up the flashlight, pointed it forward, and pulled him with her.

There were no lights in the new area, and the flashlight continued to flicker and dance as they ran. But there were no cars parked here. That, at least, made it different.

He corrected himself. There was one light. It was tiny in the darkness ahead. It took another couple of minutes of unsteady walking to piece together what they were approaching. When he finally knew what it was, he had regained a little of his hearing and a lot of his hope.

It was a glass door.

3

A dull blue glow came through the frosted glass of the single door. It looked like a typical door you'd see attached to any strip mall tenant across America. Here, it was inset into a smooth concrete face—and looked completely at odds with the mine.

Victoria swung the light from side to side on the rock, and there was a large metal door twenty or thirty feet to the left, almost outside the range of the poor light. Once she'd made her sweep, she turned it off.

It sounded distant, but Liam definitely heard her this time. Only a sharp pain remained in his left ear, but he could take it. "We need to save this light, in case we really need it."

He looked around and didn't like the fact he stood with Blue and Pink as they stared at the door. Almost without thinking, he took a step forward to be closer to Victoria—currently the only person who seemed to be doing something.

She rattled the glass door, but it didn't budge. In return, he scooted next to the door, and tried to look inside. The door revealed no clues, save one.

"There's a bar across it. Here," he said, as he slid his finger from one edge to the other, "to here. This thing's keeping it closed."

Victoria gently pushed him back a step and gave him the "shush" symbol. Her eyes conveyed a similar message.

He nodded, and tried to whisper, "Sorry." The gentle blue light illuminated the two girls—one of whom was also named Blue, which he found hilarious—but nothing beyond them. A black void enveloped everything but the door.

"Stand back, guys." Victoria's voice was starting to register at a normal volume again. As he began to turn back to her, he heard the shattering of glass. When he looked at her, she had shattered the entire pane of the door. It had splintered into thousands of fragments, many of which fell to the ground as he watched. Victoria used her tire iron to scrape the remainder from the edges—causing shards to spray all over the rocks at their feet.

Liam saw into the room. Security lights around the edge of banks of computers were bright blue. The main lights on the ceiling were all out.

Victoria stuck her head into the room, then kept going. She had to duck under the heavy steel bar that had been placed into the handle of the door on one end, and into some kind of bracket on the other side. It ensured the door could not be opened in the conventional fashion.

Here I am again, ruining someone's refuge.

He hated to admit it, but dying on the doorstep of a refuge because he didn't want to break the glass seemed like a stupid option, too. He was too important to die like that.

Too important, am I?

Was he starting to believe his own press? Hadn't Hayes said something very close to that back when they were under the Arch? He claimed he was too valuable to the research effort to waste himself fighting hand-to-hand to protect others.

He searched his feelings. He didn't think he'd told anyone to fight for him while he watched. That's how he'd know he'd gone round the bend.

As it was, he was the second person into the room, and that was only because he didn't know Victoria was going to go through before him. Pink and Blue followed him in.

The control room—he called it that, but he really had no idea what it was—had walls on three sides. The fourth side was covered by big glass windows. He walked toward it and immediately recognized he was looking through the glass at the big garage door he'd seen from outside the blue door.

"So the computer guys are in here, and the worker guys are out there?"

Victoria sidled up next to him. "What do you think they did in here?"

They'd both seen the interior of Riverside Hotel and Casino, so nothing was off the table in terms of possible uses for the place. Even so, Liam couldn't fathom the purpose of the control room or the larger facility outside the glass. A lone door beckoned them.

"We should look around here, first."

He thought that made perfect sense. Something about the blackness outside the windows made him uneasy. It was more pronounced than the fear he had for the zombies somewhere outside the now-broken glass window through which they'd entered. They were known unknowns. Whatever was in that other room was an unknown unknown. Big difference.

They realized pretty quickly the bank of computers were in power-save mode. He moved a mouse on one of them and the screen blinked back to life. The bright light from the huge monitor forced him to squint until his eyes could absorb it all in comfort.

He turned to Victoria, unable to control his excitement. He smiled, "I wonder if the internet's working?"

"I have an auction ending, would you mind checking it." She leaned to watch over his shoulder, and while there, rubbed her fingers through his hair, partly to tussle it, and partly—he hoped—as a sign of affection. But when her hand grazed his ear, he winced.

She jumped back. "Liam. There's blood."

He'd forgotten all about it. His whole head hurt already, he'd almost overlooked the pain of having his ear partially shot off.

All the girls looked as Victoria used the dying flashlight to observe the damage. She spent a lot of time prodding near the wound, and she even used her shirt to get some of the blood out of his hair and lower ear. Her analysis was that it wasn't that serious, though. The bullet had removed the top half-inch of his ear.

"My God, you were lucky." That passed for Victoria's official prognosis.

He worried a little, as he realized he could hear almost nothing out of that ear, but even that was tempered by what he saw on the computer screen.

The internet *was* up.

4

He decided now wasn't the time to worry about security. He logged into his online account, and found himself faced with pages of emails. Many had been sent in the last two weeks.

"Ha! They must have automated emails. The most recent ones showed up just today." He laughed quietly at the thought of computers continuing to send out spam long after mankind had lost the ability to receive them. He took a moment to force that into his memory; he wanted to include that in his book someday.

He cracked his knuckles, and prepared to tackle the wall of spam. He wanted to see if anything important had been sent to him by friends or family. He may never get another chance to find out where they'd all gone.

He'd just started to sort when a chat window popped up. Since he was logged into his profile, anyone looking for him would see that he was online. The words scrolled out a letter at a time. "Thank God! Worried about you, Liam."

"Huh?" He leaned back. "Look at this." He meant it for Victoria, but all the girls crowded around him.

The white box waited for his reply. The identity of the person on the other line just said, "Anonymous User," and no other information was given in Anonymous' profile.

"Who is this?" he typed back.

"Go into WOUS." The chat window showed the other person had logged off.

He turned around and pointedly looked at the broken window on the door. Somewhere out there, zombies were trying to get through the dump truck road block. Would he have time to play a silly game?

Part of him really desired to play. He hadn't touched it since just before the sirens went off. That game was, more or less, the last normal thing he did before the zombies came. After that, it was survival all day, every day.

He had no other plan, and whoever was on the other end knew who he was. That alone made it worthwhile to see what they had to say. With a few clicks, he found the game installer and had it loaded onto this computer in sixty seconds.

"Wow, this computer is fast!"

The girls continued to hover around him. Victoria's hand was on the back of his neck. He took a deep breath as he fired up the game.

He guessed none of them had ever seen it, so he took the time while it loaded to explain what he was doing. "So, this game is about..."

The words got caught in his throat. His eyes watered as emotion surged. With a cough, he tried to play it cool—he had three girls hanging on his every word—but his efforts failed. Where seconds before he was ecstatic at being able to play this game, he was now losing it. He had no idea why.

He felt Victoria stroke his back.

She can read me like a book.

The tears rolled down his cheeks; he continued to stare at the screen. It waited for his input.

"Liam?" Blue asked. "Are you cryin'?" She kind of laughed, though Liam felt his chair move and heard something that sounded like a kick.

After a short pause, she continued, "Seriously, you OK?"

Is anyone good, anymore?

The game represented an era he would never get back. It was the past, just as sure as cavemen or covered wagons. Though both, he dourly noted, would find homes in the current world more readily than a video game. He desperately wished he could jump in the game and never look back.

"I, uh," he shook his head and tried to wipe his tears like it was no big deal, "just got a little nostalgic, I guess. I played this game on the very last day of...how things were before the zombies."

As his vision cleared, he could see the game wanted his login information. He prepared himself for the laughter.

"Meat me in Yonkers? What kind of a name is that?" Blue asked.

The loading panel popped up once he was in the game world, and the three girls saw his avatar in all its glory—all *her* glory.

"What. The. Hell?" Blue actually pointed to the girl avatar.

The game designers let players build their own characters. It was very flexible, and Liam was proud he had chosen an avatar that would stand out amongst the millions of other players in the game. "Meat me in Yonkers" was a tiny young black woman, with her hair in a tight bun on the back of her head. She wore exactly what you'd imagine of a sixteen-year-old boy's imagination: black combat boots, a tight-fitting red dress cut low so her cleavage showed. He liked to think of her as part Lara Croft and part Alice, and just as tough. He'd never seen another player with the same look.

The girls were stunned to silence. He started talking to compensate for the awkwardness.

"So yeah, Yonks has lots of weapons she can use, but right now she has a Katana on her back while she holds her M16. I gave her raw meat gauntlets for her arms—the zombies bite on those if they get up on her. She's got knives and a couple of guns strapped to her legs under her dress. And—"

"Why is she black?" It was Pink.

"Yeah, Liam, why is your super-hot chicky player avatar black? Why isn't she a super-hot brunette future nurse avatar?" He could hear the smile in her voice behind him. She took things even less seriously than he did sometimes. She had described herself.

He admitted his earlier sadness was sloughing off. He turned to the pair of part-black young girls standing next to him, seeing them, not as colors this time, but as parallels to the woman he had built inside the game. A woman he admitted he found to be a very attractive, though fake, amalgam of strong females from the movies. He'd never, until that moment, thought of why he made her black, other than it made her look exotic. If he squinted his eyes, he could imagine either of the twins stepping in for Yonks. That unsettled him.

Unable to answer beyond a shrug, he turned back to the game. Inside the virtual world, the pretty young woman stood inside a convenience store.

"This is where you start. It's a safe base to stock up on supplies."

A virtual man walked in and a voice bubble popped up over his head. Yet, they heard no sounds. He turned up the volume on the computer and heard a woman's voice. No one was ever what they seemed, inside the game.

Just like the Apocalypse.

5

"—hear me, can you?" came through the speakers.

He spoke at the screen, hoping there was a microphone attached. It was too dark to see for sure. "I hear you. Who are you?"

"Don't worry about that. The less you know, the safer we both shall remain."

The woman's voice had a tinny quality to it, like it was coming from the far end of a long tube. It had a vaguely non-human quality, though he could still understand it perfectly.

"OK, then what are you doing inside this game?"

"Extra layers of protection. Your email is almost certainly monitored. Chat from there would also be tracked. I knew you had this game and while we are in here, our transmission is encrypted."

Inside the game, another text window came on screen. It was used by players who didn't have microphones, though that was so rare, he almost never used text chat. Now a text message appeared.

"Liam, continue talking. This chat window is secure."

"Seems legit. I guess. But why should we listen to you?" Liam spoke, continuing the charade.

On the screen, the words popped up as the person on the other line keyed them in. The same person, he assumed, spoke over the speakers, though he had to focus on the text to read it.

"Liam. Can't trust anyone. The triplets with you are something new. Not sure if can trust. I erased the data on the chip you got from Colonel Rufus McMurphy. If you were caught with it, you'd be shot on sight."

He was less concerned about the three girls with him being spies, than with the data chip. The colonel had entrusted it to him, and he'd allowed it to be deleted back in Cairo.

He talked, probably with inane babble, to the computer screen as a distraction while he typed. "Who is listening in?"

In seconds, a reply came back. "You met them already. They are the group most responsible for unleashing the plague on us Americans. But plague was already overseas when they did it. It was cover-up to blame others."

Liam had a hard time with the timeline of the various plagues ravaging the world. He'd need an outline when he wrote his book. Hayes and Duchesne had both agreed it was the NIS—National Internal Security—that released the plague that infected humans in such a horrific way that Liam could only describe them as zombies.

The NIS is listening.

He typed back, "All right. Nothing secure anymore. How do I know I can trust you?"

The reply came back after a delay. All the words splashed on the screen at once. "You don't. But I hope to gain your trust after I show you this. Sadly, unless you have headphones there is no way to prevent this from behind heard, and possibly recorded on your end."

The screen froze, then returned to normal. The male avatar moved inside the virtual store until he stood next to a TV on the wall. On the screen, totally incongruous with the game itself, was an image of Colonel McMurphy. When Yonkers stood close to the screen within the screen, the video began. It started with the colonel speaking into the camera. Liam recognized the backdrop as the tent at Elk Meadow—the research facility where he'd met the man.

He looked around for headphones, wondering if it was even worth it—anyone listening in would have to come deep into a mine full of zombies to give him a spanking. Before he could do more than glance around, the video started.

"Hi Susan. I hope this makes it to you. If anyone knew I made these videos, I'd probably be tossed into the zombie pen I've got out back. This is conspiracy stuff beyond anything I thought possible. I don't even know where to begin..."

At his desk, the colonel picked up a picture frame and showed it to the camera. It had a red-haired woman and a young teen about Liam's age. It was the photo the colonel would give to him later. When stuff went nutso at the camp...

"This is why I'm doing this. Why I'm risking everything. These two people right here."

He put the frame down as he spoke faster, and slightly quieter.

"Two days ago, I was shown something. I know you'll find this hard to believe, but I'm not crazy. Please know that. I...I've seen the dead walk. I mean real dead people, putting one foot in front of the other. These people, these government pinheads, think they've stumbled on the secret to immortality. Argh, how do I say this without sounding crazy here?"

The gray-haired man looked away, then back at the camera with a direct gaze at him—though Liam knew he was really talking to his wife.

"I saw a dead man rise from his pine box. They threw the lid open, and as God as my witness, something wicked and evil possessed that body and it pulled itself over the edge and it fell onto the floor. Then, with great effort, it stood on its feet and ambled toward us..."

Liam saw fear in his eyes, even two days removed from the event.

"The eyes, dear. The thing had no eyes...but it could see. I could feel its stare on me. It came for me." He laughed a nervous laugh. "But they turned on special lights which froze it in its tracks. Then they ushered us out of the control room and back to our trucks. They said we had to know what was coming so we had the stomach to do what needed doin'. I've been thinking about it ever since. Not getting any work done here, and Hayes is riding me hard to have things ready."

He again looked off camera. This time when he continued it was almost a whisper.

"Susan, I have to tell someone. I can't trust anyone here with me as it's clear Hayes has ears everywhere. I don't think he works for who he says he does. He has more power than he lets on. They have me doing research, but his team—his Riverside team—is light years ahead of the rest of us. I asked where they got the man, coffin and all, and all they said was the man did his duty for his country once when he died, and a second time when he came back to life. That can only mean one thing: they pulled him from an actual cemetery. Why would they do that, Susan? Why?"

He readjusted himself at his desk, almost pleading with his wife to believe him.

"I do know this much: the dead man was dressed in army fatigues. They were very old, perhaps World War II vintage. I think he came from the National Cemetery over at Jefferson Barracks. It's by that big quarry—"

The screen froze inside the game.

Everyone was frozen outside the game, too.

6

"Is that the answer?" Liam asked it rhetorically, though he didn't really intend to ask it at all—at least not out loud. He'd been trying to square the men and women he'd seen suffer under the effects of the zombie plague since day one. Were they dead people infected with something that brought them back to life, or were they living people so sick they appeared dead? The word "zombie" was something he ascribed to them, though the more popular, and he had to admit more accurate, term most people used was *infected*. They had been stricken with a sickness, but the disease process remained a mystery to him, even after meeting the guy who concocted the disease in the first place.

One of the plagues.

Yes, there was that. The big difficulty for them all was there were at least three different viruses involved with this devil's brew of apocalyptic pandemics. Hayes had said as much. But now, if the colonel was telling the truth, the actual buried-in-the-ground dead could also get infected and be made to rise from their graves. That, right there, was the exact definition of a zombie. The thought did not give him comfort.

He answered himself. "The answer to the big question of whether these are zombies or not."

Blue laughed, "Who the hell is askin' that question? The big question is where do we go to get safe. Does your computer friend have that answer?" She leaned toward the computer and repeated herself. "Where can we get safe, Honkey Tonk?"

Liam didn't correct her mistake. His avatar wouldn't have the answer. That honor belonged to the male avatar—Anonymous.

The woman on the audio link did respond by typing something in the screen.

"Liam. Please clear your three friends from the terminal. I have to say something for you alone. Please hurry. This link won't last forever. Once they figure out where you are, they'll cut me off."

He wanted to ask question after question, but she instilled a sense of haste into him.

"Guys, give me a minute?" He winked at Victoria, though in the soft blue light he was unsure if she caught it.

The twins mumbled, but walked away from him nonetheless, toward computers on the other side of the room. Victoria seemed less sure of leaving, but she walked several paces in the opposite direction.

The control room wasn't much bigger than his family room back at home, so they all remained close. But they couldn't see the small text on the screen, he was sure of that.

"OK, I'm alone," he typed.

"Liam. I'm being told there is someone trying to trace this connection. I've got a very talented crew working with me. I was able to see you inside the Riverside Hotel—you got my message about shutting off the power. I had hoped that by cutting the power, it would trap Hayes in the building until the good guys could get there and snatch him, but you know how that went."

Yeah, he knew. The power went out, the zombies spilled out of their cages, and he and Victoria had to rappel down the outside of a skyscraper to escape. Hayes just got in his helicopter and seemingly had it much easier. The mysterious call to Victoria's phone actually endangered him more than it ever was a threat to Hayes. But, as Grandma would say, "The Lord works in mysterious ways, or sometimes not at all." It all worked out because he and Victoria made it work out.

"We do have people on the ground near you. There's a man we've contacted on the radio named Jason Hawkes on a bluff near that mine. Get out of the quarry and find him. He can help you stay safe."

Figures it would be him.

"We walked through his camp. One of our party said he was with bad guys. Gun runners or something. He kind of creeped us all out. Should we go back?"

"Hang on."

A full thirty seconds passed as Liam stared at the blinking cursor on the screen.

"Liam, this is very important. If I get cut off, you must get out of the mine. They'll be coming."

His mind swam in questions.

"Liam, you've found triplets. You have to get them out of there. You are in great danger."

That was the second time she'd used that word. He heard a movie line echo in his head. He didn't think the word meant what she thought it did...

"Triplets? I have twins, plus Victoria. Not triplets tho."

Another long silence.

A burst of characters shot onto the screen, as if someone cut and paste a long answer. It was an email message from someone named Indigo Hamilton to "Mom."

"Dear mom. I know you'll never get this. I know you're dead. But if you ever do see this—by some miracle—I wanted to tell you I love you and I miss you. Things are getting bad in here. More infected at the exit of the mine and more people in here dying and becoming infected. I'm not sure what I'm going to do next. I love you. Love to Saffron and Azure. Goodbye for now. XX OO IH."

"We identified your two friends when you entered the mine. We've confirmed they're all sisters. The third one is in there with you, unless she died. She sent her email from the terminal you're using."

The words flew as he watched.

"Liam, someone on the outside got the idea it takes three people to study the effects of the plague. We're trying to figure it out on this end. Does that mean anything to you?"

At that moment, he remembered the words of Colonel McMurphy as he was in the throes of the virus. He said something to the effect he couldn't totally trust Liam because there were groups that would love to steal his information. That man did indeed have a lot of secret information, though in the end he did share it with Liam by giving him the data chip. Over the past few days, he'd allowed that data to fall into the hands of whoever was at the end of the digital link ending on this computer screen. Not only would it take him too long to explain everything that he'd experienced with Grandma, himself, and Victoria, he wasn't willing to trust that information to someone named Anonymous.

"No, sorry."

"OK, that's OK. Get the missing girl if you can, but get out."

His high paranoia returned. He imagined it was Hayes on the other end, or his red-headed wife, guiding him on another misadventure so that he could take over at the last second and avoid doing all the hard work. He'd done that on his initial escape from St. Louis, and he'd had Liam and Grandma jumping through hoops all the way up until the point he took her blood sample with him, after she'd been infected by him. He wanted to end the call.

"Right. So how do we get past all the zombies out there?"

"More than one exit. Schematics. You have to get out. Find Jason. He knows your Dad. Friends. Patriots. Get—"

The text just ended.

Outside the room, through the broken glass of the small door, red emergency lights began to spin. They looked like the lights you'd find on the top of a police cruiser.

Liam and the girls walked to the shattered door still being blocked by the useless metal bar. It was rust red, with a stamped badge on one end from a 4x4 company.

Sirens began to howl. First, far away in the mine. As each new horn started, he could tell they were getting closer. In a minute, a siren spun up just outside the door. The room with the dump trucks blocking the entrance was very large now that they could see it all, but remained practically empty. He already knew there was a garage door on the near wall, but he saw another large door across the vast room. Large rounded pillars of rough stone supported the ceiling throughout.

There was a missing triplet somewhere nearby.

Triplets. Three players in his weird *World of Undead Soldiers* dream. He knew now, looking back, those girls were all very similar to the two standing next to him, which meant the remaining triplet would fit into that dream too.

When he got on the bus in his dream, Grandma had wondered if he was really in her dream. What if she was in his? Both in the same dream? And, if that was true, was he responsible for bringing the girls to his side?

He turned to the cavernous space next to the control room, to peer through the larger glass windows on that side. If the third girl had been in this room, it made the most sense to think she'd continued into the adjacent room.

"Blue, Pink, you have a sister, don't you? You're triplets."

"Yeah, so?" Blue didn't seem to find it odd he would know that.

"Did you know she was here? In this mine?"

The girls walked up to him as Pink responded, "Indy? She's here?" She shook Liam's arm. "Where? Where is she?"

"That's what we're going to find out." He pointed in the direction he was going, urging them to follow. When he reached the glass door, he looked out into the still-dark room carved from stone. On the near side of the room, he saw a double row of blue string lights lying on the ground. They made a type of path into the darkness, though he couldn't see where they ended while he was still inside the control room.

"Victoria, you with me?"

"Of course. What's wrong, Liam?"

He wished he could tell her. He'd shut off the computer before anyone could see what the woman on the other end had transmitted. Someone was coming for them from outside. Zombies were blocking their escape. A set of triplets would soon be his responsibility. A mysterious typist gave him instructions he couldn't believe, not completely. And, to top it all off, the person they were trying to link up with was a friend of his dad. He didn't think it would help with morale if he dumped that on her, even if he could get her away from the other two.

He held the door handle, about to pull it, when one question popped in his head he knew had an answer. "Blue, Pink, if we do find your sister," it was completely silly to think it, and it felt silly to ask it, but he thought it was important enough to push through all that and ask, "what color will she be?"

The response was even and simultaneous.

"Black."

COLUMBARIUM

Liam wasn't surprised. There was something odd about the girls, beyond the strange way they just dropped into his life. Again, questions stacked up inside his brain. What were they doing before the sirens? How come they got separated? What were they doing in the weeks since the sirens? What made them go to the particular spot where he found them?

Not impossible. Just improbable.

Those words echoed from Grandma. What would she say about these two? Back in Cairo, she seemed to know Blue from a dream she'd had.

That's another question!

But he had to tuck all those questions into their own drawers. He was much too busy being scared. The three girls had lined up behind him as they walked into the vast chamber. The line of lights on the ground led off into the darkness. Just enough to see the way, but not bright enough to cut through the pitch black elsewhere. The reflection of blue on the rough ceiling was the only comfort. It felt like walking over a rocky covered bridge with an abyss on each side.

His brain created wild fantasies about creatures in the darkness. Here, he could see a multi-tentacled monster; there, he could see a hockey-masked murderer holding a machete. His eyes strained to see the edge, they wanted to see the edge, if only to assign the proper scale to the place. They tried, to no avail. Eventually he determined it would make him feel much better to watch his path along the blue lights and ignore everything else.

A hum came from the darkness ahead. The sound bounced off the raw earth all around them, but Liam thought he recognized the source.

"Hold up. Do you hear that?" He took a knee as he said it. The blue light was still dim, but his eyes had gotten used to it. The walkway lights were now illuminating the large cavernous room. He could see the floor and ceiling, and one rough-hewn wall was about fifty feet to his right. The left wall was still hidden, somewhere out in the darkness beyond the ability of the ambient light to reach. Or, more likely, beyond the ability of his own eyes to register. He did see great columns of rock, spaced every fifty feet or so; they held up the roof.

The girls all heard the sound, but no one offered any suggestions on what it might be.

When it arrived, it was as he expected. The drone generated a slight breeze as it hovered about five feet above them, just below the rock ceiling. Earlier in the day—or yesterday, he'd lost track of time—a similar drone had hovered above the boat. Whether it was the exact same model, he couldn't say.

"You want me to bash it in?" Blue asked. She picked up a fist-sized rock to make her point. The captain would have shot it down.

He realized he was in charge. Looking around, he saw the three girls crouched in an arc behind him. Now, seeing the formation, he was literally leading them.

Time to say something smart.

"No, whoever is using that drone is here in the tunnels with us. We can't turn around on account of the zom—infected. We need to make friends."

...or we're dead.

He thought he did pretty well.

Because he didn't know what else to do, he waved at the drone.

It hovered in place, but he knew he was being observed. He felt the eyes through the camera of the sophisticated hardware.

"We only want a place to hide. We won't take your food." It seemed reasonable to assume the craft could hear audio.

The drone tilted gently and began to move. It got lower, scooted around Liam, and seemed to focus on the girls. After a few moments, the drone moved even closer to the girls. It was closest to Blue.

"I could knock this thing out of the air...just say the word."

"No!" Liam wasn't sure what he was supposed to do, but he was confident no good could come from destroying the aircraft. "Just let it look."

It hovered for a full minute, then moved to Pink. Liam's imagination took flight and he began to fret the thing had a gun, but his rational side fought back at the notion. There were a lot more efficient ways of killing than putting a gun on a drone, especially deep in a dark mine.

Just turn out the lights.

He shuddered at the thought. They were at the mercy of the lights.

The drone seemed to finish its sweep. The fan noise increased as it tilted again and went the opposite direction—back toward the control room.

"Well, they know we're here," Victoria said with some amusement.

Blue, ever serious, replied, "We've just been checked out by a creepy machine, and you think it's funny? The captain was right about you two."

"What does that—"

The sound of the drone whizzing by cut off Victoria mid-sentence. It appeared to continue ahead, but it stopped and came back to hover in front of them. Then it jumped ahead, then came back.

"I think it's trying to tell us something," Victoria observed.

It was pretty obvious the drone wanted them to move forward. Liam stood and was ready to follow when he caught the sound of something behind them. The blue lights on the path far behind them started to wink out.

"Guys..."

They all looked behind. The lights continued to wink out, though it was random. One wink here. One there. Sometimes they'd come back on for a second, then die out again.

The drone actually bumped Liam in the back. His muscles locked up in fright, until he realized what it was.

"OK, guys. Droney says we've got to move. I'm gonna say we should run."

Blue, as if in a dream, replied, "Those are people. Heading this way."

Liam knew he had to move, but the surprise of the drone on his back and the sight of a crowd so thick it choked the lights behind them made him hesitate. The twins started to run. Victoria grabbed him by the arm.

"I'm following you," she said.

"Yeah...we should run now." He said it to her, but the words were meant for his legs. They weren't listening to his brain.

Luckily, Victoria pulled him.

They ran after the drone.

2

The cavern was immense. The large columns on the left continued as they ran. In a couple minutes, they came to the first body on the ground. Despite everything, the twins stopped when they reached it.

It was badly mangled and despite the blue ambiance, he knew the pool of liquid underneath the corpse was blood red. He'd seen lots of zombie remains over the past weeks—this one had been shot by a powerful caliber. It had ripped several holes in the torso and the killing shot was on the side of its head. A large piece of skull was missing.

On any other day, he might have lost his lunch at the sight.

This time he kept it together. "Keep running, guys."

In moments, they saw more bodies. Then scores of them. Finally, hundreds. They were piled up in an arc from their left to their right. The bodies got so thick they had to step on them to keep moving forward.

Pink whimpered as the number of bodies increased. The stink grew in tandem.

Blue seemed to take it all in stride until she had to climb on the first one. "I...I don't know if I can do this. I don't know why, but I'm..."

Liam, already on a small pile of the dead, steadied himself by holding the belt of one of them, and turned around.

He wanted to be brave, but his speech started with an involuntary shiver. "Uh...I don't like this either." A million thoughts scrambled his brain. He wondered if he should cajole them with kind words or yell at this with anger to get them moving. If he failed to inspire them, they might die. On the other hand—

"Fight or die, girls. We don't care." Victoria pushed Liam from behind. "You, too. Keep moving."

A hand reached out for his leg. When it grabbed him, he screamed like a girl.

Real smooth.

All the girls screamed in reply; Victoria recovered the fastest. She pushed him harder.

That got him moving. He fumbled with his spear, but he couldn't see the face of the one pawing at him. It would take time to find it, and digging through the bodies was low on his list right now.

He pulled his leg free, then continued across the pile of bodies. If the girls wanted to die back there, he couldn't do anything for them. His brain tried to square his feeling of wanting to save them with the reality of needing to save himself, and Victoria. The prodding of Victoria and the now-angry buzz of the drone nearby spurred him on.

The sounds of crying almost made him turn around, but Victoria whispered, "They're coming." That kept him going forward, too.

The bodies were piled two or three deep, but he saw them spread out on the ground all around. It was darker here because they had collapsed on the blue strands of light. The path continued forward; he thought he saw a shape on the wall ahead—another large door.

Several red beams of light reached out of the darkness and converged on his chest.

When Victoria caught up to him, she tried to push him. This time, he couldn't move at all.

"I've got a problem here." His voice was high-pitched, but he wasn't embarrassed. It was his extreme panic voice, though he tried with all he was worth to keep it together. "There are...lasers...aiming at my chest."

Victoria, perhaps not believing him, scrambled next to him. When she arrived, a couple of the lasers moved to her white shirt, making large red blotches in the darkness.

With the force of a fist to his face, he realized where he was. Bodies everywhere, but mostly in an even arc from left to right, as if someone had sighted in the distance and shot anything that made it into that space.

He reached over to Victoria. "Can I have the flashlight, please?"

With mechanical motions, he was able to get it from her and turn it on. At first, it refused to light, but he banged it with his hand and a tired glow came forth. He turned it on the pile of dead, confirming his suspicions.

"These people were all shot. Look at them." He panned the light on the bodies closest to them. It wasn't strong enough to see much beyond a few feet. All the bodies had terrible wounds. The amount of blood was sickening. He felt his stomach retch, though it was completely empty.

"These were zombies..." He said it almost with relief, though the implications were no less damning for them. Not with laser sights drilling into their hearts.

He turned to Victoria with the light. It was almost completely dead. In the final gasps though, he saw the recognition on her face. He felt it on his own. Together, they turned forward and screamed.

"We're alive!"

"Don't shoot!"

A few moments of silence followed.

The reply flew out of the darkness.

3

"Saffron! Azure! Get over here."

The girls, sounding distant from over the pile of bodies, shouted back. "Indigo!"

They came up next to Liam and bear crawled over the worst of the pile. He followed them with Victoria next to him. The lasers vacillated among the four, as if unsure which to choose. With certain death behind, and the possibility of death dancing on his chest, he prayed.

Please God, don't let my friends die on a pile of zombie bodies.

He'd learned a lesson from Grandma Marty about praying. She once told him she never prayed for herself. Instead, she prayed for others. Liam wondered if she really meant that, or if it was some kind of adult way of making him think of other people first. Whatever the truth, he thought it made a lot of sense as he slid across the remains of the dead.

The bodies cleared up as they moved closer to the source of the lasers. The blue lights on the floor reemerged, and the overall lighting situation improved. Liam felt he was seldom surprised these days, so it was with almost businesslike recognition he saw the big machine guns lining the wall with the door. He counted six of them, spaced about ten feet apart. The farthest one was almost invisible to his left, out in the darkness.

A young girl stood in the small doorway to the right of the larger, closed metal door inset into the rock face. It was very much like the last big room he'd been in, although the smaller door was not frosted glass —it was heavy steel. A little light spilled out from inside, setting the girl in profile for those in the darkness. Liam knew the girl even before he could make out her features. She was, after all, as short as the two girls already with him.

Blue and Pink ran ahead to their sister. Liam grabbed Victoria's hand and followed.

"Hurry guys. We have to get inside. I'll turn on the guns again." The triplets hugged briefly then disappeared from view.

Victoria had a knack for reading his mind. She voiced his thoughts with a close whisper. "Lucky that their sister is the one operating these guns, huh?"

He nodded, though she probably didn't see him in the darkness. He let her go up a couple steps to reach the doorway. When he mounted the steps, he turned around, wondering how close the zombie pursuit had come to reaching them.

He was genuinely shocked when a nearby gun barked several times as it fired. Its laser had found something at the edge of its awareness. The zombies had come very close to catching up. He threw himself through the doorway and shut it with a bang. He stood with his back against it to catch his wits, and heard more of the guns start up. The sound was muffled through the doorway. He could feel them as much as hear them.

"OK, this is too much. Who are you three?"

He was still at the door, but the three girls were nearby in front of a big computer monitor. They were talking to each other in a tight hug-huddle, apparently unaware he said anything.

The guns chugged outside the door, and he had a hard time separating himself from the metal. It was as if part of him wanted to be back there. Part of him *wanted* to get caught. He reveled in the vibrations from the machine guns.

Victoria looked lost. She stood between him and the other girls with her hands on her hips. She either wanted to peel him off the door, or listen to what the girls were saying.

Peel me off the door!

With a flourish, she turned to the big monitor near the girls. "My God. There's an infinite number of them!"

That got everyone's attention. Even Liam managed to free himself. The control room was very similar to the one they'd left earlier, though it had white lights on the walls, rather than deep blue. They seemed extra dim as if they only got half the electricity they required. Still, it was enough to see the third triplet. She was identical to the other two, of course, but was covered—absolutely covered—in dried and peeling blood. It was as if she took a bath in the stuff, and then picked off what she could from her skin, but was unable to get it out of her clothing. As he closed the distance, he thought she smelled horrible, though he couldn't say for sure as they were all covered in blood now from their climb over the kill zone.

The new girl took a moment to introduce herself. She reached her hand out to Liam. "Hi, I'm Indigo, but you can call me—"

"Black."

The girl paused her handshake. "How did you know that?" She nodded to her sisters. "They tell you?"

"Yeah." He wanted to believe they had agreed beforehand what they would call themselves in the event of a Zombie Apocalypse, but just thinking it sounded stupid in his head.

"We told him," the other girls agreed.

They all gathered around the computer screen. It displayed a view from what was apparently a floating camera in the room outside.

"Is this the drone?" Liam asked.

He shivered again, involuntarily. He wrapped his arms around himself without thinking about it.

Black happened to look at him as he did it. "Yeah, it's cold down here. I thought about going out to get some extra clothes from those people, but..."

She turned back to the screen, describing what the drone was observing. "When I first saw you, I wondered how you'd gotten through that door back there. I guess I shouldn't be surprised you broke the glass. I would have done the same. But you could have at least blocked the second door."

Liam knew they'd made a mistake.

"But that isn't the worst part. These people you see out there..." She put her finger on the computer screen to point to them. For the first time in his life, it didn't bother him. "...they came from across the courtyard."

"Oh, I guess I should explain." She punched up some keys and a map of the mine appeared. She again began to drag her finger around the screen.

"You guys came in the only door to this place. The one with the dump trucks. They get an A for effort on that one. F for delivery though." A sad laugh. "So most of the people who came down into this wing of the mine went across the courtyard area where you came in. I don't know for sure, but I was told they keep some more dump trucks and other equipment over there. They like to have backups on every level."

"*Most* went that way?" He asked.

"Yeah, a few people who work here tried to get everyone into that doorway. I wasn't going to go anywhere near a large group of people, especially not in an enclosed space. I went through the blue door. Plus, I was pretty messed up though after my—"

She looked away from everyone for a few seconds. "—my descent into this place." She stood up and turned to her sisters. "I don't think Mom made it. She...she ran to get out of the mine. I had to run the other way or I would have died, too."

Her sisters gave her a hug, and Victoria spoke up. "You did the right thing. I had to leave my friends behind. It sucked." She put her hand on the scrum of girls. A hand reached out in thanks.

Liam's eyes returned to the monitor. He sat down at the terminal and cleared the map. He brought up the screen showing the scene outside. The drone watched as more and more zombies arrived at the bodies of their friends and continued on, unaware what was ahead. A small rise of bodies formed in the middle. It created a rudimentary defilade for those coming up behind the leaders. Many of the clumsy things fell over their mates and sort of crawl-walked onto the pile. This kept them low enough to avoid the bullets of the automated guns. They sought targets elsewhere.

The guns continued to fire, but many rounds went over the backs of those slithering across the pre-sighted killbox. In minutes, those same crawling zombies crested the little rise. Some were shot on sight, but others slid down the other bodies. Even if they took a bullet, they continued—unless it was a headshot. The guns had to readjust constantly. They weren't smart enough to aim for the head, but by the sheer numbers of bullets, they often did hit their head.

The controls for moving the drone were labeled on the screen. With the mouse and keyboard, he quickly learned the basic maneuvers so he could turn the drone to face the guns. About half of them turned on their automated paths, but they weren't firing.

"Uh oh."

The girls had all turned to watch him work, and he heard mumbles of curses. They all saw how this game would end. On a whim, he asked Black if the drone had a gun.

"Nope. They told me it was just a camera."

He turned to her, looking up. Even from the chair, he didn't have to look up very far.

"Who told you? Where are they?"

Black looked at him with a serious face.

"Yeah." She dragged out the word, as if hesitant to get into it. "About that..."

4

"So, I said I broke off from the main group. I came through the blue door and the computer room there. I hid under the desks for a long time. Days, maybe. But I had to find water. I wasn't going back out the way I'd come. I was convinced there were infected just outside..."

She pointed to the computer screen with the drone footage. Only a couple of the guns still had ammunition.

"I ran deeper into the mine, and I came through *there*. But back then, there were no dead bodies. Just a couple soldiers inside this room, watching things on the outside, just like we're doing here."

The second-to-last gun dropped out of action.

"Timothy and Frank. Ha! I'll never forget their names for as long as I live. We spent days in this room. For a long time, we sat doing nothing. They gave themselves time on the computer, but they said I didn't have clearance. Sometimes they showed me the news of the plague up top from websites they liked, but mostly I just hung around. They wouldn't let me go deeper into the mine—through *that* door." She pointed to the inside door of the control room. "At least not at first."

"Days went by, but eventually the dead started to show up. The guns started to shoot. It wasn't constant, but hour after hour the guns would go off. They had a drone they used to do surveillance of the columbarium, but they brought it in so they could see into the room you just came through."

"Columbarium?" Victoria again anticipated his own question.

"Yeah, it's what they called this room." She pointed to the dark windows on the far wall. "I think it means it's where they store ashes of the dead."

Liam's dry mouth reminded him of another point. "Do you have any water here?"

Black pointed to some hard hats in the corner. "We filled up those hats with water, help yourself. There's plenty in the mine, as long as the dead aren't nearby."

The whole party drank from the hats, as Black continued.

"Anyway, they told me what was through there, but they refused to show me. They were more scared of what was back there than they were of the dead piling up at our front door."

She got up and moved to the interior door. Like the previous control room, the wall was made up of large windows, and the light of the room spilled out into another large cavern. The large metal door for trucks was just outside the window. Liam wondered how many big rooms were in the system. He didn't recall seeing many chambers beyond the first on the map.

"Then the Army came. A few days ago."

"The Army?" Blue lit up. "Are they here to rescue us?"

"I wish," Black replied. They somehow tapped into the feed on the drone and told the boys they were coming in. They got really weird though. Said I had to hide, just for my own safety. We argued, of course—I didn't want to hide when rescue was so close. But they pulled guns on me. Threatened me. So they let me out into the next room and gave me a light and told me to go find a quiet place and stay silent."

"None of it made sense. Until I heard the shooting. I saw the Army guys come through the control room. Three of them. They just kept going into this room, then they disappeared in the darkness. I haven't seen them since."

Liam realized what she was saying. "They're still here? How long ago was that?"

Black turned around, facing the room. "That was yesterday." She held up her arm and pointed to her wristwatch. "This was Timothy's. I took it from his body."

None of it made any sense.

"So the Army came through, and killed the Army guys?"

"Nope," Black replied, "they weren't Army. Neither group was, it turns out. Just a bunch of boys pretending. Doing work for their bosses up there." She pointed up, her meaning clear. "Timothy was still alive when I found him. He told me why he'd been killed. He told me what he was protecting. It was why the other group had come here." She was thumbing in the direction out the window.

"What, Black? What were they protecting in there?" Blue asked.

"It sounds cliche but you really have to see it for yourself. Words don't do it justice."

She collected herself, then made like she was going to open the door. She pulled a lever on the wall. Lights in the larger room started to spark. "It will take the lights a while to warm up. We'll get out there just in time to see them come on."

On the computer monitor, Liam noticed all the guns outside had stopped firing. Somewhere along the way, he failed to notice the lack of gunfire outside the room. But he still jumped when the banging began on the metal door.

Black saw he was looking at the drone footage. The screen showed the other side of the door. More and more zombies stacked up in the frame. The front cadre beat on the door with great force, though for once, Liam felt confident they could not break it down no matter how many were out there. Only a few could assault the door at the same time because of the small flight of steps leading to it.

Black returned to the terminal. With the mouse, she whisked the drone into the darkness and landed it. "We need to save its power in case we need it later. I don't think we can grab it through the door anymore to recharge it." She laughed a little, though the implications were anything but funny.

On her feet again, she moved to the interior door. "Hurry, guys. You've got to see this as the lights come on."

"But you said the Army guys are still out there, somewhere, right?" Liam was concerned they were about to be ambushed.

"They aren't Army. And yes, they *are* still in the room. But they won't give us any trouble. I took care of them."

Without waiting for a reply, she ran out the door.

"Come on, hurry!"

5

Liam followed Black's two sisters, with Victoria in tow. Nothing made any sense. He thought it was the lack of proper light playing tricks on his mind. Everything seemed out of balance in the darkness, low lights, and long shadows everywhere.

And the heat. The new cave was a raw shock. Hotter and drier than the summer day outside.

Ahead, Black flicked on a high-powered flashlight as she jogged. The room was larger than the last one, or at least higher. He saw the glint of metal hovering on each side of him, though he couldn't make out the shapes. On the walls and columns of the room, lights began to flicker. They reminded him of the ancient lights in his high school gymnasium. They seemed to take an eternity to light up. His teachers were always hesitant to turn off the lights for short periods of time, because they took so long to come back on.

They were coming on now.

"Hurry! We're almost there."

She was twenty-five yards ahead, but Liam saw her come to a stop. She turned out her flashlight, but there was a low light from the cumulative effect of all the lights around them starting to come on.

They arrived together in what turned out to be a large intersection in the center of an incredible interior space hollowed out of solid limestone. He was covered in sweat from just a few minutes of running.

Black spoke. "Some dumbass got the idea a quarry would be a safe place to go in the event the dead started to walk the earth. Timothy said it was because of some TV show about zombies—those fake people hid in a mine and made it look easy. But people who came into this mine never found safety." She paused dramatically, apparently because she was being dramatic. "And *this* is why."

The lights remained dim, but Liam could now see most of the cavern. Indeed, it was a cavern. It was much bigger than he imagined—hundreds of yards in every direction from where they stood. They were smack in the middle. A row of raw stone columns extended along an axis he imagined as north and south and another went east and west. They'd come up the north-south axis. The ceiling was probably forty feet above the solid rock under their feet in every direction.

And as far as he could see in every direction, the floor was crammed with tanks. Genuine armored fighting vehicles. Parked in tidy rows.

Victoria whistled.

Liam was speechless.

The lights continued to brighten. Each degree of brightness seemed to reveal another row of tanks further in the distance.

Black continued with her dramatic revelation. "Timothy told me he was part of a group fighting the people who released the plague. These tanks would eventually be used to take back the land stolen by those people. You know, so the United States could rebuild."

Liam still had no response to the number of tanks arrayed before him. He believed he was somewhat of an expert in tanks—he'd played military-themed games over the years—but he only recognized some of the models.

In front of him, he saw line after line of the M1A2 Abrams. It was the main battle tank of the U.S. military, and one of them had recently saved him and Grandma from the advancing zombies. He remembered them well. But he also saw tanks he pictured as being from World War II. Sherman tanks. They were endless. He turned around and saw other models he thought he knew, but wasn't sure. One long row appeared to be Russian. He might even see a short row of German tanks. How they were here, he couldn't even guess. To what end?

He was dizzy at the sight of the tank farm. If any Army could get all these tanks working, even if they just got the Abrams tanks working, they would be unstoppable.

A snippet of his conversation with Duchesne popped into his head. He mentioned people waiting in their bunkers until the time was right to rebuild. Government functionaries, business leaders, corporate cabals, and the heads of state. All of them were sitting in safety somewhere. Is this what they would use when they reclaimed the country?

"I wanted to kill these guys, but I didn't have it in me. The Patriot Snowballers might have unleashed the plague, but I don't think these three pushed the button to do it." She had walked toward the first row of Abrams tanks and pointed to the one on the corner. "So I put them inside and sealed up the hatches."

Liam's head spun.

"Wait a second, wait just a second. Do you mean to tell me the Patriot people released the plague?"

"Yeah, Timothy talked about it all the time. Showed it to me on his news websites. They marched on Washington D.C., and wrote out their demands. They wanted the President to give up his term. They wanted to strengthen the Tenth Amendment—something about States having more rights. They basically claimed to want to go back to 1776 and start over. Naturally, the President refused. And when he did, the Snowballers just released the plague along with their manifesto, claiming that if they couldn't have the government they wanted, they'd just blast the world back to the Stone Age so they could start over and make things better. Can you believe that shit?"

It was the exact opposite story he'd heard from Hayes and Duchesne. They had said it was the President who had released the plague, because he wanted to kill the Snowballers marching on his seat of power.

Both sounded reasonable, except for one little detail. The list of names of his family. Anyone related to Rose Peters—his grandma from Colorado. She'd helped the Patriots along. She'd—

His mind threw out a curveball. Something so far-fetched he wanted to laugh. A laugh wouldn't come out in the face of so many tanks. This had grown much bigger than a world-ending plague.

What if they targeted my family because they thought we were the terrorists.

And, taking it to the logical conclusion...

Grandma Rose released the plague, making the rest of her family enemies of the state.

It sounded absurd. But then, so did zombies. So did everything he'd heard in the past few weeks. Multiple viruses. Grandma's visions. Just being here in this room. It was all absurd for a teenager who, until recently, spent all his time playing fantasy-based video games. Now those fantasy games seemed like pale imitations.

"No, that's not right." Victoria started to speak up, but Liam caught her.

"Hey, can I talk to you for a sec?" He didn't give her a chance to respond. He pulled her backward, away from the triplets.

Over his shoulder, he called, "We'll be right back."

When he thought they had enough space, he spoke quietly.

"My dad had flags of a Polar Bear in his ammo room. That person on the computer said my dad was friends with the Patriot guy we passed on the ridge. And Duchesne admitted it was the President who released the plague on them. If we tell Black we have sympathies with the Snowballers, she might throw us in a tank, too."

Victoria's reply wasn't what he expected. "*Do* we have sympathies with them? What if Black is right? How can we be sure?"

"No! We don't—" He said it too loud, but he was angry she would even suggest such a thing.

"Shhh! Take it easy. I was only playing devil's advocate. I've met four members of your family; you aren't the type to release a plague." She laughed while holding his hand firmly.

His hackles laid back down. To be fair, he tested the devil's idea. His brain processed an image of Grandma Rose pouring out a vial of glowing green goo into the drinking reservoir of a big city. Then he tried to analyze whether it was possible. He tried to square that with the image of that same Grandma running to rescue him from drowning all those years ago. The math didn't add up.

"No, my Grandma would *never* have done that. The Snowballers have to be the good guys. And anyway the colonel said the plague started overseas. He never mentioned patriots or presidents."

A voice called out from behind them. It was one of the triplets, but Liam couldn't identify which. They all sounded the same, he'd decided.

"They got out!"

Liam found himself in a strange place. He was happy the good guys escaped, but he was cavorting with the girl who had somehow captured them. That made him a potential enemy, rather than a friend.

He felt exposed standing in the open, so he grabbed Victoria and ushered her between two of the big Abrams tanks.

Right into the barrel of a gun. It was attached to a Patriot.

6

"Don't say a word. I don't want to hurt you two."

Liam raised his arms, spear in hand. He backed up to be next to Victoria. Together, they barely fit in the space between the two tanks.

"Liam? Victoria?" A girl called loudly for them.

A long period of silence ensued. Part of him imagined the triplets running in and out of the tanks like bad-ass video game avatars from *World of Undead Soldiers*. This scenario would fit well in the game. Survive at all costs, save your captured friends. But the whole episode ended with a bit more realism than his game.

A male voice called out. "We've got them, Dave."

The man pointing the rifle at them motioned to Liam. "Go ahead, let's go see what we can see."

He grabbed Victoria's hand as they backed out. The three girls were several tanks down the row, sitting on the ground with their hands on their heads. They looked beaten.

Black saw them. "Sorry guys, I didn't know there was a hatch on the bottom of the tank."

"It's OK," Liam said. "I think these are the good guys."

"What? No! They killed Tim and Frank."

The guy behind Liam spoke loudly toward the girls ahead. "They tried to shoot us. We didn't want to kill them."

To Liam—or no one in particular—the man grumbled: "We should be killing those dead things, instead of each other."

"Amen, brother," is what came out of Liam's mouth. After he'd said it, he waited for a response. The man became quiet as they walked the remaining distance to the girls. Liam and Victoria took a seat with them.

"I heard these two talking about being with the Bears, Clarence. Said his father's one."

"We can't take a chance. Maybe it's a trick. Those last two guys almost tricked us, too."

Dave seemed uninterested in pushing the issue.

Liam was also unsure he wanted to push the issue. If they were truly Patriots, he believed they'd come to no harm. However, if they were part of the NIS, or just about any other government agency, they might come to harm for being associated with an anti-government group. Especially if the official word going around was that they were responsible for releasing the plague on everyone else. He had to admit, it was brilliant propaganda. Foment unrest against the citizens so they, the agents of the government, could swoop in and pick up the pieces. But he knew it was never that simple. There were plenty of good guys in government, too. There was no litmus test to determine the good guys from the bad, except by their actions. So far, this group of men had been treated like criminals. Would they reciprocate?

The guy who seemed to be the leader, Clarence, spoke softly to the five of them. "Look, I'm not going to do anything to hurt you kids. I'm sorry we killed your friends, but look at this place. Why do you think they were guarding this?"

Black spoke up. "They said *you* were coming to take it over."

The man released a hearty guffaw. "Me, and what army? What am I gonna do, drive each tank out of here and come back for the next. It would take me ten lifetimes. That doesn't include the time it would take to get these relics started and then clear all the cars outside."

It made sense to Liam. "Then why did you come through here, if not for the tanks?"

"Your crafty friend delayed us, but we're going to finish our mission. It's just down the road." He pointed ahead, deeper into the tank room. "I'll let you come with, but you have to surrender all your guns."

Liam looked at all the girls, settling on Black. She had to be armed, though she didn't display any weapons. How else could she have ordered these men into the tank?

Victoria let them know she was going to pull out the Glock. She set it down behind her. Liam watched as the man picked it up and stuck it into his waistband.

Black also pulled out a gun. She carelessly tossed it behind her. The leader picked it up with a quiet laugh.

"You can keep the hand tools. Never know when the infected are going to jump out. But if you try to use those on us, we won't be stingy with our bullets. Deal?"

Black seemed to speak for the triplets. She agreed with a forlorn, "Yeahhh."

Liam was quick with his own affirmation. He took comfort, no matter how small, in holding his spear.

"Then let's get started. You guys walk that way. We'll follow."

The triplets led them all. When they crossed the east-west axis, they had to step over an inset pair of railroad tracks. To the left, hundreds of yards down the tracks, Liam could see an industrial-sized metal door. To the right, the tracks went under another door in the distance. But there was a short train parked on the line. It faced the other way, but it pulled several flat cars loaded with tanks he recognized: World War II vintage Tiger tanks.

"Oh man." Liam stopped at the sight and pointed. "Those. Those tanks are *rare.*"

Clarence backed him up. "That explains how they get them in and out." He looked at Black. "Well, maybe I could finish the job of taking all these tanks if I had a train."

Liam heard her sarcastically laugh behind him.

Everyone had stopped in the main intersection of the room. Liam wore his desire to see the train on his face, and Clarence seemed to share his curiosity.

"Let's check it out."

A short ways down the tracks they passed a number of different models of tanks. Each row ended at the aisle so they could see each tank in profile. Liam hardly recognized any of them, but he knew the distinctive German Tiger. They came to a section that had been cleared out. A good number of Tigers were gone from their assigned row. Based on the numbers of missing, and the tanks on the train, more than a few had been used somewhere else...or they were being brought in.

"Where are they taking them?" Victoria asked the group, to no avail.

Everyone moved past two flatbed cars toward the engine. Liam was disturbed to see blood all over the pair of tank haulers. Like there'd been a battle here.

He walked along past the flats and saw the side of the engine. It was painted a happy bright orange and looked like the engines that pulled his train out of St. Louis. In fact—

"Damn. It says Valkyrie." He saw the name in black lettering stenciled on the side of the engine, just as it was on *his* train. This was his.

"You know this train?" Clarence seemed impressed.

"Victoria and I rode this. Well, these two engines pulled our train out of St. Louis on day three. I remember because it was named *Valkyrie*." He pointed to the moniker. "We left it at the end of the tracks at a blown bridge. Not far from here. Someone must have brought it back, and put it to work. And I think..."

He walked a few yards back to the flat car, looked, and then nodded. "Yep, these flatcars are the same. This blood is dried. It's ten-something days old."

"What's a Valkyrie? Isn't it some kind of angel?" Pink asked her sisters. They'd mentioned reading a lot, so it didn't surprise him Blue had the answer: "Valkyries are from Norse mythology. They had something to do with taking slain warriors to Valhalla, if I remember right."

"What does it have to do with a train?" Liam asked rhetorically. No one had an answer.

They spent a few minutes looking around, but the only point of interest was the large metal door far down the tracks. Somehow it had to be opened to let the trains in and out.

"All right, this is interesting and all, but we need to keep moving. I'm two days behind schedule." Clarence got them back on the main path. Ten minutes later, they had crossed the room and stood before a hole in the wall. It was about as big as pickup truck and carved right into the rock face. Vehicles had gone in and out, as the dual tracks were obvious on the ground.

"Through there." The men each had flashlights on their rifles. They turned them on as they walked out of the light of the tank room. They entered a dark chamber with a low ceiling. It was low enough Liam could touch it if he wanted, though he wasn't brave enough to try it with three guns pointed at his back. The tanks were practically cheery in comparison to the dark space they were entering.

Clarence spoke once they were all inside. "The tanks aren't why we're here. They surprised us as much as they did you. Whoever put those in here had been doing it for a long time. The Tigers on that train are from the Second World War. Many others are American tanks from that war. Probably built in factories right here in St. Louis and then stored here. But the people who put the tanks here were also playing around with something else," he added dramatically.

He swung his flashlight around. The walls were rough cut by mining equipment. The whole area looked like it was done in a hasty fashion. Large chunks of stone dotted the floor as if they'd been left in a hurried retreat. Several strange-looking pieces of digging equipment hid in the shadows in the corner. Parked until needed.

"Here we go. Here's one." Liam looked up where the man pointed his light. Something had been carved out of the ceiling. It was a hole about the dimensions of a motorcycle, though that made no sense. As the light of the flashlight bounced inside the hole, he looked up and saw a long wooden plank above, sealing the roof of the hole maybe ten feet above. He imagined he was looking up at the underside of the floor of someone's rustic log cabin.

"What is it?" His curiosity always beat out his own safety.

"Look around the room. What do you see?"

The lights of the guns swept the room. Several more holes on the ceiling were apparent. They were dark shadows dripping down into the room from above.

And yet, they were not random. Liam got his bearings and saw they made neat lines, starting with the one they'd reached first. It was a corner, just as the tanks had made a corner where the rows met.

Found him down in a quarry.

Next door to the Jefferson Barracks National Cemetery.

These tunnels go on for miles.

The reality snapped in place. Liam saw the rows for what they were.

"Oh my God."

He felt the eyes of the girls on him.

"We're underneath the cemetery. They were digging out the bodies from down here. This is just as McMurphy imagined."

To his left, the empty holes in the ceiling went on for as far as the powerful flashlight could reach.

DRAGON'S TEETH

Liam sat on a large rock just outside the room one of the men had dubbed "the drop out room" because whoever was in charge here had drilled through solid rock up to the bottoms of the military coffins in the National Cemetery, then brought down the remains.

When he discovered the pile of broken coffins and discarded artifacts of the soldiers, he couldn't take it. He had to get out, back to the light of the tank room.

At least this room makes sense.

The lights were bright enough he could see all the but furthest corners of the big cavern. Tanks of every color stared silently back at him.

"Still think the Patriots are the good guys?" It was Black. Her two sisters followed her through the gap in the wall. Pink sat on a nearby rock while Blue and Black stood next to each other. They had ganged up on him.

"They're here to find bodies in there, aren't they? They're going to use them to spread the infection. I heard what that guy said. Your dad was part of the Patriot Snowball movement. He helped kill the world."

Liam was too stunned to respond.

Blue added, "I—I appreciate what you did to save Pink. But you have to see how awful those Patriot people are."

Black seemed to think on that. Eventually she added, "Yeah, thanks for saving her. But when we get out of here, me and my sisters will be on our way. We don't want to spend any more time with y'all and *your* people."

Liam didn't know how to take that. While he fashioned a reply, Victoria walked out of the drop out room. She'd been lingering with the three men as they swept the room.

She took a knee right next to Liam, but spoke loud enough so they could all hear.

"They're still looking for something back there. They won't tell me what, but it would make sense they're looking for whatever was in those coffins that got broken open."

Liam, unable to formulate a proper reply to the girls, turned instead to Victoria. "I'm sorry, I couldn't stay in there. Someone broke open those coffins. The thought—they must have taken the bodies right out of those boxes and threw down everything else."

Noting the girls nearby, he continued, "And these three seem to believe my dad has some involvement in all this." He swept his hand between the tanks and the drop out room. "As if he could have desecrated graves like that."

Victoria turned to the other girls, but didn't say anything.

Pink spoke to the whole group. Her voice and mannerisms were more reserved than her sisters. "I want to say something. You guys wouldn't believe where I've been if I told you. I've seen zombies crush the life out of one individual and I've seen them swarm over whole crowds. I've, like, seen them scrunch themselves into small metal ducts, and I've seen them spread out across vast open spaces. I—" She choked up, and as she did so, Blue moved back to comfort her. "I'm OK. I saw those sick people slither out of a tipped barge on that muddy bank. I thought that's where I was gonna die..."

She'd been talking while looking down, but now looked over to Liam. "But those two...came along and pulled me out of that mud. They could have kept on driving and left me for dead, no questions asked. But they stopped." She smiled weakly at Liam. "And...I've been watching him every minute since then. He hasn't said a mean thing about anyone, even that icky captain guy. He treats his girlfriend with respect. He got us this far into the mine. He helped us find you." She pointed to Black. "I don't think he could have anything to do with the people who, like, released the plague and stuff."

Black stepped closer to her, and spoke quietly. "That's not what I'm saying 'sis. He may be a good guy, but his father, and those three in the other room, aren't. We gotta be Valkyries—just like the name on that train engine. Strong. Fighters. Independent. We can't be anywhere near him or them, or those guys are gonna get us in trouble. Maybe hurt us."

The two looked at Blue, as if she carried the most important vote. Liam couldn't see her expression as she was turned the other way, but he heard her soft voice. "He rescued me too. I was dead." She paused a long time. "As good as dead, I think. And Cairo was a flurry of activity with the military and people digging in to protect the town. I didn't see any Snowball people there, so they weren't the ones rebuilding. But I've not seen Liam or Victoria do anything that suggests they aren't honest people. I think he's telling the truth. At least he doesn't think his father is involved in spreading the plague."

Better than nothing.

He felt he should be doing a better job of defending the Patriots, but he had no evidence beyond what he already believed to be true. His dad would never align with any group that released biological weapons upon mankind. He'd been in the presence of two men who had every opportunity to lay blame on the Snowball movement, and both admitted it was someone in the U.S. Government who released the plague to kill the Patriot march, not the other way around. But of course he wasn't recording his conversations to be able to prove it.

Black, still conversing with her sisters, asked, "All right, so then do we stick with these people when we get out, or get the hell out of their sight? I vote we run."

The question hung on the hot, dry air.

2

The three men stormed out of the drop out room.

"Any of you kids have food? I'm starving." It was Dave.

Clarence was a few steps behind. He ignored the question. "We've got to go."

"Did you find what you're looking for," Liam asked.

Clarence stopped nearby. "Nothing's left. They took the bodies somewhere. We have to get back and report our findings."

"Can we come with?" Victoria asked. When she saw Liam look at her, she continued. "What? I want to stick by the guys with the guns." She left it at that.

Clarence ran a finger over his lips while he considered her request. "We'll get you out of the mine. I don't want it on my conscience I let five kids die, but you should consider being more careful—stick with some adults. Things are dangerous now."

Liam laughed internally at the towering irony in that statement. As if they only just now realized the danger because some older fellow pointed it out. He wanted to reply with all the dangerous things he'd survived since the sirens, but he knew it wouldn't help their plans to escape. It turns out, in this case, they did need the help of adults. Or lots of kids with guns, though none of those were nearby.

Victoria coughed, and Liam thought he detected a hint of a laugh within.

"Yeah, so we'll help you get to the surface with us, but then you're on your own. We, uhh, have somewhere to be."

"A secret meeting, huh?"

Clarence turned to Victoria. "Yeah, something like that." Then he motioned to the entire group to circle around him. He pointed to his third man. "Travis here has an idea."

Travis began. "When we came in, we had a map of the entire mine. We took it from one of the offices up top. It was a large roll with many pages. I threw out what wasn't on our route so I could keep this one."

He pulled out a folded square map that was about four feet across. He showed it to them, then walked to a nearby tank chassis so he could lay it flat on the angled front hull. They all drifted to stand in front of the display.

M60 Patton. That was the model of the tank stenciled in white lettering beneath the turret. Instead of the traditional white star of the US Army, it carried a big white "V" on the side of the turret.

Travis began by pointing to his map. "This is how we came in. If you came in through the front door, you probably came the same way." He showed them the series of tunnels, noting they were all clogged with family sedans right now.

Liam really wanted to get a tank started, roll over all those cars, and then just keep going up and out of the spiral of death. He tried to listen, though exhaustion took a toll on him, and the heat wasn't helping. Victoria's hand was on his back, propping him up, he imagined.

"And then we all came into the room blocked by those dump trucks." He pointed to the room on the map. "You can see it actually has four entrances. The first is the one blocked by the trucks. The next is the one with the blue door, where we all went through. But the next one goes deeper into the production part of the mine, while the last one—across from the blue door—is where we think we might be able to escape." He turned, pointing to the sisters. "Did any of you see survivors when you came in?"

Black, the one in the mine the longest, said the only two people she met after the initial sprint into the pit were the soldiers guarding the computer room. Everyone else must have found refuge in some of the chambers closer to the entrance. At least, that was her best guess.

Blue and Pink saw the same number of survivors as Liam—one. And he was homicidal.

"OK, so maybe we'll get lucky. If no other survivors got into that room, and if none of the infected followed them in, we might be able to escape through there." He jabbed his finger at the room. Liam noticed it was near the edge of the sheet. A dotted line continued beyond, signifying the system joined another map sheet.

"And what's beyond that room, huh?" Black asked.

"Well, that's just it. It's literally off the map. But look here." He held up the map, folding it in such a way he could look at the tiny text of the map up close. "Right here. It says 'to original mine and opening.'"

Liam saw it. They all did. Plain text and clear meaning. But he didn't like the middle part of the plan.

"So, I see where we are. I see where we need to go, but how to do we get past all those zombies sitting outside the door of the computer room now?" He explained where they'd left the horde.

Travis looked at Clarence, sharing the question.

For a long time, Clarence looked at the map as Travis held it, then he took it for himself to study it. The group began drifting apart, as if to wait for the word when they'd be summoned once more. It wasn't long.

"I'd never thought I'd say this, but I'm glad we found five healthy kids. You guys are going to save all our bacon on this."

I'm not going to like this.

3

Liam was right. As was typical for planning during the Apocalypse, the plan sucked. But, he allowed that it did make sense if they had any hope of surviving the horde of zombies now lounging with the dead machine guns.

He held both of Victoria's hands with his own. "You ready for another crazy plan?"

"There isn't one piece of the plan I like. I especially don't like the part where we separate. Please promise you'll come back to me. I can't bear to think of doing this alone."

The sweat pouring from her forehead wasn't just from the heat. She shared his nervous energy and anticipation. But, saying something positive was crucial because there was no way to sit out the escape. No rescue was coming.

"Do you remember when we first met, and I was as nervous as a new kid on my first day of school?"

"Of course. You made Grandma run over my hand and then you stammered through the next five minutes of conversation before you settled down. I thought it was kind of cute how nervous you were." She giggled softly, allowing the humor in.

"Right, well I never told you what it was that calmed me down. Can you guess? It's something on you."

She shook her head no, but looked down at herself. "I'm wearing all different clothes—thank God—so I'm not sure what it could have been."

Liam saw his opening. "Thank *God* you have one thing on the same." He pointed to her silver necklace. "This necklace. I can't explain it. When I saw it that first time, it made realize you were one of the good guys in a world gone bad. I couldn't possibly be intimidated or nervous around someone like that."

He smiled broadly at her. "Though I'm still not positive what I believe. I believe there has to be a God out there, but I'm beginning to think maybe he isn't very interested in the mess we've created here." He pointed to the nearby room. "Nobody who believes in God could have ripped those bodies out of their graves like that. I think we're dealing with true evil. Though they aren't demons or devils with pitchforks. They are people who have gone rotten."

Their eyes locked.

"Look, my point is that you and your faith were a big reason I was able to survive this far. I need you to keep that up. Keep inspiring me to look for God in all this. I need to believe this isn't all for nothing. If you can do that, I promise you I'll never stop trying to get us out of these crazy situations."

He thought she was going to lean in and kiss him. But before he could embrace her, Black interjected. "What kind of bullshit are you feeding each other? God? An all-powerful being pulling the levers and waiting for prayers just so he can answer them? Do you hear yourselves?" She laughed with definite malice.

Victoria shot back, "So what do you believe? If anything?"

"I don't believe there's a man in a chair up there, lording over all of us. I don't believe there's anything up there. It's just us. You, me, the people who released the plague. The people fighting it. Maybe this is good versus bad, but not God versus the Devil. That sound ridiculous."

She pointed to her sisters. "We were brought up to think for ourselves. Take responsibility for our own choices—good or bad—and not blame them on others, or expect others to fix our problems."

Blue nodded, though Liam thought he saw a flicker of disagreement in Pink's eyes. Still, they were getting nowhere with a religious discussion inside the Mine of Death.

"Hey, guys. Can we save this for another time? We have a job to do." He hated to cut off Victoria as she appeared to be gearing up for an argument, which he was prepared to see through to the end, but not right now.

He pulled Victoria away from the others and after a brief pause for her to catch her breath, he kept her occupied with her new job.

"So we need to go in there and get some of those wooden boxes, you ready? I can't do it without you." Something about them freaked him out.

Victoria nodded her head, then the whole group went into the drop out room and began dragging out the broken caskets. They put them in a pile very near the first row of tanks outside that room. Liam absolutely refused to touch anything else in the pile of artifacts left by those who desecrated the graves in the first place. None of the others seemed willing to test that taboo either. When they were done, they had a pile eight feet high with about twenty wooden caskets of varying quality.

"You ready, folks?" Clarence looked at the kids.

No one said no, though no one said yes, either. He took that as his cue.

He handed a lighter to Liam. "Give us twenty minutes to get to the doors, then light this pile."

"Good luck everyone." Then, with as much humor as he could muster, Clarence ended with, "Don't leave without us, huh?"

The girls might have laughed. Liam did not.

We need you guys. You have the guns.

4

Liam's brow dripped with sweat as he tried to light the fire. A small flame danced in the husk of one of the coffins. He prayed it would spread soon to the rest of the pile of kindling so they could ensure the plan would work as it was intended.

As he blew into the flames, he checked the shoes of his companions. Victoria was the most prepared. She wore her snazzy yellow running shoes she'd gotten back in Cairo. Blue had a decent pair of sneakers as well. Pink had a mangled pair of tennis shoes—she managed to keep them from being removed from her feet by the grabby mud. They looked like hell, but at least she could walk in them.

Black's shoes were the worst. Her boots were two sizes too large, and went half way up her shins.

Liam caught her attention, then nodded at her feet. "Nice boots." He forced a smile, but his concern was deadly serious. Anyone without good shoes would have trouble with a plan that included running for your life.

"I came into the mine with no shoes. My watch isn't the only thing I took from Timothy."

The fire began to catch. There was no going back. He threw some larger pieces on the fire and the dried wood caught and spread like mad. In just a few minutes, the fire had exploded over the entire pile.

Job one, done.

Far across the cavern, they waited for the next phase of their escape to kick in. And, almost as if they'd planned it, two men came running out of the dark tunnel and jumped up onto a tank, and then climbed inside. Even from hundreds of yards away, their fear was palpable.

"Where's the third one?" One of the girls spoke, but he couldn't tell who. His entire focus was on the opening.

The last man came running out of the tunnel, but he was chased by one of the fast zombies. The man ignored the tank, perhaps sure he couldn't make it to safety. Instead, he ran for the fire. In moments, the black hole belched out more of the dead. They weren't running, thank God, but there were so many, it probably wouldn't matter.

The signal fire turned out to be superfluous. The running man—he still couldn't tell which one—brought in all the zombies anyway.

A slice of panic cut through Liam. He steadied himself by looking at the fire, then he turned to the girls.

"We all know what to do. Let the zombies get into the room, let them get close to us, then get lost in the tanks and run out that door." He pointed behind him, to the door currently full of zombies.

Victoria gave a weak smile. She'd picked up a stout metal bar that had once been attached to a coffin. The other girls just stared at the doorway behind him, each holding their own hand-to-hand weapon.

His spear felt totally inadequate for what he needed to do, but at least it was something.

When he reached the halfway point across the room, Liam was sure it was Clarence. The slightly older man had slowed down considerably. He was clutching his waist as if he had a bad cramp. He turned around once, then changed course to try to jump on one of the large Abrams tanks. He managed to scramble up to the main deck, but he was unable to get the hatch open before the running zombie bounded up and sprang onto the deck with him.

He pulled out his sidearm and managed to put the zombie down with two shots. Then he crawled to the top of the turret, opened the top hatch, and fell inside. The portal was closed as the faster of the walking zombies found the tank and started banging on the exterior.

The wave continued to wash around that tank. It headed for Liam's fire down the middle corridor of the room.

"We got this," he said, mostly to seem brave.

"Just zig zag through the tanks and make your way back to safety. Easy!"

He knew that was a lie, but what else could he say. "We're all gonna get caught. Nice knowin' ya!"

He started to scream and yell at the zombies, ensuring the greatest number continued to push into the big space. For the plan to work, they needed the zombies to move toward the fire so there were fewer of them on the side with the exit.

Where did all these zombies come from?

He'd seen zombies get out of some of the cars while on the way in, but the numbers had swelled. Now if he cared to count them, he'd wager they were in the thousands. Almost every one headed their way.

They let them get to within about fifty yards. Close enough they were spotted. The zombies ramped up their moaning when they saw fresh food. They were off-the-chain loud with hunger groans and shouts. Liam felt his stomach quiver in fear, but he caught himself before he lost control.

To Victoria he shouted, "I love you!"

She replied, "I love you too, Liam. Don't stop running!"

They each took off to the right. Victoria went into the first column of tanks while he ran on the outer wall for another twenty-five yards and then stopped.

This is where I may ruin my shorts.

He waited. He could see Blue running in the opposite direction from him along the outer wall. Her job, like his, was to get the zombies to follow them up the columns of tanks so they'd get as far into the room as possible. Then all the runners were going to cut back to the door by running on the outer wall near the last row of tanks. He and Victoria had gone right. The sisters all went left.

The first zombie stumbled and fell as he got around the corner tank, nearest the fire. Liam almost felt sorry for it. It seemed to take a long time to push itself off the floor and then stand upright. With an almost comic timing, it noticed Liam and snapped its head sideways as if it was upset its tumble had been noticed. Others were soon behind it, and the chase was on.

5

Liam's plan was supposed to be simple. Run to the corner of the room, turn, then run the length of the room, turn, then run to the door. Getting to the corner was easy. With adequate lighting and his runner's form, he easily outpaced the clumsy zombies by a wide mile. But again, he had to wait so the zombies got a good look at him. He had to draw them to him.

The man who tripped had managed to stay in front of the dozens of follow on friends. It almost seemed like he tried to make up for his embarrassment by working harder than any of the others.

"Good job, runner!" he shouted. Partly to keep himself focused. Partly to encourage the zombies to go the last few yards into the corner.

He saw Victoria. She was already running back along the length of the room. No zombies were behind her, which was good. If they got between them, it would mean he was cut off.

"Got to run!"

No longer fooling around, he sprinted to catch up to Victoria. He knew she was no slouch, and in fact, had already crossed the half-way point of the room. In a few moments, he too reached the mid-point, but he slid to a stop in the dry dust and rock when he saw what was there.

The railroad tracks lay in grooves in the rock. The pair of them went underneath a huge vault-like door. The door was metallic, and bowed slightly outward. Though he couldn't see the thickness, it had the bulk of solid steel several feet thick, like the door had its own gravity. There were no hinges, no handles, and no signage. But it was a door nonetheless.

It was large enough to fit a train engine, which made sense given the fact the train tracks went underneath it. Impressive as that was, the real reason he stopped was because of the black dome hanging from an overhang a few feet above the door. In the dark recess, away from the direct glare of the powerful lights, he saw a tiny red light flashing on and off. Inside the dome, he imagined a video camera. He felt it was on and watching what was happening outside its front door.

Briefly, he waved his arm up at the camera—willing whoever was inside to open the door. But a quick look back told him his chance of getting safely inside the giant door was already past. The zombies made good time and closed in on him. More zombies walked up the middle aisle, along the railroad tracks. Yet the thing that really got him moving was seeing a zombie pop out of one of the columns of tanks in the direction Victoria had already run.

Uh oh. I'm behind them.

Sprinting for his life now, he ran directly toward the lone zombie. It was a tall, skinny man. His shirt had been ripped off, leaving his bare upper body exposed to the elements. He looked like he'd been rolling around on sharp rocks, as he was covered in scratches and smeared blood. His face was splashed with blood too, but his teeth were unnaturally white as he snarled with anger at Liam.

Meanwhile, Liam's mind constructed the most heroic action he could do: run, jump with the spear in hand, and drive the wooden stake into the brain of the hapless zombie. Then he'd continue running like he owned the place.

But that wasn't the safe way.

Rather than risk a chance encounter with the straggler, he ducked into the tanks. As he did so, another male zombie emerged to join the tall one. He didn't get a good look at it, but didn't try either. He was feeling the call of panic.

He ran into the column, ran lengthwise between two tanks, then turned right at the first row to run between the front of the tanks on the right, and the rear of the tanks on the left. He didn't recognize the models, but they looked to be World War II vintage—as if they'd been sitting in this room for a long time. The overhead lights were unable to completely pierce the darkness between the tightly packed tanks, giving a creepy aura to the steel beasts.

The cavern swallowed noise for the most part, but the drone of the zombies was steady and loud. There were far more than any of them had guessed.

Ahead, a zombie walked by. Maybe three tanks ahead. The woman didn't look from side to side. She just kept her head straight.

Liam ran. He turned as he entered the channel where he thought he'd seen the woman. She was indeed there; she had reached the rear row where white-teeth zombie had been. He only caught a glimpse of her as he ran, but he was terrified of the hand which touched his shoulder from his left side. He didn't look back. He focused on running.

Row after row of tanks were ahead of him. More zombies funneled down each column, and he knew it would only take one to block his path for good. Then he'd be surrounded—and eaten.

No, they'd only drain my blood. As if that's better...

It happened sooner than he'd hoped. A zombie ahead lazily turned the corner toward him, as if it were just wandering randomly.

Liam didn't wait, he turned to the right, made a quick recalculation, then pulled himself on top of one of the tanks. This time he knew the tank model. It was the distinctive rounded hull of a Sherman tank, white star and all.

From the higher vantage point, he saw the whole scene. The heads of the zombies inside the aisles between the tanks bobbed everywhere. They were thickest in the middle of the room, as he expected, but they were spreading out in all directions like water filling an ice cube tray. Several more had reached the outer wall behind him.

His stomach lurched at the realization he was completely surrounded while deep inside a rock quarry. With a hard lean against the turret of his tank, he took a moment to catch his breath. His mind played tricks on him as he heard what he thought was the screams of girls from elsewhere in the room.

"Liam!"

He recognized that one. He swept the ground behind his tank, but quickly grasped Victoria wasn't on the ground at all. She waved her arms while standing on the flat rear deck of her own tank. The arms of zombies reached up at her, though they had no chance to reach her as high as she was.

Not without climbing.

That got him moving. The jump from one tank to the next was easy. Much easier than jumping from one moving barge to the next with Great-Grandma on his back. The zombies couldn't see him as he jumped, and by the time he registered on their fresh food radar, he was already out of sight—jumping to the next tank. In sixty seconds, he hugged Victoria.

"Oh my God, Liam. This is unbelievable. Where did all these people come from?"

Liam didn't want to share his thoughts. Not here. On the day they'd passed this mine, a few days after the sirens, the line of cars going down the spiral road was endless. The entire highway had been blocked by the closed bridges, and the mine seemed like a place to hide. As Black had said, everyone seemed to think a quarry was a good idea, though he hoped it wasn't because of a TV show. They'd passed car after car inside the mine too, which means there were potentially thousands of survivors, maybe tens of thousands, deep in the corridors of the mines. Travis had said he threw out most of the maps because they were too bulky to carry. That could mean the tunnels went on for miles and miles in all directions...

And they were all coming here.

As more zombies spotted them on the open deck, they began to converge around the old tank. He felt Victoria tighten her grip on him, as if she was afraid she'd fall over the side into the waiting arms of the dead men and women below.

"I think we may have made a mistake coming here."

He didn't disagree, but he was silent—he scanned the room, searching for the key to their escape he knew had to be there. He was the hero, time to start acting like one.

Layers of fear mixed with panic and the reality of it all settled in.

There's no escape. Not from down here.

UNDEAD SOLDIERS

Liam and Victoria held each other as the zombies swirled about on the ground below them. The deck of the tank was higher than any one zombie, but Liam had seen enough of them to know that once enough of them got together, they would start to trample each other and climb up over the bodies of their fallen friends.

And, if they were from Chicago...

He surveyed the crowd and found one that seemed to have figured out how to scramble up the side of the tank treads, very much like using a ladder.

"That one!" He pointed to the climber. "She's climbing. We have to move."

He scanned the tank park, and focused on where he thought the first two men had gone. The plan called for them to jump into a tank nearest the exit, and then all the zombies were supposed to be drawn by the fire deep into the room. Liam and the girls were then to run around the outside of the parked tanks and meet up with the men once more, then run along the blue rope lights until they could escape. It was basically a huge bait and switch.

Only, the switch never happened because the bait was still drawing the zombies through the front door.

Liam led the way as he jumped from one Sherman tank to the next, heading in the direction he hoped he'd find the men. They scrambled, hopped, and climbed tank after tank, often only inches above the straining arms and hands of the infected horde. When they reached the last one in the corner, they had to turn to the left so they could jump the tanks in the column. That would bring them closest to the entrance, and to the place he hoped the men were hiding.

"Liam..." Victoria's voice wavered.

He leaned against the fifteen-foot long gun barrel while he looked over his shoulder. "Just keep going. Don't look down."

Victoria moved to the top of the turret, a few feet behind him. She crouched down, so as to steady herself from a terminal tumble. "It isn't down I'm worried about. It's across." She pointed to the next tank.

Unlike the jumps from side to side, the gap from the front of one tank to the back of the other was much greater. And, as the fronts dipped down, the tail ends of these tanks were blocky and high. If they were going backward, it would be a snap. Going forward was going to be a challenge.

There was no time for fancy plans. Already a zombie was grabbing the side of the tank and—no matter how clumsy the attempt—was managing to climb up the side. It seems there were more than a few people from Chicago hiding in this mine.

He ran down the short front piece of hull, placed his foot on the flat front fender, then jumped. He landed on the back deck, though he stumbled a bit on the uneven metal. He wasn't in any real danger of failing to make the jump, but they'd have to do it god-knows how many times to get where they were going.

Victoria moved to the spot he'd just vacated on the tank behind him. She smiled weakly, then made the short run and took her jump. She landed at about the same spot, and even tripped the same way he did.

"You weren't supposed to fall."

"I do what you do," she said with a real smile while she sucked in air from her burst across.

"We better keep moving."

She took his hand as they both stood up on the rear deck. "You truly know how to show a girl a good time."

"Just wait until you see how I get us out of here." Once he'd said it, he felt the pressure building once more.

Why can't I just keep my mouth shut?

He swept the room as they inched around the turret of the olive drab tank, but he still saw nothing that gave him any hope he could deliver on his glib promise to wow Victoria. The big vault door was the only thing that might give him some hope if there was any indication from within that help was to be had. His heart told him someone saw him, but his head informed him it didn't really matter because there were so many zombies in their front yard now. If they were huddled in there for protection, he didn't think now was the time they'd come out.

Another jump. They cleared the gap to the next tank, though the ground had become packed with sick-looking spectators. A few zombies had made it onto the tank behind them, though they had trouble staying upright on the uneven surface of the sloped vehicle. One fell to the side, the other made an honest effort to cross the gap behind him but he too fell into the crowd.

The next few tanks were uneventful. They were getting better at jumping and had it down to a science by the time they reached the tenth row. But then the olive gave way to tan, and the technology ramped up from mid-twentieth century to last week. They reached the first of the many rows of M1 Abrams.

Liam cleared the distance with no issues. The Abrams was slightly higher than the rear of the Sherman, but it was flatter and easier to plant a landing for him. Ahead, the deck of the newer tanks was easier to walk on and jumping would be less risky.

He turned to catch Victoria—if she needed help, which he never presumed she did—and watched as a hand grabbed her just as he planted her foot to make the jump. It stole some of her inertia and she fell a foot short of where she aimed. She landed with her stomach up against the rear of the Abrams, and let out a loud croak when she did so.

Liam was on his knees in a second, but there were so many zombies below, it would have been a miracle if she wasn't grabbed.

"I've got ya!" He had one wrist, then the other. She hung over the side and he could only watch as an ugly, broken image of a man grabbed Victoria's leg and took a bite. She was shocked and reacted with a backward kick which threw the man off. But others had her too.

Liam saw Victoria turn back to him, a look in her eyes he'd not seen before.

"NO!" He refused to yield. Whether she was bitten or not, he was going to get her onto the deck. He braced his legs and pulled with everything he had, the deficiencies in his diet temporarily ignored. Victoria, to her credit, pushed herself up the side of the armored fighting vehicle to help, though she yelped a couple more times as the zombies took their opportunities to bite where they could.

The only thing that saved her was the zombies were more interested in using their teeth, than their arms. They made no effort to pull her back into their makeshift mosh pit.

Liam dragged her as far up the deck as he could. Right up to the rear of the boxy turret.

He was afraid to look.

2

"Liam. You can let go. You saved me."

He hadn't loosened his grip, though they were temporarily safe. He was afraid that once he let go, she would start to change into a zombie, and he couldn't imagine what that meant for him. What he'd have to do...or if he *wanted* to do those things.

If she dies, I die. I knew this is how it would go down.

But he relented. Victoria pulled her arms from his, and scooched up the deck so she was leaning against the turret. Liam mimicked her by taking the seat next to her.

When they first met, he was afraid to look at her bare legs because he found her distractingly pretty. Her legs were well-sculpted runner's legs. Now, he felt the same fear at looking at her legs, though the reason was something else entirely.

Victoria pulled her legs to her and looked them over. She was wearing blue jeans—because she hated to get mosquito bites.

"I think I'm good. They bit at my legs, but they couldn't break through the material of these jeans." She pointed to the bloody bite marks, but when she pulled her jeans up to her knees, there were no abrasions—just a few ugly bruises.

She let out a fatalistic laugh. "I'll take it."

Liam's swirl of emotions got the best of him. He leaned over to her and felt the waterworks start. She seemed to take it all in stride.

"Someone's looking out for me," she laughed again, though it sounded like she was also tearing up.

"I thought we were both dead." He didn't tell her that he meant that literally, as he was ready to fight to the death against all the zombies to get away from having to kill the zombie version of her. But it was near enough to the truth.

"Well, we're not out of this yet. And maybe next time you'll consider wearing jeans too?" She said it to be funny. Something he desperately needed to hear. But there was truth there too.

He pulled back and looked at her, sharing tears. "I'm going to wear a full set of armor next time I find one."

She stood up first, and pulled him to his feet.

"Onward?"

He looked ahead once more, they had five or six rows to go. Five or six more jumps and they'd know the fate of the men supposedly leading this operation. His only hope was that they had some miraculous plan, because he still had none.

The jumps between the Abrams tanks went much faster, and with less danger. The front deck and rear deck of the modern battle tank were almost the same height, so it was practically a walk in the park to skip from one to the next, no matter what was below them.

Lava is below us. That's less scary than what's really down there.

He played the children's game of jumping the imaginary lava until they reached the last tank in the column, which was also the last tank in its row. It was the cornerstone tank where the men were supposed to be hiding.

Liam rapped on the outer metal of the turret, hoping those inside could hear it over the generalized noise of all the angry zombies humming below.

The top hatch popped open in seconds.

"Hey, Liam. You made it. There are a few more than we thought." It was Dave.

Typical understatement.

"Did you see Clarence? We saw him run into the tanks, but we had to jump in this first one before we saw where he went."

He was slightly out of breath from his tank hopping, but he answered when he could. "We saw him run into the room, that way," he pointed toward the fire, "but not sure he's still there."

Then, to the important question for the adults in the room. "So what's the plan?" He'd spent weeks thinking of plans to help people escape zombies, often drawing from his voluminous reading of zombie books. Often, he wondered why it took a teen boy to solve the problems of adults, but he'd resigned himself to not knowing the answer. It may have been as simple as he just came up with good ideas faster than anyone else, or maybe he always saw the obvious answer to the questions. Or, maybe he was just super lucky.

But this time, he literally had no idea whatsoever how to escape this fix. He wanted to dish off that problem to someone else for a change. The only problem was they were already a man down—Clarence, their leader, was missing.

He wasn't reassured by the look he got in return.

Liam was distracted by a sudden burst of noise. The zombies seemed to scream as one. He felt a hand on his back—Victoria— seeming to convey a dictionary's worth of messaging in its simultaneous firmness and gentleness. It was a caring and strength which said, "This is bad, but we're in this together."

Liam looked to the commotion. Across the wide road which marked the middle path linking the entrance with the intersection at the middle of the room as well as the drop out room, he saw three figures standing on the nearest tank. It was almost a mirror image of his own tank—currently with three forms on the top. But the three girls were distinctive with their diminutive size and fancy braids.

"They made it," he shouted.

The hand on his back passed on another subtle message. It told him to look the other way, toward the entrance. His eyes focused on a sorry-looking group of soldiers. They wore tattered uniforms, a few had thread-bare hats, but most just had ragged heads of hair. They walked as a group, as if they were still in the Army, though Liam knew it has to be a coincidence. The other zombies also seemed to give the soldiers some space, though that *had* to be coincidence.

Liam, out of ideas and attempting to counter the abject terror he felt upon seeing them, simply said, "Well, I guess we know what happened to those desecrated graves."

The hand on his back remained silent.

3

"Liam! Victoria!" One of the girls from across the aisle yelled for them.

Liam waved.

Blue shouted as loud as possible, but it barely made it across the hundred or so yelling zombies between them. She pointed into the room, toward the fire. She said something he missed, but he heard her last words, "—that way!" He gave her a thumbs up, and the three girls immediately bounded to the tank next to them.

"I guess we're going *that way*." He was talking to Victoria, but Dave heard him and shouted down to Travis they were leaving. Liam held Victoria's hand as they waited for the men to come out of the tank.

"You ready to go back in?" He wasn't. He hoped she would counter his misgivings about going back into the meat of the room they'd just spent time escaping.

She took his other hand and as they stood there in the midst of the chaos, she started to pray. She said it quietly, almost as if she was ashamed of the act. When she was done, she explained why.

"I prayed and I wished upon a star and blew out my birthday candles. I couldn't let you hear my wish or it wouldn't come true." She smiled, and Liam couldn't tell if she was serious or joking. In the end, it didn't matter. They *would* need all the help they could get.

"Amen," he said.

As was her way, she took off while he stood there with a dumb look on his face. He followed her to the next tank, though he turned back to confirm Travis had indeed come out.

Deeper into the room they went, retracing the steps they'd taken before the zombies arrived. The men caught up, their rifles slung over their shoulders.

"Look for Clarence! He has to be here, somewhere."

Liam hadn't been looking down for a while. He made his jumps, and ignored everything below. If Clarence was down there, he'd better show up. And yet, he peeked down once and came to the conclusion if the man was down there, he was already dead. The spaces between the tanks was now completely stuffed with zombies dressed like civilians of all stripes who had made a wrong turn at the fake blood factory. He forced himself to believe it was fake blood.

They reached the middle of the room. On their right was the main corridor which Liam labeled the north-south road. The *Valkyrie* was still parked where they'd left it. In front of them was the east-west road with the railroad tracks. It was about forty feet across, though on the near corner there was one of the large columns holding up the ceiling.

While the roadway was far from empty, Liam saw their chance. He waited for Travis and Dave to reach the last tank, then laid out his plan. In the back of his head he wondered if he was stating the obvious, or if it was really a good plan that the others hadn't considered.

"We have to cross this space. You two help us get across with your guns, and we'll help you get across with our—" He suddenly felt very inadequate. The men had powerful rifles, while he held a little wooden spear. Victoria held an even less beefy piece of coffin wood.

You go to war with the army you have...

He didn't give anyone a chance to think about it. Each second they delayed, the more zombies would see them and move in their direction.

He found the first zombie as he hit the rocky ground. He thrust his spear through its face, then pulled it back out with authority. The man wore a lime-green light jacket—a fact he found important at the time. Victoria hit the ground as he stepped a half a dozen steps toward the middle of the road. A small child was in his way and he hesitated for half a second before doing the deed.

I hate the Apocalypse.

Victoria surged ahead, taking the next zombie. The shard of wood she carried went into the flesh of the older woman, but she squealed at the impact, then moaned as she pulled it out. Without a sideways glance to him, she yelled, "Splinters!" and kept going.

Travis and Dave used the time to prepare their rifles. Two near-simultaneous shots rang out, downing two zombies in front of them.

Liam pushed on, keeping up with Victoria. They each cleared two more zombies, then they reached the next row of tanks. Victoria climbed up, but he stood his ground. Someone would have to—

Nope!

There were too many. He wanted to stand in the breech and clear the gap for the men to cross, but that was impossible. He scrambled up the tank and found Victoria looking back at the men, motioning for them to get across.

He was tempted to wave them off, but he knew this was their only chance. If they were really lucky, they might be able to fight their way across.

Victoria, perhaps sensing his thoughts, held fast to his arm.

He turned to her. "Not this time. This little spear can't help. If only they'd given you your gun back."

It brought him no comfort to know the men had been wrong in taking it away. No one could trust anyone these days. But in this case, it cost them.

He stared across the gap, watching as the roadway filled up with more of the infected. While he wavered between running some more or yelling something encouraging to the two men, the dead soldiers walked around the corner. They'd come down the middle of the room, and now turned down the cross street.

Liam gave the two men a lot of respect. He would be unloading his rifle right about now, but they were more restrained. "We'll catch up!" Dave yelled. They waved at Liam as if telling him to keep going. They ran and jumped along the column of tanks, headed toward the large vault door at the end. Liam wondered if it would open for these Patriots. He doubted it.

Victoria pulled him. The order of the day continued to be: run for your life!

4

They jumped tank after tank, heading in the direction given by the triplets. He had no idea what they planned to do once they reached the end of the line, but he was relieved to see they had managed to cross the wide cross street, just like he and Victoria had done.

They tried to yell out to Clarence, who had to be in one of the tanks on which they ran, but he didn't pop out. There was no way to check them all and still outpace the growing horde. Zombies were everywhere around them, but thickest behind.

And what was ahead? A stone wall with one hole that led to a room full of desecrated remains and sky lights in the rock ceiling with no view of the sky.

Still, he searched for the means of escape.

Front door was jammed with the infected. Scratch.

The back door had no exits. Scratch.

The vault door didn't open. Scratch.

The railroad tracks had to go somewhere...

He began to see where the triplets were going with this. They'd been on that side of the room. Maybe they found an exit.

He reached the last tank just as the girls dodged a zombie and ran into the drop out room.

Suicide? That's their plan?

Victoria ran up against him. She, too, saw where the girls had run. There were only a few lingering zombies in the last row. It was now or never.

In his ear, she asked, "Do we follow them?"

It was time for the hero to make his choice. He saw no reason to follow them, but he thought back to all the strange coincidences which drove them all together. He found all three sisters in mysterious circumstances. Perhaps dumb luck. Or maybe something else.

But something, for sure.

"Let's follow. Don't ask me why, cuz I don't know. Call it faith."

He was down in a moment. He speared the closest zombie as Victoria hit the ground next to him. She also used her makeshift spear, but it ran through the neck of her target. She yanked it out and pushed it away instead. They ran for the opening with no room to spare. Liam was unsurprised to see some of the undead soldiers walking down the main aisle as if they had been tracking them.

"Hurry! Inside."

The light of the tank hall reached into the drop out room, but without the flashlights of the Patriots, it was more dark than light. Liam had to do a double take when he saw one of the triplets rise up into the darkness on the ceiling.

"What the?"

He ran over to the hole, his eyes trying to adjust to the increasing darkness.

He saw the dark shapes of the three girls above him. They each straddled the rough cut hole like they were climbing a chimney. There was enough room for all three of them.

"What the hell are you doing? Is this your plan? To die in here?"

Black called down. "No dummy. There's eight feet of earth above us. We just have to dig through." She paused while she adjusted her footing and climbed another foot. "What are you waiting for? Fight or die," she said. "Start digging a grave if you want to live."

Liam was mortified. He stepped back, so he couldn't see the girls. He noticed they had a piece of a broken casket below the hole. They'd used it to climb up.

Victoria grabbed the box, moved it to the next hole, then stood there looking at him.

"What are you waiting for? I need you to pull me up."

He turned back to the opening—the soldiers ambled ever closer. Other zombies hovered behind the first cadre of the old soldiers. He imagined it was a sign of respect, but maybe they were lined up by speed.

He got up onto the casket, put his spear into the grasp of his belt, then pulled himself up into the grave with a boost from Victoria. The limestone opening was perfectly spaced so he could put a foot on each side and hold himself in the gap. Victoria stepped up on the box below him, looked once over her shoulder, then she grabbed for his hands. As he straddled the rock faces, he held her in his arms.

"Don't pull me up yet."

She hung for a second, then she used her feet to kick over the box below her.

"OK, now would be good. Hurry!"

Liam's strength ran hot and cold. He felt very drained as she hung on. But the shadows on the rocks below suggested the zombies were close. Her life was literally in his hands. He pulled with everything he had. When she was high enough, he pulled her into his chest and she grabbed hold of his body. Then she aligned her legs so she also straddled the grave.

"Climb!"

It really didn't need to be said, but he said it anyway.

They managed to climb all the way up to the wooden blockage they'd seen earlier when they had flashlights. The air was cold, like death, despite the heat of the room they'd just been in. He felt a chill rock his body as his sweat cooled on his skin.

He used his spear to pierce the wooden roof. It was very thin plywood. Within a few minutes, they had the plywood removed. It dropped to the floor, and now they had raw dirt above them. An image popped into his mind of all the dirt falling from above, pushing both of them down to the floor, but that didn't happen. It was packed too tightly.

Below, the dark shadows hovered. His eyes took time to adjust, but soon he could see the soldiers packed tight directly below—arms up, straining for prey.

Victoria took one end of the narrow grave and Liam planted himself on the other. He had his spear, and she had her makeshift wooden poker. Together they began thrusting up into the dirt. It fell in clumps on top of them, then down onto the zombies standing below.

"Uh oh. Let's say by some miracle we get through all this dirt. It's just going to make a pile below us and those things are going to climb up here and get us. Wouldn't that be a funny way to die?"

"We can't worry about it now. We have no choices anymore. Fight or die, right?"

She was right of course, though he was left scratching his head how he had allowed this to happen.

Maybe this was the only possible way out. If that was true, the triplets may have just saved their lives.

If not, at least we'll already be in our graves when we die.

Small comfort.

5

Hours ticked by, though time lost all meaning in the insufferably cramped space. With each thrust of his spear, Liam felt himself losing steam. The cool he had felt upon climbing into the upside down grave had long since given way to extreme heat. The heat of exertion, yes, but also the heat of stress and the pressure of standing with legs spread across the gap for hours on end. He'd had no water for hours, and had sweat out buckets since.

"Hey! Kid! I don't hear that spear."

He snapped out of his stupor. He'd been staring upward, but he wasn't moving his digging implement. Victoria, without knowing it, may have saved his life—again. It was becoming a regular thing with him as they pushed higher. He was drifting.

"Don't call me kid, kid." He let out a raspy laugh.

"Don't fall asleep!" She yelled it, more for the shock value than any real need. It did help him focus.

The pile of dirt below was getting higher. He could sense, rather than see, they'd made a lot of progress upward. His feet were now spread across the gap into the dirt walls, instead of the rock layers below. That at least gave his feet some relief. But not his legs. Or his arms. His arms were screaming louder than the sirens on day one.

Another heft upward with the spear released a little more dirt. He'd gotten good at closing his eyes as the debris came down, but this time he was too slow and some of the dirt got in his eyes. It surprised him he had almost no tears in his eyes to wash it away.

He coughed. There was a lot of dust in the air. The floor beneath them was hard to make out between the darkness, the dead standing there, and the dust itself.

"Hey—" He coughed violently. Speaking while inhaling the dust nearly made him fall.

When he settled back down, he finally got it out. "We uh, we might be getting close. Dry dust from up top can only mean we are reaching the surface."

"Keep digging." She sounded tired, but her voice remained strong. He could no longer see her at all, though she was only a couple feet away. He could tell by her voice she was a little lower than him, but he wasn't surprised given the low quality wood she was using to crack soil over her head. He had unwittingly taken a solid tool for the task, the sharp edge of the spear had long since been worn down.

He braced himself for another push upward.

"This is it," he said without enthusiasm.

"You've said that the last 100 times."

"And this time I'm going to be right." It was the only thing that kept him going. The supreme thought that one of these times, he was going to poke through the sod and end this nightmare.

By returning to the regular nightmare of the topside Apocalypse.

Everything is crap now.

His psyche was at low tide. Which was why he was so surprised when he felt his spear go up and out through the top. When he pulled it back down, he closed his eyes as the dirt and dust coated his head and face. Then he opened his eyes and was rewarded with the piercing ray of light coming through a tiny hole.

"Liam?" His name was an echo.

"Liam!"

"What?"

"You're staring up. Are you in there?"

With even the drip of light coming through, Victoria was able to see what she was doing and clear a section of the dirt on her side so she could reach the top. Together, they widened the hole so they would fit through.

Liam hesitated.

"What is it?"

"I don't know if I can lift my arms above my head one more time. And to get out through that hole…"

"We'll need our arms. OK, let's rest for a minute."

Liam wasn't going to argue, but he really wanted to do more than rest. He wanted to sleep. He tried to lean back against the rear wall of the grave so he could rest his upper body.

"Stay with me. Don't you dare."

"Huh?" He knew what she wanted of him, but he really needed to just take a little breather.

"Liam, dammit, stay with me!"

That got his attention. "Why Victoria, I've never heard you cuss like that." He knew that was a half-truth. She normally was very reserved in her off-color commentary, though she did lay down some foul language when they escaped the city and thought Grandma had died. "It isn't very ladylike."

He was joking with her, but he saw the smile on her face too. She pulled out the big guns to keep him awake.

"Are you ready to get out of this grave? I sure as hell am."

Liam, ever smiling, only replied with a long, "Umm," as in, "Umm, I'm gonna tell."

He had to admit, if she was trying to goad him into trying to climb, it worked. Not because of what she said, but that she'd said it at all.

Her minor breach of language etiquette told him she was seriously worried about him.

He pushed up with his legs. He would have to use his arms, but first he could position himself a little higher on the wall. He'd gotten his head into the narrow part of the hole above, not quite poking out of the grave itself, but his arms soon would be.

"Wouldn't it be funny if there are a pack of zombies above us?" He said it to be funny. His dark humor was meant to ward off the bad thoughts, as odd as that felt to him.

"I doubt zombies would hang around in cemeteries. There's no fresh victims there."

"You know, I was thinking the very same thing."

He threw his spear up through the hole, then with all the energy he had left, he pushed his arms up as well. He had to work away some of the loose dirt, but he was able to use his arms while he pulled his legs up the sides of the walls. Like some sick worm, he slid out of the grave onto his belly. The headstone was only inches away.

"Charles Everett. U.S. Navy. Blah blah blah. 1943." His eyes couldn't focus on all the words.

He slowly turned around to look back down the hole. A pretty face looked up at him.

"Victoria!"

"Yeah, I'm still here. Care to help?"

He hung his arms down and pulled up her wooden pick. What was once several feet long was now about the size of a dagger. It must have broken apart as she tore into the dirt.

"Hold on to me and use your feet to climb. The edge is too unstable to put too much weight with your arms."

"That's perfect. My arms are toast."

He knew the feeling. It took him a long time to get her out of the hole, but soon she lay next to him on the lush green turf of the cemetery.

Sleep sounded divine. As did water. A tall cool glass of Mountain Dew would be salvation.

"Liam!"

"Why are you screaming at me?"

"I called your name about five times. You aren't responding to me."

He couldn't think of anything funny to aid his defense. All he could say was, "Oh."

She continued when she had his attention. "Look, over there." She pointed, though she didn't raise her arm from the ground.

A large hole had been excavated from the grave next door.

6

He took a moment to scan the cemetery landscape. Tens of thousands of white headstones stood in martial rows on every hillside as far as he could see. They'd emerged on a flat, low section of the cemetery. Slopes rose on either side, though he literally thanked God there were no zombies anywhere in his field of view. That, at least, gave them some time to rest.

The girls were nowhere in sight. He figured they made good on their plan to separate from him.

He rolled over toward Victoria. She was filthy. Her face was covered in dirt and mud, like she'd been at an expensive spa and had it caked on. Her white top was now mostly brown from all the dust and dirt that mixed with her sweat. The bottom half of each of the legs of her jeans were well-soiled with mud. That was from planting her legs in the muddy walls for—

He looked at his watch. It was late afternoon, but he had no idea how long they'd dug. He didn't think to check the time when they started out. For every minute of however long they were in the grave, he thought the climbing zombies were going to come up and grab him, but they never did. The creepy soldier guys just stood vigil, moaning and clawing upward, but the dirt that fell on them was spread out and compacted.

In the bright light, he could hardly believe such a scene was mere feet away. The sounds from below were muffled by the soddy edges and thick earth in the hole.

"Where do you think they went?" He could hardly talk.

"Where did they come from...where did they go?" She let out a giddy laugh, though her voice was dry like his. "I think I'm finally going crazy, Liam. I really don't care. I just climbed out of a grave! They saved us."

"I thought that was my job?" It came out in a whisper.

She looked at him. He only saw her pretty eyes.

"You did your job. You got us out of there." She nodded to the hole.

He was too tired to argue. Instead, he stood.

"Come on. We need water." He enjoyed being on his feet, thankful that his arms hung to his sides at rest, while he looked for his target. "This way."

He had gone ten paces when he remembered Victoria.

Good boyfriends help their girlfriends.

But she was already on her feet. He absently thought she was stronger than he was. She was more likely to pull him to *his* feet. This time was different because he was insane with thirst, and had a touch of delirium.

My excuse. I'm stickin' to it.

As he expected, the low point of the cemetery contained a small creek. He stumbled into the rocky depression—it was more of a drainage ditch than a natural creek—but it contained his prize. Years of Boy Scout warning blared in his head about drinking untreated water, but he threw all the books into the fire of his thirst. He was not going to be denied by science.

He nearly fell as he bent down to stick his face into a particularly deep section of the creek. He took long, dangerous gulps. The water filled his stomach until he could feel its weight inside him.

Victoria put her head in next to his. All was quiet for a long time.

Liam, finally sated, used the water to wash his face and eyes. When he was done, he felt like the proverbial million bucks.

Down the creek, and beyond the cemetery, he could see the dingy brown of the Mississippi. They had almost gone full circle.

He grabbed her and pointed where he was going. He was too tired to explain.

They stumbled through the cemetery, wary for the dead, and the undead. He was careful to go around the plots, as if to atone for the desecration they'd inflicted upon the robbed grave sites.

You had no choice.

Well, other than death.

He had no energy for moral dilemmas. He'd done what was necessary to survive, though it didn't sit well with him once he'd made the realization. How many men and women used the same excuse in his zombie books? The one excuse that seemed to always exonerate any crime.

He hopped over the low stone wall marking the boundary of the cemetery. He then crossed the railroad tracks next to the river, and scrambled down the rocky bank. In moments, he stood alone at the edge of the wide river.

The quiet was only broken by small ripples along the shore, or birds in the distance. A woodpecker far away registered as the loudest noise until Victoria came tumbling down the rocky bank. He watched her on unsteady feet as she closed the final few paces to stand beside him.

"Are we safe? What do we do now, swim?"

He thought that sounded exactly perfect. He swooned a bit at the thought of the cool water around him. He'd last felt it jumping in to save Pink.

"We'll find some driftwood and float away," he finally replied.

Overhead, far across the river, he saw the movement of a drone.

He pointed. "Can't we get some peace and quiet?"

Victoria said nothing.

Minutes later, still waiting for driftwood to float by, Liam's phone rang in his pocket. He'd absolutely forgotten about it since he pulled it out in the boat, not wanting to risk getting it wet when he jumped overboard.

From inside the plastic bag he could see the data. It was a text message from the same 435 area code that sent them to the quarry. It was brief and to the point. "Now you know truth. Swim away."

He didn't bother replying. The person on the other end knew he was alive. That was all that mattered, for now. Patriots. Villains. Cures. Plagues. Life. Death. These all swirled through his exhausted mind.

"We're going to wait until a large tree floats by, we're going to grab on, then float with it until we find the boat parked downriver. If it's there, we're going to take it. If not, we keep swimming. They told me to find Jason up on that cliff, but I'm going to Camp Hope. I need to find my parents. My dad. I need to know if he knew about this place. I need to know—"

He spoke so only the two of them could possibly hear. "I need to know once and for all if my dad had anything to do with the Patriot Snowball movement. Maybe he knew the men who died helping us escape."

"I'm with you. Always."

She grabbed his hand and they steadied each other as they watched the water flow by. They'd jump when the time was right.

Together.

EPILOGUE

For once, things went exactly as Liam planned. They'd found the boat left by the captain. They had no way to know if he was coming back, but they left a note sticking out from under a rock saying where they were going. It said they were coming back.

The powerful boat made short work of the smaller Meramec River. It took less than an hour to speed up the increasingly narrow river until they reached the same point he and Victoria had first arrived at the river after leaving the Beaumont Boy Scout Reservation a week ago. From there, it was a mile walk to the front gate of the camp.

When he arrived, he was recognized by the Scouts defending it. His spear matched many of the spears carried by the guards. The Hope Spears were a specialty of the place. He was excited to tell tales of what his spear had seen and done recently. But first, he had to find his parents.

He vaguely recalled the cheering crowds. The fawning younger Scouts. The pats on the back. The camp had been emptying out when he left, but now it was back to its former size—and looked to be growing even larger.

Must find parents.

His dad had broken his leg, so the natural place to find him would be the infirmary. It was where he last saw him, though on the day he left, he only said goodbye to Mom because Dad was so badly injured and couldn't come out to see him. Though if he'd told them he was leaving the camp, he thought his dad might have tried to come out to stop him.

Word spread rapidly. His mom found him.

"Liam, thank God you're all right. Where have you been?"

The age old question. In the Old World, he saw the question as an invasion of his privacy. Where are you going? Who will you be with? Are girls going to be there? All the things that used to make him upset were tossed aside. Now he was glad to share his tale, because he'd made it back to tell it.

Finally, after all his "missions" to save Grandma and help find the cure, he would offload the task to someone who could actually make things happen. If anyone was more prepared for the Apocalypse than his father, he hadn't found him.

"Hi Mom. We found Grandma in the city—"

They hugged while they spoke.

"We left her in Cairo, Illinois, she's safe there."

His head was dizzy at the feeling of security he felt in his mother's arms. But it couldn't last. He released her.

"We figured out something important about the plague." He scanned the area, wondering if he would be shot by a mysterious assassin for revealing the secret. In the end, after all he'd been through, he fought away the fear. "It affects the dead. It apparently lasts forever. Like, literally forever."

He conducted another sweep of the nearby camp. "Where's dad? I need to ask him some important questions right away. He may be in danger."

He began walking to the bullet-ridden and boarded up administration building, as he assumed he'd be inside. When his mom didn't follow, he motioned for her to come to him. When she demurred, he turned back to face her.

"He's somewhere else?"

Her eyes were sad. Like she'd been crying a lot.

"The survivalists came back?"

A head shake no.

"Zombies?"

Another head shake.

He tried to force something positive into the mix. His heart warned him not to do it, but he wasn't going to listen to the warnings of his brain.

"He went to a hospital?" His voice was tentative, as if he knew it was a lie.

Her tears answered his question.

It was unfair, but anger spilled out, rather than sadness. "What then? Where the hell is he? I've survived a lot of stinking death out there. I climbed out of a freakin' grave. I really need to talk to him. The fate of the country is at stake. Maybe the world!"

His mom cried freely. It was obvious to any bystander why.

Still, Liam pushed. "Where is he, Mom? Where?"

2

His dad's grave was just a stick in a muddy mound on top of one of the nearby hills. The camp made a best effort to bury all the people who died during the recent attack by the survivalists. An attack made to find *him*, he was sad to admit.

I ruin every safe space I encounter.

Victoria walked with him up the hill. His mom followed too, but she remained behind—she seemed hesitant to get too close to Liam in his condition. The only thing she'd gotten out was that he died because of the wound on his leg. He'd shattered a leg bone and without proper antibiotics it had become infected and he'd caught something which made him burn up. He died suddenly, not long after Liam left the camp.

"Why! Dad, why?" He was mad now. A visceral anger at the suspicion his dad knew more than he let on, but more than that, he was mad his dad didn't trust him with that knowledge. It could have made all the difference in the effort to fight—

For what? The truth? For the cure? What could he have known that would have made any difference in the fact there was a massive cavern with hundreds of tanks in it? Did he know about that? Wouldn't that have been the first place he'd taken the family if he did?

He ran through a multitude of possibilities, but the only thing that made any sense was that his dad really didn't know about that place. Whoever was behind that great steel vault had to be someone other than the Snowballers.

He fell to his knees at the grave. Vertigo struck as he looked down at the ground.

Is he clawing up through the mud, like I did?

Without thinking about it, he moved backward on his knees. Just a foot. Enough to not be in the way.

"Dad. I really needed your help." He said it with resignation. Victoria took it as her invitation to kneel next to him. She put her hand through his arm, and held him.

He was reduced to tears. At some point, his mother closed the distance and stood next to him. She looked down at the grave with him.

"He was very proud of you, Liam. I think he knew he wasn't going to make it. He made me promise to tell you of his pride in you, though I refused to listen to him. I never saw the end coming."

Liam realized he'd been a jerk. He'd lost a father. She'd lost her husband. If he lost Victoria now, it would destroy him. He'd been very nearly ready to kill himself back in the tank room when he thought she'd been bitten. His mom was stronger than he was. That became apparent once he took five seconds to think about it.

He stood to be next to her.

"I'm sorry, Mom. I had no right to yell at you."

He held her, just as Victoria had held him. After a long period of silence, his mom spoke.

"Liam, your dad left you some notes I think you're going to want to see."

The anger burst out, totally outside his control. "I knew it! He *was* involved."

"Liam, before you say anything else, you need to see them. It's not what you think."

He could think of a lot. His dad worked for the bad guys. He was part of the government conspiracy. He was part of the Patriot Snowball plot, and he *did* release the plague. He was in league with Hayes and Duchesne and everyone Liam hated right now. He stood against everything he'd taught Liam since he was a baby. The bad thoughts flowed like the river. His exhaustion, grief, and sour mood wouldn't harbor any thought his dad was really a good guy.

Was he good or bad?

He wouldn't be able to rest until he knew the truth.

"Let's go," he said in a spiteful voice. Then, upon seeing Victoria's silent rebuke, and realizing he *was* being a complete jackass, he softened it.

"Please, Mom, I have to know."

###

ACKNOWLEDGMENTS

Thank you for reading *Last Fight of the Valkyries*! I'll be working on book 5, *Zombies vs. Polar Bears*, by the time you're reading this message.

If you've read this far, I think it's safe to say you qualify as a "superfan" of my books. Seriously, whether you loved them or merely survived them, I want to take this opportunity to shake your hand in appreciation. The series has taken on a life of its own and brought me to places I never imagined just a few short months ago.

For one, I had no idea these books would sell beyond a few copies to my mom. I wrote them mainly for my own enjoyment and even a few weeks after I hit the publish button on book 1 in December, 2015, I still wasn't thinking of them in terms of making money. I just wasn't wired that way.

However, about a month after the launch of book 1, I put the finishing touches on book 2 and hit the publish button again in January, 2016. Suddenly I had two books in the marketplace and a few people started to notice. A trickle of people read through book 2 and had pre-ordered book 3. It was slated to come out in the middle of February, 2016. As the weeks went by, more readers pre-ordered book 3 and it dawned on me they were buying all three books in quick order. One of those early people was probably you. Yes, you—reading this, right now.

Because of *you*, I decided to write a book 4. I spent the month of March doing almost nothing but writing *Last Fight of the Valkyries*, and I loved the directions it took me. I don't want to give anything away on the off chance you're reading this before reading the story, but there were things in the ending that even I didn't know were going to happen until they took place far into the writing process. It has truly set things up for an exciting book 5!

Now, as I release book 4, and as I'm talking to my best and most endurance-oriented fans, I'm going to look back on some of the reviews for my first book and add commentary in the form of replies. You see, as an author, I don't feel it's right for me to comment on reviews directly on the site where they appear, because reviews are a way for readers to talk directly to other readers. I don't like to get in the middle of that natural process.

However, in my own book, I feel free to highlight some of the reviews which interest me, and, if you'll indulge me, show my thought process as I read and respond to some of them.

First, I'd like to take a minute to address, in bulk, the several people critical of one key aspect of my books that honestly caught me by surprise. It seems obvious in retrospect, and shows my lack of experience as an author, but I had no idea Grandma Marty's religion would be seen so negatively by some reviewers. I've touched on this in some of the "acknowledgments" sections. Marty was based on my own grandmother. It's hard for me to visualize my own grandma in those situations, because although she was far more religious than Marty, she wasn't one to proselytize. So, while it's safe to say my grandma was very religious, she was not a Bible-thumping, in-your-face, follow my religion or go-to-hell type of woman. She was a Christian, and thus I wanted to write Marty in the same spirit. See what I did there? Haha.

They say you can't please everyone, and that's reasonable. However, I take reviews seriously. I re-read my own books looking for places where I made religion in-your-face or otherwise out of place with the story. Anything that would cause such negative reviews. I really couldn't find anything that I, as a reader, felt was pushy or showy about religion. I describe Grandma's prayers, her belief she was seeing an angel in her visions, and Victoria's cross necklace and her desire to find a Bible in various places throughout the book. Any of those could have been substituted for non-religious counterparts. Grandma could have been meditating. She could have thought Al was a ghost. Victoria could have been wearing an Ankh. I could have then pleased those who gave me a negative review and been on my way to author greatness.

But that's not how I heard the story. Part of being an author is writing from the heart. I listen to my characters, and when I'm really lucky, I can see them. I imagined Victoria when Liam first met her. He was nervous because she was a cute, older girl in a pretty dress. But, and who knows where such things come from, I saw her with that cross necklace. As the author, it gave me comfort that here was a girl who might bring something to the table. I felt she had some gravitas, despite her age, because she sees something larger than the current catastrophe surrounding her. Liam took comfort from that, and was one facet of his later attraction to her. Could I have used an Ankh? Absolutely. But it would have been fake. A cop out. It wasn't what I saw. Besides, at the time, I only considered my own writer's voice, not the voice of dissenting reviewers.

One other reviewer mentioned religion in the negative, and suggested that there was no way Liam would have tried to grab a Bible for Victoria while under threat of the zombie horde. Everyone is entitled to their opinions, but I have to ask what fifteen-year-old boy DOESN'T do stupid stuff to catch the eye of a girl he fancies? I did plenty of doozies in my day, mostly while cruising the town in fast cars. I saw nothing in that act tied to religion. He did it to impress a girl, which is pretty much the most important reason to do anything as a teen boy! He even says as much later in the story. He'd been looking for that Bible since they'd met. It's one of my favorite scenes, and I'm quite happy with how it's written.

To counter the above, many reviewers appreciated the religious element present throughout the books. In fact, the great majority of my readers seem to appreciate the inclusion of religion, not as a central theme to the story (e.g., this isn't Christian Fiction) but as something that would naturally happen if the world suddenly found itself overwhelmed by zombies. To ignore religion—any religion, it just so happens this character is a devout Christian—would be a gross oversight. Liam is less of a believer, at least at first, but his struggle to understand what's happening with the world would be, I think, what most normal human beings would experience. If there were no religion at all, I happen to believe things would devolve to a Mad Max level of barbarism much faster. That isn't to say it couldn't happen otherwise.

There are many details of the reviews that I found thought-provoking.

One reviewer took offense to the fact Liam was an asocial gamer who lived in his parent's basement. I don't see Liam that way at all. In fact, he normally plays his games with his four or five friends at one of their houses, but since he was spending the summer with his great-grandma, and since he had no choice but to live in her basement and hang out at the library, he ended up appearing as the "typical asocial teen gamer." Also, I should point out I was a somewhat asocial gamer in my younger years, and I did spend some time living in my parents' basement. Funny how life experiences can make it into a book!

Bollocks! That's a word Liam uses at one point, and a reviewer found that to be unnatural for an American teen. Again, this is a life experience thing. I grew up watching Benny Hill, Blakes 7, and Doctor Who. I was enamoured with all things British. Today's teens (and I know a few) are also hooked on British television, including the new version of Doctor Who. They also enjoy the British teen story about the boy called Harry Potter, though I don't recall if anyone said bollocks in those books. In short, I don't think it's a stretch that Liam would use that word. We could argue whether the "average" American teen would use that word.

Other reviewers have described Liam both as too smart for being fifteen and too dumb for being fifteen. I tried to balance his youth with his deep understanding of the zombie plague itself. When I was fifteen, I could have recited useless stats from *Dungeons and Dragons* manuals. I read and studied those books all the time (to the detriment of school). I could tell you how to fight hundreds of different monsters—their strengths, weaknesses, etc. I'd like to think if I ever came across a gelatinous cube in a dark alley, I'd know the secret to defeating it: step out of its way. Thus, I felt Liam would understand the global ramifications of the zombie apocalypse, even if he didn't really know how to properly use a radio. In the end, I'm glad there are complaints of both as it suggests the truth is somewhere in the middle.

I believe Liam would also have advantages over adults in some situations because he'd read about similar things in his zombie books. I'm fascinated by zombies in our culture. For one thing, we've all agreed that zombies are killed by hitting them in the head. But if zombies actually stumbled their way into reality today, how many people still wouldn't know how to kill them? It seems incredible, especially for people who regularly read and watch entertainment about zombies, but most people probably don't have that deep background in zombies. In that light, Liam could appear to know more than his years suggest when he is helping with zombie-related lore. This would include the basics—arm up, aim for the head, find and secure shelter.

There are lots of other little things that have been mentioned in the 80+ reviews for book 1 that I could discuss at length, but I'll just breeze over them to wrap this up. There are some complaints about not enough cussing in the zombie apocalypse. Personally, I don't mind cussing in books, but when I wrote this, I didn't feel any need to overdo it. Call it a residual effect of using my grandma as an archetype for Marty. She wouldn't want needless cussing in "her" story. My grandma never used a harsh word in my presence, much less cuss words. I generally don't talk that way around my family, though I have plenty of friends who do. I'm ambivalent on the issue, but for my book I did what I felt was true to the story. Of course, many others responded that they appreciated the story was on the clean side, and in fact I let my ten year old read the first book.

Someone mentioned the one-dimensional racial makeup of the story. I have to wonder if that person even read the book though, as one of the central characters (Officer Jones) is clearly described as a big black man. As you readers know, book 4 has three major characters of "color." Also, though I don't make a big deal out of it, Phil's last name is Ramos, suggesting he is Hispanic. I honestly don't know that it does anything to advance the story besides give him some depth beyond what I've written. I think my characters are concerned with larger issues. When my wife first read book 1, she imagined Victoria was also Hispanic, even though I don't recall any indication of race. Go figure.

Well, that's all the highlights of the reviews for this edition of my ramblings. If you care to add creative reviews to any of my books you've read, I'll mention them in the notes of my next book! Thank you, truly, for being a reader!

E.E. Isherwood, April 17, 2016

ABOUT THE AUTHOR

E.E. Isherwood is the New York Times and USA Today bestselling author of the *Sirens of the Zombie Apocalypse* series. His long-time fascination with the end of the world blossomed decades ago after reading the 1949 classic *Earth Abides*. Zombies allow him to observe how society breaks down in the face of such withering calamity.

Isherwood lives in St. Louis, Missouri with his wife and family. He stays deep in a bunker with steepled fingers, always awaiting the arrival of the first wave of zombies.

Find him online at www.zombiebooks.net.

BOOKS BY E.E. ISHERWOOD

E.E. Isherwood currently has six books in the *Sirens of the Zombie Apocalypse* universe. Visit his website at www.zombiebooks.net to be informed when future titles are launched.

The *Sirens of the Zombie Apocalypse* series

Since the Sirens

Siren Songs

Stop the Sirens

Last Fight of the Valkyries

Zombies vs. Polar Bears

Zombies Ever After

Book 1: *Since the Sirens*

When fifteen-year-old Liam goes to stay with his ancient great-grandmother for the summer, he immediately becomes bored around the frail and elderly woman. He spends most of his time at the library texting friends or reading dark novels. But one morning stroll changes everything as the Zombie Apocalypse unloads itself directly into his life. Now he and his 104-year-old guardian must survive the journey out of the collapsing city of St. Louis while zombies, plague, and desperate survivors swirl around them.

Book 2: *Siren Songs*

After escaping the chaos of the collapsing city, teens Liam and Victoria are faced with a difficult choice. Do they try to find Liam's parents or defend their suburban home from refugees and the infected? They find new allies to hold things together, even as the government appears increasingly impotent in the face of a mutating virus. And why is a representative of the CDC trying to enlist Liam's 104-year-old grandma to his cause?

Book 3: *Stop the Sirens*

Liam and his parents are reunited at last, but the matriarch of their family has been taken to a covert CDC location for medical experiments. Liam wants to mount a rescue operation, but they must first reach a refuge, endure warring government agencies, and learn Grandma's location—not to mention survive a world awash in zombies. With Victoria at his side, Liam finds his fortitude bolstered by her faith. Together they begin to unravel the mystery of the zombie plague.

Book 4: *Last Fight of the Valkyries*

Liam, Marty, and Victoria are rescued from St. Louis. Now safely in the defenses of the town of Cairo, IL, they are once again free to look ahead—into the headwinds of the Zombie Apocalypse. Liam is separated from his parents, Mel and Phil are missing, and Grandma's status as a sane person is very much in doubt in their new town. But when Liam finally realizes what's on the chip given to him by Colonel McMurphy, he sees the way forward. Always with an eye toward saving civilization, he takes his first steps in that direction.

Book 5: *Zombies vs. Polar Bears*

Liam is more resolved than ever to solve the mystery behind the zombie plague. He now has several clues—some gleaned at great personal cost—about the zombies, although he remains unsure who's behind the creation of the plague. Was it the secretive National Internal Security division as he was originally told, or was it the Patriot Snowball movement as reported by remaining government officials? Everyone has an opinion, but the truth might lurk within his own family. Meanwhile, Grandma Marty remains in Cairo, Illinois. She is confused by her strange dreams by night, and afraid of what she hears over the great defensive levees of the town by day.